REVENGE ON THE DEVIL

STEAMY REGENCY ROMANCE

VILLAIN'S REDEMPTION
BOOK THREE

WREN ST CLAIRE

Note: this book contains content that some readers may find confronting. Turn to
the next page if you wish to read the trigger warnings. Skip the next page if you
don't want any spoilers.

❦ Created with Vellum

CONTENT WARNING

This book contains references to domestic violence and miscarriage and depicts on page murder. If you find these topics triggering you may not wish to read this book.

This one is for my dear husband Joe, who always believed in me even when I didn't.
This book helped me hang on to my sanity through your illness my darling. I will always love you. I will always miss you.

Joseph Brian Campbell 26 May 1950 - 17 July 2023

CHAPTER 1

*J*une 1815

Genevra Tate looked up from her vigorous polishing of the beer engine handle, as a new customer strolled into the tap room. Welcome summer sunlight streaked through the mullioned windows across floorboards worn and grey with scrubbing, taking the morning chill off the air. It was mid-morning and only a handful of the regulars were present, muttering into their tankards of porter or sharing a coffee-pot and late breakfast.

She tracked the stranger as he wandered in, looked about and spied her at the bar. He smiled, drawing an answering smile from her. He was tall, well-made and handsome, with unfashionably long dark hair and a dark stubble on his jaw. His clothes were casual but of good quality, he had eschewed a hat, jacket and neckcloth in deference to the summer heat, and wore only a shirt and waistcoat with well fitted breeches and boots.

"Good morning, sir," she said. "Would you care for a drink?"

"I would at that me darlin'," he said with a striking Irish accent. As he came closer, she got the full effect of his startlingly dark blue eyes. "A half pot of porter," he said leaning on the bar and smiling with blatant admiration.

Genevra fetched a pewter pot and pulled the handle of the beer engine to dispense the porter, the dark liquid forming a thick, delicious, creamy head on top. Pausing at halfway to let it settle, she looked up at her customer and said encouragingly, "Would you like a bite to eat with that?"

"No, thank you sweetheart. I've just eaten."

She topped up the rest of the pot.

"Ah, thank you," he said, receiving the pot from her and taking a long draught. "That's a fine drop."

"Whittaker's" she said, flicking a stray strawberry blonde curl behind her ear as she wiped down the bench.

He nodded. "Would Jacob Tate be around me darling? I've a mite of business with him."

Genevra's heart skipped a beat. "What would your business be with Jacob?"

"That would be my business, love. Can you direct me to him?"

"He's buried in the St Giles Church cemetery six feet under!" she said with perhaps more venom than the situation warranted. *After all the man was dead and couldn't hurt her anymore.*

Her customer pursed his lips in consternation. "Can you tell me who the publican of this fine establishment might be then?"

"That would be me. Genevra Tate. Jacob's widow." She held out her hand. "And who might you be?"

"Connor Mor at your service ma'am. Delighted to make your acquaintance. Forgive me manners, I tort you was the bar maid."

"It's a common mistake Mr Mor, how may I help you?"

He leaned in and said softly, "It's a matter of some delicacy, you may want to do this in private ma'am."

She eyed him suspiciously for a moment and then waved him round the bar to the office behind it. She showed him into a small square wood panelled room, dominated by a scratched desk and two battered chairs.

"Well?" she said, her arms crossed.

"It's a matter of some debts," he said apologetically, and her heart sank. *She had enough debt as it was. What had Jacob done?*

"How much? And to whom?"

"The debt is owed to Mr Garmon Lovell, of Lovells' gaming hell in St James Street." He handed her a slip of paper he had taken from his waistcoat pocket.

She took it with a hand that trembled slightly and opened the paper. She couldn't believe what her eyes were seeing.

"Five hundred pounds?" Her voice squeaked in outrage. She thrust the paper back at him. "I do not believe you. My husband could not have incurred such a monstrous debt."

He refused to take the paper. "I assure you that he did Mrs Tate."

"Where's the proof?"

He took another piece of paper from his pocket and held it up for her to read. It was an I.O.U. signed by Jacob for five hundred pounds to Garmon Lovell and dated to January 9th, 1815. It was undoubtedly Jacob's handwriting. She groped for the chair behind her and sat down heavily. "My God," she whispered. "It's a fortune!"

"You note the date Mrs Tate. That is six months ago. Mr Lovell has been very patient, but he really must insist the debt be paid in full by the end of the week."

"The end of the week?" she jumped up. "That's impossible! I had no notion of this debt until this very moment. I cannot summon five hundred pounds out of thin air! You must give me time- I -"

"As I pointed out Mrs Tate, Mr Lovell has been very patient. He requires that the debt be paid immediately. I will call again at the end of the week." His expression had hardened, and she shivered. "I can assure you, that should you not have the required funds Mr Lovell will take steps to recover the amount from you by means you will not like." He shook his head. "I should not like to see violence perpetrated against such a lovely lady as yourself my dear, but business, as they say, is business."

She shuddered, terror slicing down her spine. "Get out!" she said, pointing to the door.

He bowed. "Good day to you Mrs Tate. Thank you for the fine porter. I will see you on Friday."

He turned to leave the room, and she followed him. "It's four pence!" Holding out her hand. He turned, fished in his pocket and dropped the coins into her palm.

"Good day ma'am."

He turned and sauntered out, cool as you please. She fumed and then reaction set in, her knees gave out, and she went back into the office, collapsing into the chair shaking with terror.

The look in Mr Mor's eyes as he threatened her with violence just brought it all back. She bit her lip hard, to stop its trembling, and blinked back tears. She would not cry, *damn it!* Jacob was dead and could not harm her anymore. Yet he could reach beyond the grave to haunt her with his unpaid debts, bringing terror and financial hardship to her door. *When would it end? When would she be rid of him? He was like a curse.*

"Mrs Tate?" Annie one of the barmaids called out from the tap. Pulling herself together with an effort, she plastered a smile on her face and went to the door.

"Yes Annie."

"There you are! Joe says can you come down to the cellar, something about rats?" Annie shuddered. "I'll mind the tap for you."

"Thank you, Annie," she said wearily and headed towards the cellar to manage the immediate crisis. Mr Lovell's debt would have to wait until she had a spare moment to address it.

CHAPTER 2

A **few hours earlier**

The room in which Mr Garmon Lovell sat, was quite pleasant, particularly given its location in Monmouth Court, Saint Giles in the notorious district of Seven Dials. A fresh coat of paint to the walls, panes of glass in the windows and a sturdy door with a lock, did much to restore the room to its former glory. As had done the coat of paint and new windows to the building in which it was situated above a bookshop and printers. The renovations gave it a certain éclat in the rather run down environs of Monmouth Court.

The row of urchins before him certainly thought so and were suitably overawed. This collection of the urchins of the street were, to a child, small, under-nourished, filthy and scabrous. They also stank of the Thames in which they spent quite a bit of their time. That notwithstanding, they were valuable to Garmon as the cogs of his vast information network. He paid them five pence a day and a meal, to fatten them up, but he suspected most of the money and the food went to their families, because the little varmints continued to be skinny and malodorous no matter his efforts.

Having briefed them for their day's work, he dismissed them. He listened to them pad downstairs on dirty, bare feet and into the street where they would disperse to their posts for the day, returning at dusk to receive their wages and meal and be replaced by the night shift.

The idea of using street urchins for his spy network was not his. He had learned it from his mentor, the Chevalier De Salle– purportedly a French émigré fled the terror in Paris -, on the streets of Brussels, where he served an apprenticeship as a youth and young man; learning the ways of an adventurer, which included aping the manner of a gentleman, as well as how to fleece an ignorant nobleman and survive the brutality of Brussels' backstreets.

De Salle owned Brussels in those days, much as Garmon now owned London. He wondered if the old reprobate was still alive. He'd lost touch with him when Brussels was annexed by the French in 1795, and they were forced to flee the city. He returned to London, De Salle's intention was to go to Italy. He had been tempted to go with him, but a strange homesickness sent him back to St Giles to find his own way.

Dismissing the reminiscence, he returned to his work of sifting through titbits of information that he had gleaned from his various sources, putting together connections and opportunities which were his stock-in-trade. This was his new enterprise, having been robbed of his gaming hell by the Duke of Mowbray. He still had every intention of getting the hell back, now that he was healed of the bullet the Duchess of Mowbray had put in his back. She had damned near killed him with that shot, if it weren't for Connor he would have died of the fever.

Vengeance was a dish best served cold, and Garmon's fury had cooled to arctic temperatures by now. He meant to exact a price against his treacherous niece and her iniquitous husband that neither should ever forget and get his hell back in the process. They would both learn the price of crossing Garmon Lovell.

The door opened to admit a swarthy man of solid, muscular build, escorting none too gently, a thin man in a jacket shiny with age and a battered crown beaver hat. He removed it at sight of Garmon, revealing a thinning crop of greying hair, combed over his balding forehead. His eyes watered behind their spectacles, and he clutched his hat nervously. Garmon nodded to Rooke, who released the thin man's arm and stepped back, blocking the exit with his large frame.

"Mr Whiteside, it is quarter day. Where is my money?"

"Mr Lovell, Sir, I just need a little more time-"

"How much does he have Rooke?" Garmon asked.

Rooke stepped forward and laid a roll of bills on his desk. "Just shy of fifty pounds by my reckoning."

"It's all I have Mr Lovell!"

"But not enough..." Lovell counted the bills rapidly and shoved them in a drawer of his desk. "Rooke, retrieve whatever you can to make up the shortfall. The house if necessary. Good day Mr Whiteside."

"Not the house—where will I live?"

"Not my problem, Mr Whiteside." Garmon returned his attention to the pile of documents before him.

"Please Mr Lovell, I'll do anything, just don't take the house-"

"You had your opportunity; I have been more than patient. Mr Rooke, please remove Mr Whiteside from my presence."

Rooke stepped forward and seized the man's arm as he cried out a protest. Rooke hustled him towards the door and the man's glasses fell off in the scuffle, clacking on the floorboards. "Please! Wait! I–I have something you may want-"

"I want my money," replied Garmon.

"I have information!" The man tried to pry his arm out of Rooke's grip, but the attempt was futile.

"Well?" Garmon sat back sceptical. "Out with it."

"You will leave my house alone?"

"Depends on the value of your information."

"I want a guarantee-"

"You're in no position to be making demands Mr Whiteside. Leave here with your information and without your house, it's all one to me." He waved a hand. "Rooke." The big man seized his arm again and Whiteside began to babble.

Garmon listened to him for a few minutes and then waved him away. "I already knew most of that, and the rest is incorrect. Take him away Rooke and bring me the title to his house. Send the men in to sort through what is there, anything of value bring to me, the rest they can have."

"Yes Mr Lovell." Rooke bundled up the still protesting Whiteside and manhandled him out the door. His protests could be heard all the way to the street. Garmon shook his head and returned to the pile of documents before him.

A LITTLE WHILE later Mr Rooke came back with the title deeds for the house and a collection of valuable trinkets.

Garmon shoved the deed in a drawer, sorted through the trinkets and instructed Rooke to exchange them for money from Old Harry in Bent Street.

Rooke nodded. "Cruikshank's been spotted over at Temple Bar this morning."

"Good send a couple of lads to fetch him, I want a word."

"Already done, Mr Lovell. He should arrive at any moment."

"Excellent, escort him in, will you? He might need a little persuasion."

"Yes sir."

He came back shortly with a very tall, very thin man dressed rather dapperly in a coat of navy blue over fawn-coloured pantaloons and a floral waistcoat.

"Ah Mr Cruickshank, nice of you to drop in," said Garmon with heavy sarcasm.

Straightening his neckcloth and shucking his cuffs, Cruikshank grimaced. "There was no need for violence Mr Lovell. No need at all."

"There was every need Cruikshank. You've been evading my men for weeks. You owe me one thousand pounds. Pay up!"

Cruikshank eyed him with mild alarm, nowhere in proportion to the fear he should be feeling. The man had the hide of a rhinoceros.

"We are both businessmen, Mr Lovell. You know full well you can't expect a fellow to produce a sum like that out of thin air."

"You have had several months to make good on your debt Cruikshank, do you fancy a spell in debtor's prison?"

"Now do be reasonable -!" He said visibly blenching.

"I have been more than reasonable Cruikshank." he advanced on the man and despite Cruikshank being several inches taller, he shrank back from Garmon's menacing glare coming up against Rooke standing like a brick wall behind him. He glanced up at Rooke and gulped.

"Mr Rooke, I think Mr Cruikshank is unaware of the seriousness of the situation. Perhaps you could enlighten him?"

Rooke reached a big hand around and gripped Cruikshank by the throat and squeezed. The man's face began to turn purple, and he uttered some choking sounds, his hands scrabbling in effectually at the hand on his throat., his feet dangled a few inches off the ground. He wasn't taller than Rooke.

Just as he judged Cruikshank was losing consciousness, he waved at Rook to ease his grip, which he did.

The man coughed and wheezed for a bit, while Rooke kept him upright.

"I trust I've made my point?" Garmon leaned against his desk watching this display of distress dispassionately.

"You—have that!" wheezed the other man.

"Good, next time it won't be you my men bring me, but your son. How old is he? Eight? Ten? Just the right age to be a mud lark. Don't you think? He'll have to earn his living somehow, as he will be an orphan by the end of the week."

"No! You wouldn't!"

"You know better than that. How many men have wound up in the Thames who crossed me? Care me to list them?"

Cruikshank swallowed painfully. "No."

"Good, then pay up by the end of the week, or you'll be joining that illustrious list!" Garmon smiled, but he knew it didn't reach his eyes, it was a grimace, designed to put the fear of God into anyone who witnessed it. He'd practised it for years in his teens and got so good at it, he'd induced many men to lose control of their bowels on sight of it.

"And if you think to disappear, think again. Your son is sojourning with us until you pay up in full."

"He's not! he's with his mother in S-"

"Soho. Yes we picked him up this morning. Don't worry we will take very good care of him. Won't we Mr Rooke."

"That we will Mr Lovell," rumbled Rooke in Cruikshank's ear.

He jumped and shuddered. "You're a cruel man Mr Lovell!"

"I'm a businessman. Which you also claim to be . But unlike you, I pay my debts. Now, do you require any further persuasion to my point of view?"

Garmon advanced on him again and grabbed his hand, twisting the fingers. "I understand you're fond of playing the piano, Mr Cruikshank. Difficult to do with broken fingers."

Cruikshank yelped and whimpered. "I understand Mr Lovell. Truly. You'll get your money. I promise."

"Don't promise, just deliver. You know what will happen if you don't." Garmon let his fingers go.

"I do. I do." He nodded cringing and holding his fingers.

. . .

SOME HOURS later the door opened again and Connor ambled in. Garmon looked up, taking in Connor's casual appearance. Garmon sat back in his chair. "Well did you get the money?"

"Not yet. According to his so-called wife, Tate is dead. I told her I'd be back on Friday to collect. Naturally she claimed not to have the money."

Garmon waved a hand dismissively, he had more things on his mind than another petty debt. "I want you to take a note to Diana from me."

"Alright, but why?" said Connor with a puzzled look.

"I have a plan to get the hell back and this time it's going to work!' He glared at Connor.

Connor flushed. "It wasn't my fault Diana smelled a rat. I did warn you she wouldn't fall for it."

Garmon got up from his desk and paced to the window and back, too restless to sit still. Just thinking about that devil Mowbray and his wretched little ungrateful witch of a wife made his blood boil.

"So, what is the plan?" asked Connor.

With his back still to the room Garmon said, "I plan to lure Diana to the hell ostensibly to meet me. Instead, I want you to kidnap her. We will hold her to ransom until Mowbray surrenders the title deeds to the hell. He dotes on her; he'll do anything to get her back."

"No."

Garmon rounded on Connor. "What do you mean, no?" His heart thudded in his chest, two parts fury to one part anguish at this betrayal.

Connor looked at him steadily. "I mean no. I won't do it. I'll do a lot of things for you Garmon, I've even killed for you. But I won't do this. She's your niece for fucks sake!"

Garmon strode over to the desk and pounded on it with his fist to stop himself hitting Connor with it. "Yes, my treacherous, ungrateful niece! The little bitch betrayed me!" He breathed hard, his vision blurring.

"She's happy Garmon. After everything she went through I'd've thought you of all people would be happy for her. God, have you got no heart? I thought you cared for her!"

"Clearly you do!" Garmon's eyes narrowed.

Connor flushed. "Yes, I do, and there's no need to glare at me like that, it never went further than the odd kiss, she wasn't interested in me and whatever you might think of me I don't force myself on unwilling women!"

Garmon's shoulders twitched and a pang from the bullet wound made him wince. "So, I should fucking hope. You knew what my rules were about Diana, no one was to touch her and that included you! If I'd known, I'd've, had you fucking flogged!"

Connor's face twisted into a grimace. "Yes, you always hide behind your bully boy's, don't you?" Connor shook his head, turning away. "Since you lost the hell, you've lost your mind! I've about had enough of your obsessive madness." He turned back. "I won't let you hurt Diana anymore. Find another way to get the hell back, but don't use her to get it!"

"I'll do as I see fit, and you'll do as you're told!" snapped Garmon.

Connor smiled and it wasn't pretty. "I'm not eight years old any more Garmon, you can't beat me into submission. Get someone else to do your dirty work from now on. I'm out!" he turned and slammed out of the room, his booted feet loud on the wooden stairs. The bang of the back door slamming out into the street left Garmon shaking with rage. He almost went after him, but pride held him in place. *He'd be back. Connor wouldn't leave him. Connor was loyal.*

He swallowed the hard lump in his throat and went to the locked cupboard against the back wall, taking out a key with hands that shook, he fetched out a bottle of whisky and a glass, poured himself a generous tot and tossed it off in a swallow.

Connor's voice echoed in his head: *since you lost the hell you've lost your mind*.

It was true he hadn't been himself since then. He had lost a piece of himself. He wasn't whole without the hell. It was his identity. *Fuck!*

A shudder, remnant of the old fear ran through him, and he reached for the bottle. A second glass steadied his nerves and he put both the bottle and glass back and relocked the cupboard.

CHAPTER 3

 **ive months ago**
        "Jacob!"

The voice behind him made him stop and turn. Moonlight shone on the water of the Thames lapping against the embankment. It was late and he was drunk. He peered at the man walking towards him. He looked eerily familiar, but it couldn't be. He was safely locked up in prison, where Jacob had put him! He took a step, listing with the slope of the embankment. *Fuck he was drunk!* Jacob staggered trying to recover his footing.

The man came to a stop in front of him and the moonlight revealed his features, familiar as his own.

"Elijah!" His heart thudded uneasily in his chest. He forced a grin. "How did you get here?" He put out his arms to hug his twin and Elijah grinned back, a baring of teeth, more than a smile.

"I escaped, no thanks to you! Prick!" Elijah's fist connected with his stomach and sent him flying backwards into the mud.

Pain and nausea swamped Jacob's body, and he turned, struggling to his knees, and vomited into the mud.

Elijah's laugh brought him to his feet with a roar of rage, and he swung wildly. Elijah dodged and laughed again. Jacob staggered after him, sobering by the moment, his vision narrowing to dark, red rage.

"You gave me up, you bastard!" yelled Elijah. "I'll kill you for it, you drunken, sodding fuck!"

Jacob fumbled in his coat pocket and brought out a knife, flicking it open he advanced on his brother. "I don't think so Elijah!"

Elijah closed with him trying to wrest the knife from his hand. The two men swayed and scrabbled, scuffling in the mud, each trying to overbalance the other. Elijah twisted Jacob's arm up his back and with a cry he let go the knife before the bone snapped. Elijah got his arm over Jacob's throat and squeezed.

Jacob's head pounded as he gasped for breath. He stomped on his brother's in-step with his boots and wrenched himself out of his grip. Turning he punched him in the stomach and Elijah stumbled backwards with an ooff, tripped over some driftwood and fell backwards into the water.

Jacob waded in after him. Pulled him up by his shirt and hit him square in the face. Elijah's eyes rolled back, and Jacob let him go. He flopped back into the water, and his head hit something with an audible crack. His body rolled sideways in the water his head going under.

Jacob stood, his head hanging while he tried to bring his own breathing under control. He grasped Elijah's shirt pulling him up again and shook him. His head lolled drunkenly, bloody water streaming off his collar length hair. Jacob dropped his hand into the water and found the rock his brother's head must have hit.

"Fuck!" Jacob howled. He dropped to his knees in the water and shook his brother again, but there was no response.

Panic skittered over his skin, and he looked around. He didn't think anyone had seen what happened. Feverishly he tore his brothers tattered and filthy clothes from his body and stripped off his own. Dressing the other man in his clothing took some time, and he kept looking around to ensure no one was about.

When he had dressed his brother in his trousers, shirt and waist-coat, he towed the body out further into the Thames, where the current caught it, and it floated away from him.

He watched a moment or two, then sniffing, he sloshed back to the shore and put on his brother's wretched clothes, a stained and tattered shirt, and breeches, not much better. He had kept his signet ring, boots and his purse.

He turned and hurried from the embankment up the steps and into the darkness. He needed to find a boat to take him up the river, away from here. Between this accident and the debt to Lovell, London was too hot for him just now. Better to lie low for a bit.

CHAPTER 4

June 1815

Generally, after a day of back-breakingly hard work, Genevra fell into bed and slept like the dead, but thanks to the Irishman's visit, sleep eluded her. The worry she had managed to keep at bay for the rest of the day, spiralled out of control as she fell into the pit of dark despair at 3:00 am.

The night terrors she used to suffer when Jacob returned drunk from some spree with his mates, returned with a vengeance, and she lay shaking under the covers, rigid with fear, a prey to a rigour mortis of panic. Unable to breathe, unable to move, she rode out the attack which left her limp and sodden with sweat and tears.

She fell into a deep slumber just before dawn and was awoken by the clatter of the dray horses on the cobbles beneath her window, bringing today's deliveries.

Dragging herself out of bed, she washed hurriedly in the cold water and scrambled into her clothes, shivering. Bundling up her hair into a knot on the top of her head she bolted downstairs to receive the delivery and thus her day started all over again.

As the day wore on, her determination that she would not

surrender to the terror again grew. She had to be free of this insidious creeping fear before it stole her sanity and her life. And she had to find a way to stave off the debt to this man Lovell. She didn't have five hundred pounds to pay him and even if she did, she had other debts to service as well.

The Tavern was doing relatively well as to daily trade, but Jacob had mismanaged the funds so badly, that when he died, she had discovered a drawer full of unpaid bills. And of course, as soon as word of his death got out, every supplier to whom they owed money had begun to dun her. So, she had done the only thing she could do, turned to her wretched stepfather for a loan. Which he had gleefully agreed to provide, in return for exclusively selling her father's brew, Whittaker's. The move had at least consolidated her debts, but it hadn't made them go away.

She was whittling the debt down, but she wasn't out of the woods yet. Just as she was beginning to think she could be free and clear inside of six months, if trade continued as it was, or sooner if trade improved, this wretched debt from Lovell came to light. She had to find a way to buy time to pay the debt. *But what did she have to barter with?*

She had never heard of Lovell, but a casual enquiry of her tapster, Joe, elicited some disturbing information.

"Lovell?" said Joe pausing in the act of connecting the hose pump to the cask of beer. "Aye I've heard of him. The hell is popular with the swells. By all accounts he grew up in St Giles, son of a prostitute or some such, but his talent for cards earned him enough to set up the hell."

"How old is he?" Genevra stopped stacking bottles of wine to push the pins back into her bun which was threatening to fall. She was wondering if the Irishman was actually Lovell himself, under a false name.

Joe shrugged. "Forty maybe?" *No, the Irishman wasn't that old, closer to her own age she guessed.*

"Does he have a family? A wife?"

"Not that I've heard of. Why do you ask?"

"Jacob had some dealings with him, I was just curious," she said carelessly.

"Well, I'd stay out of it. By all accounts he's a dangerous man to cross, with a long reach as I understand, and a might of men at his beck and call to do what he wants. He's not the sort you'd want to be mixed up with," Joe said, straightening and giving her a fatherly look of concern.

She forced a smile. "Thanks Joe, I appreciate the warning, but I'm not about to tangle with him," she lied. "I was just curious when I came across his name in some of Jacob's papers that is all."

An idea, distasteful as it was, was forming in her mind. There was one thing she could offer that might persuade the man to give her more time. *Could she, do it? The idea of offering herself to man of violence...* She shuddered and swallowed as her stomach knotted up. *No, she couldn't, anything but that. Perhaps there was some other service she could perform for him? But what?*

She would first try to play upon his good nature, if he had any. Joe's words and the words of the Irishman, suggested that he didn't, *but no man was all bad, was he?*

Except Jacob. Her heart sank. In a world in which Jacob Tate existed, good men were few and far between. It was probably too much to hope that Garmon Lovell had a smidgen of compassion in his apparently ruthless heart, but she had to try to find it if he did.

She would leave it until Thursday night to pay him a visit and hope her courage didn't fail her. She had to save the Tavern; not only her own livelihood, but those of her staff, depended on it. If Lovell should foreclose on her, she would lose everything she had fought so hard to retain and could end in debtor's prison. It didn't bear thinking of.

But then neither did offering her body to a man she didn't know. One who was likely to be as bad, if not worse, than Jacob. *No one could be worse than Jacob, could they?*

If she had survived Jacob, she could survive this. One night in exchange for financial freedom, what could he do to her in one night that was any worse than what she had been subjected to for years? It was worth it. It had to be. If her courage held... Was she brave enough or would fear continue to control her? Take away her choices? She could do it. She had to.

TWO NIGHTS LATER, Connor hadn't returned, and Garmon's temper was at breaking point. He had sent his boys out to find Connor, and they had come back saying no one had seen him since Monday. He hadn't returned to his lodgings, nor had he been seen at his usual haunts, such as the Bucket of Blood.

Garmon's shoulders twitched, and his wound ached. *Where was he? Had he left London altogether? And if so, where could he have gone?*

A pain in his chest persisted, and he blamed it on the stew he'd eaten for dinner.

He couldn't wait any longer to execute his plan against the Mowbray's. It would have to be tomorrow night.

DIANA, Duchess of Mowbray, received the note from the hand of a dirty urchin in the middle of Bond Street, and the creature was gone before she could question him, leaving her with a grubby piece of paper and the lingering odour of the Thames in his wake. *One of Uncle Garmon's mudlarks.* Opening the crumpled sheet, she read the note and then stuffed it in her reticule.

"Who was that, your Grace?" asked her maid.

"No one my dear," said Diana frowning. *What was Uncle Garmon up to this time?* She debated whether to show the note to Anthony and decided against it. She could deal with Uncle herself. If she brought Anthony into it, he'd likely kill Garmon (or die trying), and she wasn't about to let that happen.

GENEVRA SURVEYED her appearance in the glass. Her deep blue eyes seemed too big, dominating her face. *Did the weariness in her bones show in her eyes?* She tried smiling to dispel the heaviness in her quaking heart. *She would not be afraid. She had to do this.* The alternative was unthinkable. *One night wouldn't kill her. She had survived much worse.* She straightened her shoulders and smiled again, bobbing a curtsy to her reflection. Her heart lifted a little, but she was still conscious of a brittleness in her nerves. *She was afraid, but she wouldn't surrender to it.*

She had donned her best gown, a cream satin that complimented her creamy skin and gave her hair a luminous glow. Romantics called her hair colouring strawberry blonde, she had always just thought of it as carrot coloured, she wasn't accustomed to thinking about her appearance a lot. But looking in the mirror she had hopes that she was tempting enough to persuade Lovell to look upon her situation with compassion. Not that Mr Mor had shown any. *Like master like servant?*

It was a gown she hadn't worn in a while, *when did she have time for evening gowns these days?* And the bodice was a little tight, causing her breasts to appear as if they were about to burst from their confines. Which, given the nature of her errand, was probably not a bad thing. All the same, it made her distinctly uncomfortable. She wasn't a whore and behaving like one, even for a cause such as this, didn't sit well.

Her mother would be mortified and her stepfather–the thought of Hiram's face if he should get wind of this escapade made her smile and strengthened her resolve. If there was one thing she was determined on, it was that Hiram would not continue to exert control over her future. She would pay his blasted debt down as soon as she possibly could, and if getting a stay of execution on this one from Lovell would allow that, she could do whatever it took to achieve it.

What she refused to think about was what her real father would think of this. On that thought, she very firmly shut the door. Papa wasn't here to save her. He was dead and gone these many years. There was no one to look out for her except herself, and she had people she was responsible for. *She could do this. She had to do this.*

A simple gold locket that her parents had given her on the occasion of her marriage, and her only piece of jewellery, nestled just above her cleavage and drew further attention to the generous pillows of her breasts.

Her heart quaked, and she wondered briefly if she should change into something less blatant. But her experience of men told her that the more alluring she looked, the more likely she was to get what she wanted. Men were incurably weakened by female charms. Even Jacob had been vulnerable to seduction unless he was so blind drunk or furious that nothing and no one could reason with him.

She had dressed her strawberry curls in an elegant knot on the top of her head, but try as she might, she couldn't prevent the wisps of curls falling round her face. Her gloves, were grubby and had holes in the fingers, so she couldn't wear those. Her reticule was still clean and intact, but her evening slippers had also suffered some accident while stored, the ribbons were ruined and the fabric stained, forcing her to exchange them for a sturdier pair of kid boots.

She flung her cloak over the ensemble and strode purposefully towards the door.

Half an hour later she stepped down from the hackney carriage in St James Street and approached the discreet entrance to the four-story mansion that was, she was reliably told, Lovell's gaming establishment. The building was well maintained and lights in the windows told her that it was occupied. She paused looking up at the entrance.

A carriage drew up behind her, but before she could even turn to see who it might be, an explosion of pain to the back of her head made everything go black. The last thing she remembered as she crumpled towards the pavement was of hands grabbing her round the waist and lifting her bodily off her feet.

DIANA WAS ATTENDING the theatre with her husband and the Stantons that evening. So typical of Uncle Garmon's arrogance that he thought she could just drop everything to obey his summons. With his note burning a hole in her reticule, she vowed to deal with him tomorrow.

GENEVRA WOKE to a thumping ache in her skull and the realisation that she was bound to a chair and gagged, with a musty hessian bag over her head, through which she could see nothing except a faint light from candles. She made a noise in her throat and pulled at her bonds, shaking the chair in her efforts to rise, which failed. Both her wrists and ankles were tied, and she was, in-turn, tied to the chair. The gag tasted foul and for a panicked moment she thought she would be sick and choke to death.

Just then a door opened, and a man's voice said, "Good God!" the next moment the bag was ripped from her head and a brown haired, handsome male of forty-something years, judging from the grey at his temples and the lines round his hazel eyes, was glaring at her.

He was of just above average height and moderately broad through the shoulders, he was dressed casually in shirt, beeches and boots. With his sleeves rolled up, his magnificent forearms were on display and the open collar of his shirt showed his throat and a glimpse of a hairy chest. His masculinity and power fairly screamed at her. Whoever this was he was not a man to cross, that was obvious. He rounded on the two men behind him.

"You imbeciles, it's the wrong woman! Fuck, do I have to do everything myself!" He turned back to survey Genevra, and she made an urgent noise in her throat. "Ungag and untie her for God's sake and get out!" the men hurried to obey him, muttering profuse apologies.

"Sorry Mr Lovell sir!"

So, this was Garmon Lovell. Why had Jacob been so foolish as to get himself into debt with such a man?

Her heart thudded in panic, fury poured off the man in waves, *why had he had her kidnapped? But he'd said she was the wrong woman. Why was he kidnapping women off the street?*

She took a deep breath when the gag was removed. Which made her cough and the sore spot on the back of head throb. As her hands were freed, she brought them to her face to cover her mouth, embarrassed.

"Get out!" said Lovell, his eyes flashing green in the candle-light. She jumped, then realised he was speaking to his men and waving them out as they obsequiously backed out and shut the door.

His mouth compressed in a line of consternation and his brows drew down in a frown as he regarded her distress. He turned away and got out a decanter and glasses pouring out two generous tots of golden liquid.

"Here," he said, handing her a glass. "I'm sorry."

She wiped her streaming eyes with a handkerchief from her reticule and sniffed the glass cautiously. *Whisky.* This had not gone at all how she had imagined. She glanced around the room, *where was she? In the gaming hell?* Her heart was still thudding hard, and her nerves were jangled to pieces. *What now?* How could she recover from this? She felt all off kilter.

She swallowed a mouthful of the whisky and discovered it was a good drop. It burned all the way down but settled her nerves in the process.

"Thank you," she said putting down the glass on the low table to her right and taking a better look round the room. Apart from the chair and table beside her, it contained a desk with a chair and cabinet against the wall. It was very plain, not the sort of room she imagined would be inside a gaming hell like Lovell's.

"My apologies ma'am, you were in the wrong place at the wrong time, and I employ fools!" He said, casting his eyes over her. It was difficult to discern what he was thinking. His eyes appeared more green than hazel in the candlelight now. *What would he do with her?*

His scrutiny was thorough and unsettling.

Her skin prickled as she wondered if he was looking for injuries or appreciating what he was looking at. She pulled her cloak over her exposed bosom, suddenly conscious of her assets being in full view.

"May I know your name?" he asked.

"Mrs Tate," she said and waited for him to connect the dots.

"Mrs-" He frowned in an effort of memory. "Ah Jacob Tate's widow I presume?"

"Yes," she said.

"And what were you doing outside Lovell's at 8:00 pm in-" He paused and took in her appearance. "An evening gown?"

"Calling upon you Mr Lovell," she said striving for some composure. If she was to present her case she needed her wits about her. "Before I was assaulted by your men. Do you make it a habit to kidnap women off the street?"

"No, I do not. As I said, you were not the target of my men. They mistook you for someone else."

"My misfortune is some other lady's fortune then?" she said with a slight edge to her tone.

He raised his eyebrows. At least his temper seemed to have cooled somewhat. Her skipping pulse settled down, and she took another sip of the whisky. He filled a glass for himself and offered to refill hers. She held it out and let him. She needed all the Dutch courage she could get in this situation. *He didn't seem inclined to throw her out, so perhaps she would have an opportunity to ask for clemency after all?*

She took another sip of the really quite excellent whisky and tried for a nonchalant tone, "I certainly didn't expect to be ushered into your presence bound and gagged."

He smiled at her mild joke and bowed his head, "you have my deepest apologies. Were you hurt?"

"I received a blow to the back of the head, which is somewhat painful, yes."

He frowned and set down his glass, stepping towards her and skirting behind her chair.

"Tip your head forward," his voice was crisp with command, and she obeyed without thinking. His fingertips touched the back of her skull lightly and a shiver prickled over the nape of her neck and down her spine. A whiff of his scent, something woodsy and spicy assailed her nostrils. A finger trailed down her nape and her whole body jerked in reaction as an unaccustomed heat bloomed between her legs. She gasped and the finger withdrew abruptly.

"I apologise for my men's brutality, but I doubt that the blow has done any lasting damage." He moved back to the desk where he resumed his glass of whisky.

Perhaps it was the scent of his cologne or the effect of his touch, but the man before her was suddenly better looking than she could have hoped for and the way he was looking at her made her pulse dance in nervous anticipation.

"What were you wanting to say to me?" He leaned on the edge

of the desk and crossed his ankles, a slight smile curved his lips, and her heart skipped a beat for an entirely different cause than fear.

She swallowed and summoned her best smile. "You must understand, Mr Lovell, that I had no notion of the debt my husband owed you until Mr Mor came to see me the other day."

"So, you say, but what proof do I have that your husband is dead? Perhaps he sent you here in the hopes that you will soften me up?"

"I can assure you my husband is dead Mr Lovell." she said through clenched teeth. "If you wish me to furnish you proof, I will gladly take you to the St Giles Church cemetery where you can view his gravestone. He was unequivocally dead as a door nail when they drew his body from the Thames with his face half chewed off!"

He raised his brows at this graphic description but seemed unmoved by it. *But then if he'd grown up in St Giles, he would be used to such horrors daily.*

He bowed politely. "You have my condolences Mrs Tate."

"Save your breath! I was never so glad of anything in my life!" she said frankly.

"I see. How long has he been ah–dead?"

"I don't know precisely. He disappeared back in February. They fished his body out of the Thames just over three months ago. I was able to identify him by his clothes, what was left of his face and the general shape of his form, despite its bloated condition. His signet ring was missing, but no doubt the assailant who killed him stole that."

"I see. And might I enquire why you were so elated to be rid of him?"

"I'd rather not go into that, suffice it to say that I was not happy in my marriage Mr Lovell."

"How long were you married for?"

"Five years." She swallowed, her jaw clenching.

"I see the subject is distressing for you," he said quietly. "Perhaps we should return to the point at issue?"

She took a breath and shook her head to shake off the memories and straightened her shoulders. "As I said, I am not in a position to repay such a huge sum immediately. If you will give me some time -"

"The debt is outstanding by several month's madam." His voice was gentle, but it held an implacable note that sent a tendril of fear skittering down her spine.

"I know, but as I said, I wasn't aware of it until the other day." Time to implement her plan, if she dared. Panic rippled through her body and her stomach knotted, her hand clenching on her glass. *I can't do this!*

But then she thought of the Tavern and her staff and everything she had worked so hard for, and stubborn resolution came to her aid and stiffened her backbone. *At least the man wasn't ugly, old or obese. In fact, he was quite attractive, decidedly masculine. Something in the way he handled himself called to her at an elemental level, drawing a response from her body, that nullified her fear. She could do this. She had to.*

She set the glass down on the table and undid the clasp of her cloak, letting it fall back over the chair and rose.

"Surely you must agree that to find such a vast sum as that is not possible in the twinkling of an eye. I have a business to run, and if you will but give me a few months -"

"What business?"

"The Globe Tavern on Brewery Yard, I thought you knew that was my husband's business?" It was the business she was trying to save, if he foreclosed on her, she could be declared bankrupt and sent to debtor's prison. She suppressed a shudder at the thought.

Yes, she had to do this, that alternative was worse, far worse than whatever Mr Lovell could do to her. He was more attractive than she could have wished for and if his temper was uncertain, she could only hope he wouldn't turn it against her. She wasn't sure what she would do if he did and at all costs, she must not show her weakness.

His eyebrows rose and a thoughtful expression came over his face. She wasn't sure if this was a good or a bad thing.

"My business is reasonably profitable sir, I can, if you give me sufficient time, repay the debt either by installments or if you wish to wait, the full sum in one go. But it will take me some months to accumulate such a large amount." She waited with bated breath and a fast-beating heart for his reaction.

He pursed his lips and regarded her with a sapient eye. "And why would I do you this favour?"

Because your men assaulted me in the street and kidnapped me! But she knew that even if she took the case to the magistrate she would be unlikely to get any redress. Joe had made it clear the Mr Lovell's power reached far and wide, including Bow Street. She swallowed and straightened her spine, taking a steadying breath.

This was it, she had better make it convincing. Putting up a hand to the locket, she toyed with it lightly, drawing attention to her breasts and like an obedient dog, Mr Lovell's eyes followed her fingers and snagged on her cleavage. She took a breath, heaving them slightly and glanced at him under her lashes. She dropped her voice a little and said softly, "Perhaps we could come to some arrangement?"

He put down his glass and rose, stepping towards her, and she discovered that he was a full head taller than her. Since she was tall for a woman this was unusual and gave her an oddly vulnerable feeling.

"And what arrangement might that be Mrs Tate?" he asked. Like hers, his voice had dropped, and his eyes had taken on a smoky look. *So that frisson of attraction she had felt when he touched the nape of her neck was returned?* She glanced down and was pleased to see a slight bulge in his breeches. The crackle of tension between them suddenly went up a notch and a rush of heat flooded her body, pooling between her legs with a pleasurable buzz. The intensity of it took her breath away.

She licked her lower lip and opened her mouth to reply and was stopped by his descending on hers. They pressed, warm and soft, creating a tingling pleasure she had never experienced before. His lips moved over hers, teasing and inciting. His hands held her face gently, guiding her where he wanted her.

Her body reacted like tinder to a flame. Her lips parted instinctively to take his tongue, and she arched her neck to get closer as he explored her mouth with a thoroughness that turned her insides liquid with unwonted desire. Jacob had never kissed her like that, if he had perhaps she would have been a more willing bed mate.

When he broke the kiss, they were both breathing quickly, and she had her hands on his shoulders for balance, because her knees had gone to jelly. The fiery tingle between her legs was something that she hadn't felt in an age, and made her stupid for a moment, she just gaped at him.

"Did I misunderstand you Mrs Tate?" he asked with a smile that made her nipples go taught. *Oh God, this man!*

His hands dropped to rest on her waist, warm through the fabric of her gown, they squeezed gently, the thumbs tracing circles on her belly. Tendrils of sensation coursed through her body; this she hadn't bargained on. Suddenly the price she would have to pay to save the Tavern seemed far more attractive than she had thought it would be.

She swallowed. "No, I think you have taken my meaning very well Mr Lovell. I will spend the night with you in exchange for a stay of three months to enable me to pay the debt."

"A month for two nights," he responded promptly with a wicked smile that made her heart flip and her body tremble. Shaking her head to rid it of the ridiculous impulse to agree to any terms he nominated, she summoned her anger instead.

"That's outrageous! Certainly not!"

"Seven nights -"

She gasped and he went on, "and you can have three months clear, and a further three months to pay the debt down in full."

She stared at him mulling this over. "Three months, before I need pay anything at all?" she queried.

"Yes, and six months from today's date to pay it in full."

That would give her time to pay down some of her debt to her horrid stepfather before she need address this one. "Done," she said holding out her hand.

He grinned and shook it, then he kissed it. His lips were soft and warm on the back of her hand and sent a tingle all the way to her core, causing her cheeks to flush.

"I want that in writing," she said swiftly, making a recover.

"You're a shrewd businesswoman Mrs Tate, I like that." He turned to the desk, drew a sheet of paper from a drawer and taking up a pen he swiftly wrote the terms of their agreement on the page, signed it, and dipping his signet in the ink pressed the design into the page. "Your signature madam," he passed her the pen, and she dipped it in the inkwell and read the terms before signing.

He took the pen back from her and drawing her into his arms he said, "And no time like the present, to begin."

CHAPTER 5

Garmon held her gaze with his as he lowered his head to kiss her again, very well pleased with the bargain he had struck. From the moment he clapped eyes on her, Mrs Tate had exerted a certain fascination. Those eyes, so deep a blue, seemed familiar in some way, but for the life of him he couldn't think why. And when he touched the back of her skull through those impossibly ginger curls, and caught a whiff of her natural perfume, he hadn't been able to resist touching the nape of her neck. It had taken some control not to touch his lips to that tempting creamy skin, then and there.

Whether it was her vivid blue eyes, creamy skin with a hint of freckles, her luscious strawberry blonde hair that was threatening to come undone round her beautiful face, or her generous breasts, he didn't know. But when she made it clear she was prepared to horse trade over the debt, he'd known then he wanted her.

That kiss had seared his bones. It had admittedly been a while since he'd been with a woman, and abstinence always did lend a spice, but even so, he couldn't recall a kiss that had burned hotter than that one, and he was eager for another and more of Mrs Tate. *What was her cursed name?*

"By the way, what is your name?" he asked, his mouth hovering over hers.

"Genevra," she said her voice husky.

"Genevra," he repeated, liking the taste of it. "Mine is Garmon, if you care to use it." And then he closed the gap between their lips and plundered her mouth with his tongue.

His hands running over her back, moved down to grasp her generous bottom, the perfect complement to her bounteous breasts. He liked a woman with curves and Mrs Tate–Genevra–had them in abundance. And she was tall enough that he didn't need to stoop to kiss her, yet she was small enough to fit perfectly into his embrace and remind him she was everything a man could desire.

His cock, which had hardened the moment he touched her delectable nape, was rigid and demanding now, but he intended this encounter not only to satisfy him, but her as well. She deserved that at least, his men had used her badly and almost more than what she had said, it was what she *hadn't* said about her husband that told him she deserved a little pleasure, and it was no hardship to him to give it to her.

Nothing was more arousing than a woman in the throes of lust and if he didn't miss his guess, Genevra was swept away as strongly as he was by the connection between them. It was rare, this kind of physical attraction, and he meant to make the most of it, as long as it would last. It would burn itself out, he had no doubt, *but while it burned...*

He reached up to undo the buttons on the back of her dress, intending to loosen her too-tight bodice that showed her undoubted assets to such advantage. But as his hand touched the buttons he felt her stiffen and caught the soft inhale of apprehension. Finely attuned to female fear from his youth growing up in

a brothel, he sensed the sudden wave of resistance in her and
stilled his hand.

"Hush," he murmured into her hair, bringing her close against
and stroking her back soothingly. "You have nothing to fear from
me, I won't hurt you. I derive no pleasure from hurting women, I
promise you. On the contrary, it is their pleasure I crave." He
soothed her like a startled mare until he felt her relax in his arms.
Smiling into her hair his cock twitched. She smelled delicious.

"Alright?" he asked softly.

She nodded, her face against his shoulder.

He resumed undoing the buttons on the back of her dress as
she leaned against him, and slid the short, puffed sleeves off her
shoulders. Leaning back so that he could see her bosom as it was
revealed he rubbed his thumbs over the soft creamy skin in the
hollow between shoulder and breast, and pushed the fabric down
slowly to reveal more of her breasts.

He glanced at her face and registered no further sign of
apprehension, just a kind of dazed fascination.

Reassured of her willingness to proceed, he bent and kissed
the smooth warm expanse of bosom, his tongue traced a pattern
over her skin, dipping between the swell of her breasts into the
valley of her cleavage. Her natural scent wafted up to him and
made his aroused cock twitch. He loved the scent of her, clean
and pure and sweet. He swallowed an involuntary groan. Desire
for this woman invaded every sense, tightening the muscles of his
body with want.

He eased the fabric down further, revealing the pink circles of
her aureole and finally the pert nubs of her nipples, tight and
proud against the white skin of her plump breasts.

"Beautiful," he murmured running his tongue over one nipple
and feeling her jerk in reaction, listening to her intake of breath.
His skin prickled reciprocally, and he grinned suckling the
nipple, cupping a round globe, and enjoying the heft of it, the soft
fullness in his palm. Engulfing the other in his left hand, his

fingers and thumb rolled the nipple and elicited another reaction from her. She leaned in closer, her hands grasping his shirt, a little whimper escaping her lips. His cock jumped again in sympathy. Want heated his blood.

Such sensitive nipples! Not all women had them, but Genevra, certainly did. He filed the information away for further reference. One of his ambitions was to make a woman come from playing with her nipples alone. *Could Genevra be a candidate for that particular fantasy?*

He transferred his mouth to the other nipple and suckled and licked it, enjoying the little gasps and twitches that told him she was enjoying this treatment.

Finally, he raised his head and kissed her mouth again, and she pressed closer, her arms going round his neck and her body plastering to his.

His arms held her close as he deepened the kiss, tongue and lips devouring. His hands roamed over her back and descended for another hard squeeze of her bottom, pressing her into his aching cock. *God, he wanted her!*

He swung her round and propped her bottom on the edge of the desk. Pushing up her petticoats, he ran his hands up the inside of her thighs, easing them apart and positioning himself between them.

Her breath hitched as he watched her face, her eyes wide, her lips swollen from his kisses.

His thumbs rubbed circles on her flesh at the top of her thighs, running along the crease, skimming the curls covering her intimate flesh.

"Lie back," he murmured. She eased back onto her elbows, watching him warily. *What did she think he was going to do?*

His thumbs edged upwards onto her labia and pulled the soft flesh apart with deliberate slow circles. He dragged his eyes from hers, he wanted to see what he was doing to her flesh. He pushed her skirts up higher and viewed her mound, covered in strawberry blonde curls slightly darker than the ones on her head. He smiled.

He moved a hand to spear her lips with his finger. She was slippery satin; he pushed his finger down parting her pink dewy lips and listened to her gasp. He reached the entrance to her body and swirled around the place, feeling the wet heat of her on the pad of his fingertip.

Her sweet musky scent wafted up to him, and he swallowed another groan as his cock twitched and leaked behind his falls. His balls tightened, aching with need. He ignored the urge to take her swiftly. She needed more, to make her ready. *But when she was ready...* he swallowed the saliva gathering in anticipation.

He drew his finger back upward towards the nub of her most intense pleasure, listening for her reaction, watching her flesh twitch and weep as he traced up and down between her lips.

This time she groaned, and his stomach muscles contracted in sympathy. *Fuck this was fun. When was the last time he'd enjoyed arousing a woman this much?*

He continued to move his finger up and down between her lips and listened to her moans and panting breaths, watched her flesh twitch and her thighs tremble. Reaching her entrance, he pushed a finger inside her and delighted in the tight, wet heat of her.

God yes, he wanted his cock in there.

He slid in and out of her, added a second finger and listened to her panting breath.

Slowly he knelt and bent forward setting his lips to her flesh, inhaled her scent. He speared her with his tongue, and she jumped under him, uttering a strangled noise.

"What, ohh..." her voice disintegrated into something incoherent, and he licked her sweet silky flesh, she tasted delicious.

Settling to his task, he licked and suckled, sliding his fingers in and out with increasing speed, adding a third finger to stretch her, make her ready to take him.

Her breathing accelerated, accompanied by little moans and incoherent noises, her hips rolling.

His cock jerked in his falls leaking more fluid, and he judged she was ready for a thorough fucking, because frankly he couldn't wait any longer.

"Ready, Genevra?" His voice came out husky, he couldn't remember when he'd last been this aroused. "I want to *fuck* you." His tone going gravelly on the word, his muscles pulling tight with the need.

Her eyes were wide, the pupils blown, her lips swollen and red. Her body tightened in response, *she felt it too, the urgency, the ache of wanting!* He clenched his teeth against a groan.

She swallowed and nodded. *Thank God she hadn't changed her mind.* He'd never forced a woman, but his level of arousal would be hard to step back from at this point. *He wanted her. Savagely.*

He rose, scrabbling urgently at his falls with his left hand, and released his rigid aching cock. His pulse thudded in his ears, his breathing kicking up in anticipation.

Straightening, he removed his fingers and lining up his cock, he pressed the head to her entrance. Pausing to savour the moment, he then pushed forward firmly and slid effortlessly inside her, she was wet and open, taking him easily.

For a moment he held still, swallowing the groan that threatened to burst from his throat and just absorbed the searing pleasure of being engulfed in tight, wet, heat. He leaned forward and found her eyes again. Wide and shocked, her cheeks pink, her lovely breasts heaving with every breath, her hair a tangled pink halo round her head. *Deliciously fuckable!*

"Good sweetheart?" he asked, panting in anticipation of what was to come. He certainly hoped so, good was a poor word to describe what he was feeling, *bloody fucking marvellous might come close.*

She nodded again, and he gripped her hips and began to stroke inside her, slow easy thrusts designed to make this last as long as possible. *God, it felt so good.* He closed his eyes to savour the pleasure wafting over his skin and sinking into his bones.

After a few strokes, she began to move under him, her hips responding to his thrusts and disrupting his steady rhythm.

"That's right," he muttered. "Fuck me!" he thrust harder, deeper.

Her gasps became louder, and she moved more frantically, her panting became mingled with moans and other noises that set his blood racing. He moved a shaking hand from her hip to swirl over her place of pleasure and bring her the satisfaction she was clearly craving.

His body was wound tight as a coiled spring, his breathing laboured, and his pulse thudded hard in his ears and chest. The pleasure fuddling his senses made it harder to concentrate on hers, and he lost his rhythm, his strokes and caresses becoming erratic. His balls pulled tight, and he groaned helplessly, losing control.

"God Genevra!" he ground out. His voice gone gravelly with deep, bone aching desire.

She cried out and her body arched under him, shuddering and the avalanche of pleasure he had been trying to hold at bay, broke loose and rolled over and through him.

He groaned, balls deep, unable to keep it in. The flood of hot pleasure took his breath away. He groaned, grunted and cursed. His cock jerked and loosed his seed in four strong jets, tumbling into a series of smaller rippling aftershocks. Poleaxed by the trembling pleasure, he collapsed slowly on her body, breathing hard. "Fuck!" he whispered.

God yes! That was how a fuck was supposed to feel! He closed his eyes absorbing the pleasurable aftermath of lassitude flowing through his body and weakening his knees.

He laughed with the sheer joy of it, a feeling of euphoria he had not felt in a long time flooding his body and mind.

Yes, that was a glorious, stupendous fuck!

With an effort he lifted his head and looked down at her. "God, I hope you enjoyed that because I sure as hell did."

She lay with her hands above her head a look of dazed relaxation on her face. She licked her lips. "Yes," her voice was husky. "That was incredible."

He lifted himself on his hands. "Don't tell me that was your first release?"

She flushed. And shook her head. "No, just the first like this."

"The first with a man?"

She nodded, closing her eyes as if ashamed. Which he found strangely touching.

"Hey sweetheart, that's not your fault. It's his." He stroked the tendrils of hair off her face. "Look at me."

She opened her eyes and blinked at him, and he kissed her, a soft touch of the lips. "Thank you," he murmured and then rising he disengaged their bodies and rebuttoned his falls.

She sat up and pushed her skirts down, pulling up her bodice.

"Here let me do you up," he said as she slid off the desk. He buttoned up her bodice and rested his hands on her shoulders. He felt an unaccustomed tenderness towards her, following that intense release. Normally he could wait to be rid of the whore he'd fucked, but Genevra wasn't a whore. It was different with her.

"I will send you home in my carriage."

"You have a carriage?" she asked looking round at him.

He smiled. "Yes, I have a carriage. I will send it to pick you up tomorrow night."

"Send it at eleven, the bar closes at ten and that will give me time to close up and for the staff to leave. Only Mrs Bell, the cook and her son Neil, live on the premises with me. Joe and his boys and the bar maids all live elsewhere." She was all practicality, he liked that. A business woman through and through.

"Eleven it shall be. I look forward to it." he said with a smile, already thinking of things he wanted to do to her, share with her.

WREN ST CLAIRE

Clearly her experience of pleasure was limited. Her husband had used her badly from what he could gather. The thought made his blood surge with anger towards the deceased Jacob Tate.

She nodded looking down.

He kissed her hair and murmured in her ear. "We have a week of delights ahead of us, Genevra. Tonight, was just a taster." He'd not even thought of using a French letter, he'd been too eager for her, and he didn't think he could bring himself to do so going forward, it would mute the pleasure too much. *If she came here with the intent to let him fuck her perhaps she took precautions? Used a sponge or oils? If she hadn't...*

He would speak to her about it next time. If there were consequences he would take care of her, it would be worth it for a week of the kind of pleasure they had just shared. His body was still tingling with it.

She nodded again and moved out of his embrace to pick up her cloak. She seemed a bit subdued.

He looked at her with some concern. "You're not regretting it are you?"

She looked up as she flung her cloak round her shoulders. "No. I'm just realising what I've been missing," she said with that devastating frankness he found so refreshing.

He smiled and kissed her forehead. "Plenty more of that my dear." Her words confirmed his suspicions and he resolved to make this week a journey of discovery for her. By the end of it she would be mistress of her body in ways she couldn't even imagine yet.

And along the way he would explore and exploit every last drop of pleasure she could offer him. His cock twitched at the thought, and he fleetingly thought of keeping her here for another round.

He looked at her face and traced the weariness there. *No, she'd had enough tonight. It would keep until tomorrow night.*

. . .

40

SHE STEPPED up into the carriage and was surprised at how luxuriously appointed it was. Relaxing back against the squabs she reflected that the evening had turned out far better than she had hoped. She had secured a stay on the debt with the time to repay it and enjoyed a very pleasurable interlude with an exceedingly attractive man, who for all his fearsome reputation as a violent brute and bully, had been both considerate and tender in a way that she was completely unused to.

For the first time she truly understood the pleasure to be had between a man and woman. Her experiences with Jacob had been brutish and short for the most part. Even in the beginning of their marriage when she still fancied herself in love with him, before he grew violent and hurt her, their encounters had never gone on long enough to bring her to fulfilment, had never been preceded by enough kisses and caresses and strokes to sufficiently arouse her, or to prevent it hurting when he took her.

In fact, she generally got little warning of when he wanted to take her. He would grab her and fondle her breasts briefly or push up her skirts and push his fingers inside her, mutter something obscene and moments later he would either bend her over some convenient piece of furniture, push her up against a wall or throw her to the bed or the floor and push himself inside her. If she resisted, he would slap her and hold her wrists until they bruised.

If he was drunk, he might punch her if she tried to evade him or fought back. He was big and much stronger than her, and it always ended with her getting hurt if she tried to resist him, so she learned not to. She learned to take it in silence, but her lack of responsiveness would often displease him too, and he'd curse her and slap or punch her for not enjoying it.

The contrast between her previous experience and tonight's interlude with Garmon was so stark, it had her in shock. *For a start he kissed her and oh God what kisses!* For those alone she would have let him do anything to her that he wanted, they melted her bones and set fire to the place between her legs in a way no man ever had.

Then he'd licked and fondled her breasts extracting such tingling pleasure from them, she had never known was possible, and finally he touched her between her legs eliciting a fiery pleasure from her sticky swollen flesh, so sharp it almost hurt. His touch was even more pleasurable than she was able to achieve herself.

And then he used his mouth on her. She sighed with the memory. She had heard of such a thing, other women talked of course, and men made lewd suggestions and gestures with their tongues, but she had never conceived of it being so extraordinarily delightful. Combined with his fingers inside her, it had brought her perilously close to exploding. And then to her frustration he had stopped.

But then when he took her, filled her, stretched her and instead of it hurting, it had been divine. Right. As if he belonged there inside her. She sighed again. And his strokes drove her towards the pinnacle again and this time when she reached it and went over, it was marvellous. So deeply pleasurable she wallowed in the memory of it.

And the double pleasure of feeling *his* release had been a surprise too. She had not known it was possible to derive pleasure from the sensation of a man's releasing his seed, but the hot rush of it triggered a second smaller wave of pleasure in her and a bone deep satisfaction followed in its wake. As if something primal and right had just been achieved. As if she had experienced something for which she had been born to accomplish.

Which was absurd. Wasn't it?

The prospect of a week of such pleasures made her laugh out loud for sheer joy.

CHAPTER 6

our months ago
      Jacob got off the ferry at Richmond and wandered up the High Street in search of a drink.

The Red Boar Tavern had a familiar hops and malt smell that welcomed him. He ordered a pot of porter and a meal. The bar keep eyed him askance because of his clothing but when he produced the coin, he served him.

He sat at the bar on a high stool and drank and ate, watching the bar maid circulate the room dodging gropes and lewd comments from the clientele. She was built on generous lines, which her old-fashioned bustier cut low across the bosom accentuated. Her hips swayed as she sashayed her way round the room. His cock stirred as she bent over to retrieve some empty pots and return them to the bar, giving him a nice view of her cleavage.

She returned to the bar with her tray of empty pots and picked up another load of full ones. He leaned over and smiled. Jacob knew how to be charming when he needed to be.

"Those men giving you any bother sweetheart?"

She glanced at him and wrinkled her nose. He didn't look or smell good at the moment; he knew that his brother's clothes stank. "Forgive my attire, I gave my clothes to a poor beggar who needed them and took his instead. I'll buy myself some new ones in the morning."

"Why would you do that?"

"The fellow came to my aid when I was set upon by thugs," he waved at the bruising on his face and knuckles. "I wanted to reward him."

"Oh," her face softened, and she smiled. Leaning in and giving him an even better view of her lovely bosom, she said softly, "I can handle the men, but thanks for asking, my name's Maggie by the way."

"Jacob," he said, raising his pot in toast to her and smiling at her over the rim.

Her smile widened, and she swung away to deliver her next round of drinks. He sat at the bar and bided his time, exchanging glances and smiles with her every so often.

The patrons were getting drunker and more troublesome by the hour. When one of them lunged at Maggie and tried to pull her into his lap, Jacob rose stepped towards them. "Let go of her!"

The drunk, a wolfish man with a beard and a torn and stained waistcoat over a potbelly and broad chest, laughed. "Whose gonna make me, you?" His expression of contempt took in Jacob's clothes and battered appearance. "Looks like you've been in one fight too many already," he added clamping Maggie more tightly as she wriggled in his lap. "Sit still sweetheart, or you'll feel the flat of my hand!"

Maggie elbowed him in the stomach, and he let her go with an "oof". She leapt to her feet and Jacob closed in, gabbing the man by the throat and hauling him out of his seat. The man wrenched himself out of Jacob's grip but not before he had bruised his throat. The man swung wildly, Jacob dodged and landed a punch to his jaw, the man went down heavily.

His friends all rose and converged on Jacob and the publican yelled sharply, "take it outside, or I'll call the constable!"

The man Jacob had knocked flat sat up groggily and was helped up by a mate. Holding his jaw, he threw Jacob a sour look and limped out of the Tavern with his mate. The other men resumed their seats with some venomous looks and mutters in Jacob's direction. Maggie returned to her rounds and Jacob went back to his third pot of porter.

A little while later the men got up and left.

Eventually Jacob rose and went out to the alley to take a piss. He was tired to the point of exhaustion, his body and particularly his head ached, he itched from the flea ridden smelly clothes and his stomach was sour with the events of the night. Leaning a hand on the wall he aimed at the brickwork and let go, closing his eyes.

The hot slice of a knife in the ribs came out of nowhere. He tried to turn and received a blow to the head that sent him down with a crash. He knew no more.

June 1815

Garmon, arriving at his place of operations in St Giles and having discovered that Diana had not responded to his note, sent a second one, with more persuasive language, alluding to Connor's disappearance and requesting her to come to see him as a matter of urgency.

He then dealt with the pair of idiots who had kidnapped Genevra instead, not, as he had initially intended, with undue harshness. They had after all done him an accidental favour. He was still experiencing little thrills from last night's encounter and looking forward to the evening with heightened anticipation. In fact, his humour was considerably improved, and he found himself frequently distracted during the morning by thoughts of the lady and what he wanted to do to her when she was within his reach once more.

In between fantasies, those blue eyes teased him, where had he seen them before? The mystery eluded him, but he would solve it, he didn't like mysteries. Blue eyes and red hair were an unusual combination.

HE WAS THUS in a more conciliatory frame of mind when Diana appeared at his door in the middle of the afternoon. She strolled in wearing a very fashionable ensemble in leaf green, complete with parasol against the summer sun.

"Good afternoon, Uncle."

He looked up from his desk, jerked out of a pleasant daydream concerning Mrs Tate. He rose and came around the desk to kiss her cheek, having rapidly re-thought his strategy.

"Diana. How kind of you to come."

"I thought I had been summoned?" she said kissing his cheek and taking a seat in the guest chair.

"I thought you were ignoring me."

"I had an engagement last night," she said, removing her bonnet. "Now, what can I do for you?"

"I don't know that you can do anything, but I thought that you should know. Connor is missing."

She jerked and frowned. "What do you mean missing?"

"He left here on Monday around midday and hasn't been seen since. I can't find him. Have you seen him at all?"

"No. Not since-" she stopped and waved a hand. "I shot you." She pursed her lips and added. "I'm glad you have recovered."

"Kind of you," he smiled but suspected it was more a baring of teeth.

"I had to stop you somehow. I couldn't let you kill Anthony."

"So, you thought you'd kill me instead! Your own flesh and blood!"

She widened her eyes and shook her head. "I never intended to kill you."

"The shot itself wasn't fatal, but the damned fever almost was."

She lost some colour at this and said with what appeared to be true contrition, "I never intended or wished you harm, but you must understand that I cannot allow you to hurt Anthony!"

"Then persuade him to give me back the hell!"

She shook her head. "I can't."

"Nonsense, he dotes on you! If you asked him-"

"I won't!" she interrupted him. "He needs the income from the hell to restore his estates and clear his debts."

"I'm getting my hell back. You can help me or suffer the consequences!"

She rose. "In that case I will bid you good day Uncle."

"Damn it! How much does he need?"

She widened her eyes at him. "More than you could afford to pay I'll warrant."

"How much?"

"Over half a million pounds!"

"My God!" Garmon sat back in his seat winded. "The hell can't make that much profit."

"Not all at once, but over a number of years it can."

"But isn't the debt pressing?"

"He needs the steady income to feed the estate. The sale of his mother's property has covered the immediate debts and provided enough to begin repairs to the estate. The rest will have to wait until the hell begins to pay."

"Got it all worked out then?"

She smiled wryly. "Anthony has, yes."

"Damn it! It's my hell. I built it from nothing..."

"Then you shouldn't have staked it. You were losing that night."

"I never lose!"

"But you did," she said quietly.

He sunk his head in his hands. "Yes, I did."

"What possessed you?"

He shook his head. "I don't know. The conviction that I never lose I suppose. I refused to believe that he could beat me." He looked up. "Will he play me for it?"

"No." She shook her head.

"How do you know?"

"I know." She smiled a secret smile, her gaze losing its focus. "He made me a promise."

"And you believe him? Devil Harcourt?"

She blinked and refocused on him. "Yes. He's changed."

"Leopards don't change their spots."

She retied her bonnet and picked up her parasol, turning towards the door. "He loves me Uncle, and I love him. But I don't expect you to understand that. Have you ever loved anyone?" She reached the door and paused, looking back at him. He didn't answer and she left, closing the door quietly behind her.

He stared at the door for a moment and then picked up the ink well and threw it at the door. The glass bottle smashed, and ink splashed all over the door panel and dripped onto the floor.

After a moment the door opened and Rooke stood there, his large form filled the door frame. "Is there anything wrong Mr Lovell?"

"Yes, damn it there is! Put the word out. I want the Duke of Mowbray. Get him for me! And get that mess cleaned up!" He waved at the ink and shouldered past Rooke heading for the stairs.

THE DAY PASSED for Genevra in a kind of euphoric fog. Her distraction and apparent happiness drew comments from her staff, and Joe in particular, twitted her on her evening at the theatre. She had told her staff that she was attending the theatre the previous evening with her family, to account for her going out in evening dress and leaving them to run the Tavern for the night.

As evening approached a nervous thrill had her stomach in a flutter, and she was so preoccupied over what to wear she mixed up two food orders and forgot to charge someone for their beer. Fortunately, Joe caught it and apart from throwing her a puzzled look didn't say anything. She blushed and took herself sternly to task.

Ten o'clock finally crawled round and the last of the patrons left the premises, she told the staff they could leave and that she would close up. Mrs Bell and her son had already retired to their rooms for the night, so she was able to scoot round and hurriedly clean and tidy up ready for tomorrow morning and then fly upstairs to dress.

She dithered between her blue silk and block printed muslin and finally chose the blue silk because it laced at the front, and she could get it on unassisted. In her haste to get rid of the staff she had forgotten the logistical problem of dressing herself. Her day gowns all laced up, but the more exotic gowns for afternoon and evening wear, required assistance. The other advantage of the blue silk was the way the colour matched her eyes and gave her figure an alluring line due to the old-fashioned lacing.

Washed, perfumed, primped and dressed, she made her way downstairs to wait for Garmon's carriage, her heart skipping and her body buzzing with nervous excitement. The sound of an equipage pulling up in the street sent her to the door to check. Letting herself out and locking the door with her key, she allowed the servant to help her up into the vehicle, and she sat back feeling like Cinderella going to the ball to meet her prince.

Which was such an absurdity it made her laugh.

The laughter relieved some of her nervous tension, and she peered out the windows to observe the route they took. Immediately she realised it was a different one than last night and wondered where the carriage was taking her. Not to Lovell's nor to the house she had left from the previous evening which had housed a bookshop and printery.

Twenty minutes later, the carriage drew up to a narrow four-story house in Hart Street. The servant who had conducted her into the carriage, now helped her down and up the steps to the house. The door was opened by another servant who led her up a flight of stairs to a first-floor apartment and the door was opened, this time by Garmon himself. She was so pleased to see him, she couldn't stop smiling.

He paid the servant with a coin and took her hand.

"Come in my dear," he drew her into the apartment and shut the door. The room was elegantly furnished and finished with fresh paintwork, curtains covering the windows and a large Aubusson rug over the wooden floorboards.

The room was well lit and warm from a fire in the grate, the furniture elegant if masculine in style.

"Welcome to my current abode," he said taking her cloak and hanging it on a coat tree near the door. "Would you care for a drink?" He led her towards two comfortable looking armchairs drawn up to the fire.

"Yes please," she said suddenly shy. After thinking about him all day, she found herself unaccountably thrown off balance to be in his home. After all, despite their physical intimacy last night they were virtual strangers. She sat, and he brought her a glass of red wine, offering his own in toast.

"To a night of pleasure my dear." She clinked her glass with his, and blushed.

She caught his smile of amusement, and it made her pull herself together. *She was behaving like a schoolroom miss instead of a mature businesswoman. This was a business transaction after all and not some romantic adventure. She'd really had her head in the clouds all day, and that would not do.*

"I haven't been able to stop thinking about you all day," he confessed sitting in the chair opposite. She noted that he had dressed more formally tonight, wearing both a jacket and neck-cloth as well as shoes, with his shirt, waistcoat and tight-fitting pantaloons. His clothing was of excellent quality and cut, and fitted him to perfection. He could easily pass for a gentleman on Bond St. "It seemed an age until this moment." A pause and then he added as if compelled to fill the silence, "Your dress becomes you very well."

"Thank you," she said, husky voiced of a sudden. She drank some more of her wine and noted that he swallowed his in three mouthfuls. Putting down his glass he reached for hers and set it with his empty one on the table between them. Rising he drew her up into his arms and said softly, "I think we both have other things on our minds, hmm?"

She blushed again and he grinned. "Your blush shows your freckles." Then he kissed her, and conversation was no longer needed.

He tasted of wine and smelled of soap and sandalwood, he had bathed and shaved for her, his face smooth to touch tonight. He slid an arm round her waist and drew her against him, his other hand cupping her skull gently and guiding her where he wanted her, to deepen the kiss. The back of her head was still a little tender from the blow she received last night, but he handled her gently and his kiss was so distracting she didn't care.

She wrapped her arms round his neck and pressed as close as clothing would permit. She wanted every inch of him as close as she could get him. Returning his plundering kiss with a ravenous appetite of her own, she wasn't holding back anything tonight. She fully intended to reap as much pleasure from the encounter as she possibly could.

When he broke the kiss, they were both panting, and she knew her face was flushed, because all of her was flushed and tingling, just from his kisses.

"My God, Genevra," he said with that gravelly tone that set off a shiver over her skin and a twitch between her thighs.

Then he made her squeak by picking her up in his arms and carrying her into another room. This proved to be his bedchamber. Dominated by a huge four-poster bed, draped in blue velvet and a matching coverlet, with the sheets turned back invitingly. Like the sitting room, a generous fire had warmed the room to perfection.

He set her on her feet beside the bed and tugged at the laces of her bodice, tracing kisses down her neck, his lips were soft and warm and left a tingling in their wake that set tendrils of pleasure through her body. She reached up to tug at his neckcloth and he let her pull it from his neck. He then stepped back a moment to remove his jacket and cast it aside.

Returning to her lacings, he pushed her gown off her shoulders and down to her hips, then set to work on her corset which he removed swiftly and flung to floor. She wriggled out of her gown which slid off her hips and pooled round her feet, then raised her arms as he pulled her chemise up over her head and revealed her naked, except for stockings and boots.

"God in heaven you're beautiful," he whispered, pulling her in for another kiss, holding her face and teasing her lower lip with his teeth, pushing his tongue into her mouth and working her lips with his. The effect on her body of this oral assault was electric.

"Garmon!" She gasped, leaning into him, reaching for the buttons on his waistcoat, she fumbled them open and helped him take it off. He reached behind his head to pull off his shirt, and she was able to see and touch his chest and torso for the first time. His chest sported a good crop of brown hair, as did his forearms, and she took a moment to appreciate the texture and the muscular form beneath.

He was taller and leaner than Jacob, who'd been broad through the shoulders and densely muscled with an insulating layer of fat overall.

She ran her hands over the swell of his pectoral muscles and the curves of his shoulders and biceps, his skin was warm and smooth beneath her fingers. His stomach was lean and ribbed with muscle, the whole of his upper body tapering nicely to his waist and hips.

She leaned in and placed a kiss on his left pectoral, rubbing her face over the hair that curled over his skin and sliding her hands appreciatively down his stomach.

She pressed her breasts against the roughness of the hairs on his chest and her nipples pulled tight in response, her arms going round his body. She wanted to say something but seemed to have forgotten how to speak.

He pulled her against him and kissed her again, seemingly their unspoken communication was sufficient. His lips and tongue plundered her mouth and his hands roved over her back and down to her buttocks, which he seized and squeezed with almost brutal roughness.

Releasing her abruptly, he knelt to remove her boots and then ran his hands up her thighs to her garters, swiftly rolling down her stockings and removing them, his lips tracing patterns down the inside of her thighs with warm damp kisses. His fingers reached for the soft flesh of her inner thighs, and he leaned in to kiss her mound, his warm laboured breath on her flesh made her shiver. A finger speared her with one searing swipe that made her gasp.

"Sorry sweetheart I can't wait," he gasped, rising he unbuttoned his pantaloons and shucked them, along with his shoes, and bore her down onto the sheets and pillows in a tangle of limbs. He drove his cock, hard and hot, against her flank, his breathing loud in her ear as his hands ran all over her body in a fevered rush as if he couldn't get enough of her.

His mouth traced kisses over her face and neck and breasts, and she returned them, kissing whatever part of him she could get her mouth on, chest, shoulders, neck.

He rolled her under him and pushed her legs apart abruptly

with his hands, spreading her wide. It occurred to her that she ought to be alarmed by this show of roughness, but instead she was aroused by it, he was clearly out of control with lust for her and her own body clenched on emptiness, she wanted him inside her. Memories of how it felt last night flooding her and making her wet with anticipation. She moved her hips in invitation and he groaned.

"Genevra!"

"Yes Garmon, please," she panted.

Surging forward, he speared her with his cock and after a moment's resistance the full hard length of him slid inside her, filling her up and making her cry out with the pleasure of being stretched and filled.

She lifted her legs to take him deeper, as he plunged again and again inside her. His arms holding her tight, his face buried in her neck. The thrill of the movement of his body within hers, built, and she clutched at him, writhing her hips to increase the pleasure, sounds coming from her throat that she didn't know she was capable of making.

His thrusts became wilder and faster, deeper and harder and her body revelled in this rough taking, rising to meet each plunge with gathering desire.

Her breath came in pants to match his own laboured breathing, and she tore the pleasure from his body with frantic twists and rolls of her hips. His body plundered hers, and she loved every moment of it. Feeling the tremors, the tensing and rising of his pleasure in every part of her, he was nearing his crisis, she could feel it, rising like a wave, gathering with each fervid thrust.

He stiffened on a loud groan, and she felt the quiver and hot rush of his seed within her as his body let go of its tension in a fountaining rush.

Like an electric spark, arcing from one point to another, her own release was triggered, and the pleasure exploded through her body. She arched into him with the force of her release and shuddered through endless moments of bliss so intense, the scalp on her head and the soles of her feet tingled.

She collapsed back against the sheets, panting as a blissful lassitude took her, and she felt him likewise subsiding into a loose mass of lax muscles above her, crushing her to the bed with his weight, his panting breath hot against her neck.

Eventually he moved, lifting his head, gazing down at her, his face flushed and sweat dewing his brow. "I'm sorry, sweetheart, that was not how I intended this to go. I simply couldn't wait to feel you again. To be inside you."

"That is perfectly fine Garmon," she said, stroking his cheek. "I was as eager as you for that fulfilment, and it was-" she shook her head at the impossibility of describing that explosive rush of pleasure that flooded her whole body.

"Yes, I agree, words fail me too." He smiled and kissed her forehead. Disengaging and rolling off her, he hopped out of bed and disappeared into the other room, returning with the bottle and glasses. He put them on the bedside table and went to the dresser. He poured water into the basin; he washed himself quickly and brought a damp cloth back to the bed and offered it to her.

While she used the cloth, he topped up her glass, poured one for himself and handed hers to her.

He dropped the cloth back in the bowl and climbing back into bed, he banked the pillows and reached for his own glass across her. Offering her a second toast, he grinned and said, "To even more pleasure."

She laughed and clinked her glass.

After a moment or two of savouring the wine, she said, "I had no idea it would be like this."

"What?" he asked watching her from his banked pillows.

She slewed round a bit on the pillows to face him, enjoying the soft crispness of freshly laundered fine cotton sheets and pillowcases.

"When I was contemplating making you my offer," she felt her face flush. "I thought it would be unpleasant and degrading at best and painful and dangerous at worst. I didn't expect I would enjoy it." She smiled at him shyly.

"There is no point to sexual congress if it's not enjoyable," he said.

"For the man yes, but for women-"

"Women are as capable of enjoying it as men, if the men will let them." he interrupted.

"Yes, so I have discovered." She paused chewing her lip. "Thank you."

He took her hand and played with her fingers. Something in his expression made her heart skip a beat. "There is no need to thank me for something that is your right. And in any case, I am quite selfish in the matter. A large part of my pleasure is derived from my partners'. A woman who is aroused, arouses me!"

He kissed her hand and then took one of her fingers in his mouth and ran his tongue over the pad of it. The sensation was so delicious and unexpected she gasped, rubbing her thighs together in reflex. He gradually let her finger fall from his mouth. "Like that," he said softly.

Putting his glass and hers on the bedside table, he took her in his arms and kissed her.

With the pillows behind her and his arms around her, his bare chest pressed against her and his tongue plundering her mouth she felt cocooned in warmth. Wrapped in a kind of decadent pleasure she had never felt before.

When he raised his head to gaze down at her, she ran her eyes over his face looking for clues as to what he was thinking.

"I am going to enjoy teaching you pleasure. It is clear to me that you have not had enough of it in your life. And quite selfishly I shall derive a great deal of pleasure in return. Your body is heaven Genevra. Let me demonstrate."

CHAPTER 7

*G*armon slid down the bed, to commence what he planned to be a thorough exploration of Genevra's delightful body. He began with the ravishing of her breasts. These luscious globes made him salivate with longing, and he had entirely neglected them earlier, driven by an over-mastering desire to just get inside and fuck her.

The problem had been his inability to stop thinking about doing precisely that all day. Despite the slight distraction of his unsatisfactory meeting with Diana, he had been walking around with an erection for the duration, remembering and anticipating.

Having her back in his arms had completely destroyed his plans for a slow seduction, especially when she responded so immediately and wantonly to his kisses. It was obvious she wanted the same thing and from that point on it was a frantic rush to the finish line. He was pleased and mildly flattered by her response. A mutual attraction this strong was rare and to be savoured and enjoyed to the full.

His mouth made a meal of her hard nipples, nibbling, licking, sucking first one and then the other. His hands cupping, squeezing, stroking and caressing the lovely, round, soft flesh. Her legs moved restlessly on the bed, signalling her arousal from this treatment. *Could he? Would she?* He decided to try.

Lifting his head he said, "Spread your legs and keep them spread. Wide as they will go."

She gaped at him.

"Trust me," he said coaxingly.

She nodded and obeyed. He looked down and groaned at the sight of her spread out before him, her breasts lolling heavy, with her nipples jutting up pink and hard, her stomach a lovely curve and her quim revealed to him in all its pink, satiny glory, damp and dressed with strawberry curls.

"Now, no touching yourself unless I say so, hmm?"

She nodded, and he grinned. "I am going to play with your breasts, just your breasts. And you are going to keep her thighs spread wide and clench your inner muscles as I do so. You understand what I mean by that?"

"I think so," her voice was a husky croak. She swallowed, her tongue licking her lower lip.

"The idea arouses you, doesn't it?"

"Yes," she whispered.

He pushed a finger inside her. "Try to clench," she obeyed, and he groaned, imagining what it would feel like if she did that while his cock was inside her. "Yes, like that." He withdrew his finger and licked it grinning at her. Her eyes widened and he kissed her lips. "Now clench and release while I play with you."

He bent his head to her breasts and nuzzled and licked and kissed one mound while he cupped and squeezed and fondled the other. He kissed and suckled, using his tongue to swirl over and tease the hard nub, feeling her arching up into his mouth as he widened and took more of her breast, sucking harder.

She whimpered, her hands clutching the sheets, and he transferred to the other breast giving it the same treatment, soothing the first with his fingers. He sucked hard on her nipple, pinching the other at the same time. Then soothed and repeated the process, each time getting a little harder.

Her sounds got louder and more urgent and her hips rolled, her thighs trembled and her back arched. A deep groan tore from her throat and she cried out panting.

She collapsed back on the bed trembling her thighs snapping together and rubbing, her panting breath audible. He kissed each pink breast soothingly and sat up, his cock jutting up hard against his belly.

She lay limp and pink against the pillows a dazed expression in her eyes.

"I didn't know that was possible."

He grinned. "I told you I would show you pleasure you have never dreamed of." He leaned over her and kissed her, slow and deep. He couldn't seem to get enough of her mouth. Sitting back on his haunches he said, "Would you do me a favour?"

"Of course, what?"

He waved at his belly. "Suck my cock with that luscious mouth of yours?"

She smiled and sat up. "I'd love to."

He groaned again. "Genevra I'm going to die of pleasure, and it will be your fault!"

She laughed and leaned forward.

"No stay there I want to-" he moved to straddle her. "Lean back against the pillows." She obeyed him, and he knelt before her, resting his hands against the bedhead behind her. He leaned forward, and she circled his girth with her fingers, and pulled down the foreskin to reveal the head of his cock. She took him in her mouth, and he groaned at the sensation of her tongue against his flesh and the hot wet cavern of her mouth.

He closed his eyes the better to appreciate the exquisite sensations and thrust slowly in her grip, driving himself deeper into her mouth, careful not to choke her.

He savoured the experience for several minutes mindful not

to push beyond a certain point. This was purely for the pleasure of it, he had no intention of ejaculating yet. He wanted a lot more pleasure before he reached that point. An advantage of having climaxed so quickly the first time was that he could delay the final event for longer now, allow them both to wring the most from the experience.

He thrust into her mouth with agonising slowness, teasing himself and resisting the urge to go faster. *God that was good!* Her tongue swirled over the head, sending shivers through his body and tightening his balls. He panted, groaning softly. *So good...*

*Too good...*Pulling out of her mouth with a muffed groan, he sat back on his haunches and regarded her.

"What's wrong?" she asked.

"Nothing, I don't want you to make me come yet. That was a pure piece of indulgence."

"You like it?"

"Oh yes, very much," he leaned forward and kissed her again. "Now I'm going to pleasure you."

"But you already have," she protested.

"Not half, sweetheart. You won't be able to walk by the time I've finished with you," he said, moving down her body until he was between her splayed legs.

"That will be very awkward, I have to work tomorrow," she said playfully. Then she jumped and uttered a kind of squeak as he plunged his face into her delicious fragrant cunny and licked and kissed her. Spearing her with his tongue and lapping at her flesh.

He worked her relentlessly until she was feverish with wanting to come, writhing and clutching the sheets while he pushed his fingers in and out of her and lavished her bud with licking, sucking and kissing.

"Garmon!" She pushed up into him frantic, panting, moaning. His cock twitched and ached forcing to him bear down into the mattress with his hips to ease the aching.

He renewed his assault on her flesh and pushed her ruthlessly over the edge into a climax, savouring the cries of her pleasure and the pulsing of her flesh under his tongue.

Barely allowing her a moment to recover, he pushed her again to the peak and through another fall with his tongue, and his fingers. More gentle but relentless he pushed her into another and another until she was panting and limp and cried out in protest.

"Garmon please!"

He raised his head and grinned. "Had enough?"

"Please," she put out a hand.

He shook his head. "I don't think you've had enough yet."

"I have really!" she protested breathless and trembling.

"You want my cock? You want me to fuck you?"

"Ohh!" she collapsed back on the pillows, her legs falling open. "Yes! Yes! Fuck me!" she said to the ceiling, her lovely neck arched and her breasts on full display.

His cock leaked copiously at this display of debauched wantonness, his balls already tight, throbbed painfully. He rose over her, grabbing a pillow to fit under her bottom and gripping her hips, he speared her hard with his cock. She lay splayed below him, while he fucked her with hard deliberate strokes, his eyes feasting on the sight of her laid out and helpless in his grip.

"Do you like it, Genevra?" he asked his voice cracking with barely controlled lust.

"Yes!" she rolled her head on the pillows and clenched the sheets, her breasts bouncing with the movement of his thrusts as he jarred her whole body with the force of his fucking.

"God, Garmon, yes!" her voice rose, and then he felt it. The clench of her inner muscles as she strained against him, arching her back. He moved one hand to rub roughly over her bud to bring her off and the result was spectacular.

Her muscles pulled taught, and she groaned loudly, her body shuddering and the internal clenching became a ripple that made him groan helplessly and his cock quiver, teetering on the edge of coming.

He wrenched himself free of her grip, squeezed the base of his cock hard to stop himself coming and panted, watching her roll slowly sideways off the pillow, her legs coming together as she curled into herself moaning softly.

He leaned over her, stroking her hair off her face. "Are you alright?"

"Hmm," she nodded, her body writhing on the sheets.

He smiled. He recognised the signs. She had reached that point of over stimulation where her whole body was afire. He had hoped to achieve that with her but was surprised it had happened so quickly. He rolled her gently onto her stomach and pushing her tangled hair aside, kissed the back of her neck, which made her moan and writhe on the bed.

"It's all right sweetheart, I know what is happening. Your skin feels hypersensitive, doesn't it?" He stroked her back gently.

"Hmm." She rubbed her face into the pillow, pushing her bottom up.

"You feel all coiled up inside, don't you?" he swallowed the groan the sight of her wet swollen peach pushed up into his view provoked.

"Y-yes," her voice breathless, broken.

"Oh Genevra," he groaned leaning over her and kissing her back, her shoulders her spine, his hands caressing her skin. He gently lifted her beautiful round bottom up and placed the pillow under her tummy. Her hips writhed on it, she seemed almost insensible of what he was doing, lost in some erotic dreamscape of her own body's sensations.

Her breathing came in erratic pants, punctuated by little mewls and moans that made his sorely tried cock leak and twitch. Moving between her writhing legs, he slowly lowered his body on top of hers and slid the head of his cock along her wet swollen flesh.

He groaned with the pleasure of the sensation, and she jerked beneath him and gave an answering groan. Pulling back a fraction, he found and notched the head to her entrance and pushed gently but firmly inside her. She gasped and her back arched, he groaned and gripped her hips, kissing her back and then stretching forward and taking his weight on his hands and knees he lay on her full length. Rocking slowly, he pushed into her, leaning down he found her mouth, and kissed her. Then he reached under her to rub her gently while he slid in and out of her slowly and she moaned helplessly into another climax.

"That's it," he whispered kissing her neck and her cheek and her shoulder, rocking himself inside her and swirling her inexorably into another peak. She shook beneath him, her limbs tensing and going limp and tensing again as he wrung yet another surge of pleasure from her. She was panting and their skin was slick with sweat where they touched. The slap of their flesh meeting was audible between their laboured breath. He was perilously close to losing all control.

It was time, he couldn't hold back the nagging ache to come any longer. He gripped her hips and pulled back onto his haunches bringing her up with him onto her knees.

He massaged her gorgeous bottom, enjoying the feel of her buttocks in his hands, his thumbs separating them so that he could see himself pushing in and out of her wet cunny. His cock was red and glistening wet, swollen and veined and so fucking hard it hurt.

He pushed deeper, gripping her hips again as he sped up his thrusts, *God yes!* The pleasure, held at bay for so long, surged up and up and wound itself into a tight knot of exquisite, agonising, ravening, joy. And burst. His cock jerked within the confines of her hot tunnel and spilled his seed in a series of blissful shots that left him gutted and limp, collapsing on her back and pushing her back down onto the bed in a panting heap.

. . .

63

SHE WAS RUINED. She couldn't move. He rolled off her and lay panting beside her. But she couldn't even turn her head to look at him. What he had done to her, she couldn't begin to describe, or comprehend. Her body was jelly, boneless. Her lady parts were mashed, wet, swollen, beyond tender.

His hand on her back made her flinch. "Genevra?"

She swallowed. Her throat hurt.

"Genevra, sweetheart?"

She opened her mouth, but nothing came out but a huff of breath.

He removed the pillow and her body collapsed onto the mattress. He turned her over, and she flopped onto her back.

His expression of concern made her force out. "I'm all right." Her voice cracked.

He stroked the hair from her face, and then he disappeared from her view. She felt him get up from the bed, but she couldn't summon the will to turn her head and watch him.

He returned, sitting down on the edge of the bed and lifting her head with one hand, he offered her a drink. It was whisky, potent and fiery, it caught the back of her throat and made her cough. But the spirit brought some sense back to her limbs and when she had stopped coughing, she took another sip. He eased her head back onto the pillow and stroked her cheek.

"Better?"

"Hmm." she cleared her throat. "Yes. Thank you."

"I did warn you; you wouldn't be able to walk." he said with a smile.

"I didn't think you meant it literally," she said, attempting to match his light tone.

He put the glass on the bedside table and kissed her forehead.

He then climbed back into bed and eased her into his arms. "I think you have earned a rest."

She huffed a weary laugh, resting her head on his chest and closed her eyes. "I have to leave before dawn, my staff..."

"Hush, I'll make sure you get home in time, rest."

"Hmm..." sleep took her over the edge into darkness.

GARMON LAY awake for some time listening to her breathing and wondered how a week was going to be enough to explore everything he wanted to with this woman.

He woke at half past two. A habit he had formed in childhood, when sleeping was hazardous at the best of times, was the ability to wake at a time he nominated to himself. Getting out of bed quietly, he pulled on a robe, poked up the fire and set a kettle on to boil some water.

He returned to the foot of the bed and watched Genevra sleeping. She lay on her back, her glorious light copper hair, a tangled halo round her head, her face relaxed. He would wake her at three. That would give her sufficient time to get home before her staff arrived.

Glancing at the clock he moved quietly into the sitting room where he rekindled the fire that had gone out and picking up the novel he was reading, he sat and lost himself in the fantasy world of Mrs Gaskill's Mysteries of Udolpho for twenty minutes.

Putting the book aside and rising at just before three, he went back into the bedroom. The kettle was boiled and taking a cloth he poured the hot water into the basin and turned to the bed. Sliding under the covers, he watched Genevra's sleeping face for a moment longer. A flash of his childhood surfaced, of his mother sleeping exhausted and of his reluctance to wake her as instructed. Pushing the memory aside, he bent his head and kissed Genevra's lips gently.

She woke with a start, her eyes springing open in alarm.

"Good morning," he said with an amused smile at her shocked expression. He could see the moment she recalled where she was and how she got there and what had transpired before she slept.

"What time is it? I have to go-"

"It is 3:00 am, and you have plenty of time." He watched her scrambling out of bed and added, "There is hot water in the basin."

"Thank you," she said going to the basin and making a hasty toilet, shivering slightly despite the fire.

While she was doing that, he gathered up her strewn garments and when she turned from the basin he said, "Let me be your maid." He had done this often enough as a lad in the brothel for the girls and his mother.

She stared up at him, slightly dazed and watched as he knelt to offer her a stocking. She put out a foot, balancing herself with a hand on his head. His fingers lingered momentarily as he fastened her garters into place. And he resisted the temptation to kiss her sweet mound. If he started, he might not be able to stop, and she really had, had enough tonight and besides he didn't want to make her late.

Rising he helped her on with her chemise, laced up her corset and then her dress, knelt again to help her on with her boots. She clutched at her hair. "Do you have a comb?"

He nodded and produced a comb and brush, when she went to take them from him, he said, "Let me."

She turned her back in acquiescence, and he carefully worked the tangles out of her hair before plaiting and pinning it for her. Dressing a lady's hair had been another of his duties. "There, perfectly respectable," he said turning her to the mirror on the dresser, his hands on her upper arms.

She looked up at him over her shoulder. "Thank you."

He smiled and kissed her hair. "You're welcome. My carriage will pick you up at eleven tonight. You will find it out the front now waiting for you."

"You—you want to continue, tonight? You wouldn't prefer a break?" she said turning towards him.

He shook his head. "No, but we will explore other things tonight, I shan't tax you so, I promise."

She nodded, lowering her head.

He tipped it up, with a finger under her chin and kissed her lips gently. "Thank you."

She swallowed. "Thank you, I didn't know- I've never-"

"I know. I'm sorry if I pushed you too far-"

"No!" she put a hand on his chest. "No, it was wonderful, just overwhelming. I feel strange this morning, light and sort of out of kilter. I can't explain it."

He kissed her forehead. "You had better go before I forget my good intentions. Until tonight." He cupped her face and kissed her mouth again. Letting her go reluctantly, he stepped aside and escorted her to the door. He helped her on with her cloak and then escorted her down the stairs and out into the street, where he handed her into his carriage. He watched the carriage turn the corner before he went back inside.

He had a great deal to accomplish today, because he had achieved fuck all yesterday, he'd been so distracted by thoughts of Genevra. Today he would do better.

He didn't.

CHAPTER 8

*T*hree months ago
Jacob woke to the feel of a soft mattress under him, he was face down and someone was wiping his back with a damp cloth. Pain radiated outwards from his right side in hot waves. His head ached and throbbed with his pulse. An excruciating pain ran up from his right leg when he tried to move it, making him cry out. Nausea roiled in his gut. He moved his head and miraculously a hand with a bowl appeared in time as he vomited over the side of the bed.

A feminine hand. She murmured something he didn't catch, being distracted by the heaving of his stomach. When it finally settled, he muttered his thanks and flopped back on the bed, closing his eyes. A moment later she offered him water to rinse his mouth and he peered up at her bleary-eyed. Maggie.

After he took a couple of sips of water, he tried to smile. "Maggie. Thank you."

"Someone stabbed you; I think it might have been one of those men." She bit her lip, her brow creased and blinked her eyes, they were grey blue in the lamp light. Dawn was breaking through the window behind her, it had been a long night. "When you didn't come back inside, I went to investigate and found you bleeding on the ground."

He tried to move and winced with the pain, it hurt like the devil!

She placed a hand on his shoulder to stay him. "I've sent for the doctor. I think your right ankle is broken."

"Where am I?" His voice croaked.

"My room at the Tavern," she flushed. "You defended me, I couldn't let you bleed to death in the alley." She swallowed.

He nodded and tried to take her hand, but his arm felt like lead. Pain pulsed through his body from multiple sources, he was one big ball of agony. His eyes closed, willing it all to go away.

SHE WAS LATE! Garmon looked up from the book he was trying to distract himself with and glared at the clock on the mantelpiece. It was a quarter to twelve. With a growl, he discarded the book and got up to pace to the window, peering out into the street, but there was no sign of his carriage. He couldn't believe that she would renege on their deal so early on. But she had indicated this morning that she was reluctant to come back tonight.

It had been an unsatisfactory day all around. Upon further consideration of his meeting with Diana he had concluded that really there was only one course left to him, reluctant as he was to take it. He had threatened this course when Mowbray first seized the hell but had not followed through. Mostly because Connor talked him out of it. He now knew why, Connor's partiality for Diana extended to a desire to protect the duke. Not from any fondness for the man personally, but because to harm the duke would cause Diana pain. Truth to tell that had been a consideration that weighed slightly with him as well. Yes, he was angry with Diana for her betrayal. But despite the promptings of his darker self, he had some scruples over pursuing a course that would bring her such heartache.

But really, he had no other options now. He must recover the hell and there was only one way to do it. It had to be the duke. So, he had put the word out today. An attractive bounty to ransom the duke for the hell. No easy feat, the man was much hedged about with security. Even so, a clever or desperate man might accomplish the impossible for a sufficiently large inducement.

The undertaking sat ill with him. Was he developing a conscience? That was a luxury he couldn't afford. And yet the doubts still persisted, no matter how much he tried to silence them. His temper already raw, was tinder sharp and Genevra's failure to show up made it even worse.

He paced away, annoyed with himself for being so put out by her defection. His body tensed with frustration. The truth was, he hadn't had anywhere near enough of Mrs Genevra Tate, and the thought that she would pull back from their agreement, not see it through, was disappointing in the extreme. He was cranky to begin with, this made it worse. He really didn't give a toss for the money, beyond the principle of the thing. He had plenty of avenues for recouping funds. But Genevra, what she offered, was unique, and he realised, with a jolt that brought him to standstill in front of the fireplace, one that he craved with the same kind of hunger he had once craved the excitement inherent in the turn of a card.

He wanted her and his thirst, his hunger, was not satiated yet, not anywhere nearly enough. What he had planned for tonight was different, and his plans were now in ruins. The disappointment was sharp like a pain to the chest. He felt like a jilt at the altar waiting for a bride who wasn't coming.

An idiot in fact, for investing so much in an ungrateful conniving little bitch! His fists clenched and his teeth ground together. *Well, he would make her pay! Did she think he would consider the past two nights sufficient to stave off the debt? That wasn't the deal sweetheart! He would make her sorry she had crossed him. He was not a man to cross and however pretty and beguiling she might be she wasn't going to get away with-*

The sounds of a carriage drawing up outside, arrested his vengeful thoughts and took him to the window in time to see a cloaked figure descending from the carriage and a glimpse of light-coloured skirts. She disappeared from view, and he heard the front door open and footsteps on the stairs.

He straightened his neck cloth, attempting to compose himself and pack all that ire he had stirred up away. Going to the door as a knock sounded, he opened it to reveal a flushed Genevra, escorted by the man he paid to act as porter and ensure the security of the house. He passed the man his coin and held the door for Genevra. She slipped passed him, removing her cloak as he shut the door. He took it from her.

"I'm so sorry I'm late!" she said pushing tendrils of hair off her face and trying to subdue them with pins. "A couple of patrons refused to leave and in the end Joe and his boys had to throw them out for me."

"Joe?"

"My tapster." She smoothed her gown and glanced round the room, catching sight of the table laid for two. "Dinner?"

"Supper, I have sent Burridge out for it. He will be back soon. Would you care for some wine?"

"Yes please," she came further into the room, and he got a better look at tonight's gown, which was an embroidered muslin. He thought of the three he had seen so far; this one became her best. It was simple in style and cut, with a white satin ribbon under her breasts and the embroidery on the sleeves and hem was its only ornament.

He poured her white wine and passed her the glass. A knock

71

at the door sent him to answer it and let Burridge in with the covered tray of the meal. He let the man arrange it on the table and returned to pouring himself a wine. Burridge bowed himself out, and he waved to the table.

"Would you care to eat?"

She smiled moving to the table. "How did you know? I missed dinner and I'm famished."

"Good," he ensured her chair was pushed in sufficiently and joined her on the opposite side of the small table.

She surveyed the dishes laid out and exclaimed, "This is marvellous, thank you!"

He shrugged; it was simple enough fare. Sliced cold meat, a selection of cheeses and fruit with fresh bread, oil, salt and honey to drizzle and dip. He waited until she had made her own selection, before filling his plate and watched with quiet amusement her delight over the food. His earlier fury disarmed by her evident pleasure in being here with him, and her quick apology for being late. *He should have considered that she might have difficulty getting away on time every night. After all she was running a service business, and as he very well knew, customers did not always behave the way you wanted them to.*

When she popped a piece of soft cheese in her mouth and closed her eyes in ecstasy his cock twitched. And when her tongue scooped up a drip of honey from her lip, he swallowed a groan. *She would be the death of him, and she wouldn't even know it.* Her bodice was cut low enough to show her generous bosom and cleavage to advantage, and he had to keep dragging his gaze away from that fascinating prospect.

Forcing his mind away from her assets, he said by way of polite conversation, "Tell me about your family."

"My father was George Whittaker of Whittaker's Brewery; you've heard of it?"

"In Great Russell Street?"

She nodded. "I have two sisters, Mary and Beth. I'm the

middle daughter, and we had a brother Johnathon, but he died when he was twelve, and I was eight. Without a son to carry on the business, my father came to rely on me to help in the Brewery and I learned everything about running it. My eldest sister, Mary, is too refined to work in the Brewery and Beth, the youngest, caught scarlet fever when she was five and almost died. Her health has been precarious ever since and besides she was too young. Papa relied on me." She looked down at her plate, toying with the piece of bread. "He died seven years ago, and my uncle tried to take over the brewery, so Mama married again to–to stop him."

"I gather from your expression this didn't please you?"

"My stepfather and I do not see eye to eye. We clashed from the first. Suffice it to say that he is the type of man who assumes a woman is too feeble-minded to understand even the simplest of tasks. That she is incapable of doing anything but genteel things such as embroidery and ordering the servants. That she could never possibly know the first thing about business or-" She stopped, her hands clenching, her face flushed.

"I see, very trying for one of your ah- capable disposition, no doubt."

"He makes my blood boil!" she burst out. "He drove his own brewery to the wall with bad business decisions, and it is only by a miracle that he has not done the same to Whittaker's. He is a pompous, vain, narrow-minded, idiot! I loathe him."

"I see." He kept his face straight with an effort. The matter was clearly one about which she felt passionately, and he couldn't help but admire her spirit. *She would be an excellent wife, supportive and strong, capable and dependable. As well as passionate and desirable.*

She sighed. "I married Jacob Tate to get away from him and fell from the frying pan into the fire." She took a sip of wine. "Jacob owned the Globe Tavern. I thought it was the perfect match. He was handsome and charming enough before we were married. I thought we would be partners in the business and expand it together. I nursed dreams of running my own brewery you see." Her mouth twisted. "But Jacob didn't want a partner, at least not in his wife. He wanted a drudge he could fuck when he felt like it, and heaven forbid if she ever voiced an opinion or had ideas of her own!" She blinked, and he caught the glisten of unshed tears in her eyes.

"You were wasted on him," he said quietly. He was glad the man was dead for he would have killed him if he wasn't.

She smiled through the tears, wiping her cheeks. "Thank you." She took another swallow of wine, and he topped up her glass. "So, you see, I was over the moon when he turned up dead. I'd been living in dread of him coming back, although the longer he was away the more hopeful I grew that he wasn't going to."

She nibbled at a piece of fruit and looked across at him. "So there, you know my life history now. What about you?"

"I have no family," he said abruptly.

"What none? Are you an orphan? Do you not know who your parents were?" The sympathy in her voice almost undid him. *Damn!* He looked away a moment wondering how she had managed to pierce his armour so easily.

"My mother was a prostitute, at least she died as one. She was an Opera Dancer. She always insisted my father was a lord, but I never believed her until, on her deathbed she finally told me his name. I don't think I believed her even then. I always thought, growing up, that my father was Samuel Gatwick, her Pimp." He grinned, but he knew it was more of a grimace. "Gatwick was an unmitigated arsehole. I hated him." He paused, wondering if he could tell her the rest. She was watching him with sympathy, and irrationally he wanted to wipe that look off her face, make her realise he wasn't a worthy recipient of her sympathy. "I killed him—eventually."

She swallowed and her cheeks lost some of their pink bloom. "How old were you?"

"Twelve."

"You were a child." Her hand reached out and then retracted to a fist.

"I was never a child. I'd just bedded my first whore, and I figured I was man enough to confront him. I was skinny, but I was strong and quick. He was drunk and stupid. I stabbed him, he tripped and fell, hit his head."

"It was an accident."

He shook his head. "No, the wound was fatal, he would have bled out in seconds. There was blood everywhere. Never seen so much blood, before or since. But I was rid of him and so was Mama, and that was what counted."

"Who *was* your father then?"

"Lord Phillip Lovell. I didn't know this until later, but he had paid for our upkeep for the first few years of my life, but I was too young to remember any of it. Then he died and the money stopped. That's when Mama took up with Gatwick and became a whore. She died when I was fifteen, but I was twenty-five before I tried to find my father's family. By then I was earning a fair living from my gambling, playing in hells, finding innocent young lordlings to fleece.

"I wanted to open my own hell and I figured the Lovell's owed me, so I went looking. To be honest I didn't expect a warm reception, but I wasn't above a bit of blackmail if it would get me what I wanted. Turned out I didn't need it.

"I discovered I had a half-brother, the legitimate son of Lord Phillip. Peter his name was. He was unaware of my existence until I called on him. Decent fellow. He paid me what he figured his father would have done, had the family not cut me and Mama off after the old man died. It was enough, combined with the money I'd made from gambling, to open my own hell."

"Lovells."

"Yes."

"You've never married?"

"God no."

"Children?"

"Not to my knowledge. If I did, I'd take care of them." He paused and reached across the table to take her hand. "We never discussed this, but I'd take care of you and the child if-"

Her face twisted and she looked away. "There's no need. I can't, you see-"

"Oh. I wondered why you didn't seem concerned." He knew an irrational moment of disappointment. *He should be relieved; he didn't want to father bastards. He didn't want his sons to suffer as he had. In fact, he'd do his damnedest to ensure they didn't, but there had been none that he knew of. Perhaps he was incapable?*

He dragged his attention back to her, aware suddenly that she had risen from the table and walked to the fire. Her back was to him, but it wasn't difficult to figure out she was upset.

He got up and went to her, put his hands on her shoulders. She was shaking with silent sobs. He pulled her back against him, wrapping his arms round her tightly and murmured, "I'm sorry Genevra."

"It's not your fault!" she gasped. "*I'm* sorry for behaving like a watering pot!" She took a breath and said as if the words burst out of her. "I lost two! The doctor said I'd never have another."

His heart, the thing he didn't think he had, jerked at that, and he turned her in his arms and held her tightly. She leaned into him, her face buried in his shoulder and wept. "I'm sorry love," he whispered. "So sorry."

"He did it," her words were so muffled he thought he'd misheard them.

"What?"

She lifted her head, her face streaked with tears, her eyes red. "He did it. It was his fault. It's why I hate him. I could probably have forgiven him all the rest, but not my babies. He took -" her voice became suspended with tears for a moment. "He took my babies from me!"

"How?" His voice sounded hollow to his own ears. His vision tinged with red.

"The first time, he punched me in the stomach. I began to bleed the next day and the babe was born too soon, she was blue and only took a few breaths before she–d–died. I named her Grace."

"And the second?" His voice croaked.

"He pushed me down the stairs. It ruptured something inside me. There was a lot of blood. It was far too soon for this one, but it was formed enough to tell it was a boy." She wiped her face and her eyes flashed with fury. "He was upset about this one. He blamed *me* for killing his son!"

Garmon stared at her through a narrow tunnel of black and red as a flash of incandescent rage poured through his body, demanding an immediate and effective outlet. He spun away and punched the wall beside the door. The plaster cracked under the force of his fist and rained down on the floorboards in flakes and pieces. He was dimly aware that he made a sound, a roar of rage. He was shaking.

He punched a second hole in the wall beside the first, and a third, before he was able to control the rage enough to stop.

Leaning on the wall he gasped for breath, fighting flaming anger and incongruous tears. He closed his eyes and breathed, listening to his heart thudding in his ears and pounding in his chest. He gasped, wiping his face and noted the swelling on his knuckles, and gradually he became aware of the pain in his hand and of a noise behind him.

He turned to find Genevra backed against the farthest wall, her face white as a milk, staring at him in horror. She was visibly shaking and even at this distance he could see the tears rolling down her cheeks.

He swallowed and cleared his clogged throat. "I'm sorry!" he took a step towards her, and she cringed away, looking around her for some way of escape or for some method of defence, he could read it in her eyes and posture. The woman was terrified. And no wonder. He cursed his own temper and lack of control.

"Genevra don't be afraid. Please, my anger was for Tate, not you. I would never hurt you. If he wasn't already dead I would kill him for you, for what he did. He is an animal who doesn't deserve to live!" He cleared his throat again, his voice husky, his throat tight.

"Please..." He stepped towards her, crossing the space between them slowly. His right hand hanging at his side throbbed.

He stopped a couple of paces away and waited for the sense of his words to sink in. He could tell when she mastered the terror and came back to herself. She slumped back against the wall behind her, her hands pressed flat to the wall by her hips.

Her lips twisted in a tremulous smile. "Thank you." Her voice was husky, broken.

She licked her lips and nodded at his hand. "You've hurt yourself."

"It's nothing, just a bit of bruising , some swelling."

"Let me see," she held out her hand, and he stepped closer letting her take his injured hand in hers and examine it.

"I should bathe it for you, since you were injured in my cause." She smiled wistfully, her fingers tracing a gentle path over his bruised and swelling knuckles.

"It's nothing, really," he repeated.

"Do you have some arnica?" she asked.

He nodded and fetched the little pot of it from his bedroom, setting it on the table. Then he poured himself a scotch and downed it. "Do you want some?" he offered.

She looked up from the pot of arnica. "Yes, thank you." He poured her a drink also and let her smooth some of the ointment on his knuckles. It stung a little, but he was more engrossed in her gentle touch and concern and barely noticed. He was not in the habit of being doctored or cared for, it gave him an odd tight feeling in his chest.

"Thank you," he said with a smile and pushed a lock of hair back behind her ear where it had come loose from her bun. The tear tracks still showed on her cheeks, and he used a thumb to wipe them away.

"No one has wanted to defend me before," she said quietly bending her face forward as if to hide. His chest tightened, and he swallowed an unaccountable lump in his throat. He felt as if someone or something had opened up his chest and tried to pull his innards out. Raw and unstable was how he felt.

An instinct to comfort stole over him, and he took her into his arms and kissed her hair. She wrapped her arms round his torso, and they stood thus for several minutes, the only sounds in the room the crackle of the fire and the ticking of the clock. Finally, he stirred and said softly, "Come to bed, I just want to hold you."

She let him lead her to the bedroom, and they undressed each other in silence. Crawling under the covers naked, he pulled her into his arms and settled her head on his chest. Her arm draped over his stomach and her leg looped over his, she nestled in and murmured, "Thank you."

"Hush, go to sleep."

She did, but he couldn't. The images her words had conjured in his mind were too graphic and too haunting to let him sleep, so he stayed awake and held her and wondered what next in this strange odyssey he had begun with Genevra Tate.

He saw her home himself, accompanying her in the carriage and seeing her to the door of the Tavern. He waited until she was safely within before jumping back into the carriage and giving a peremptory order to return home, his thoughts dark and angry.

GARMON SPENT the following day stewing on what Genevra had told him. It didn't improve his temper that there was no outlet for his impotent rage, and he eventually turned to contemplating what he could do to make Genevra happy instead.

~

GENEVRA'S DAY was much like any other on the surface, but the passage of last night played on her mind, colouring everything. Raking up the past was painful, but Garmon's reaction, his rage and tenderness in the face of her distress, had been wonderful and terrifying. She had not shared the truth of what happened with her two pregnancies with anyone, both had been ostensibly caused by falls on her part. She rather thought Joe suspected, but he never said anything, and she had never been able to bring herself to speak of it. Instead, she buried it, hid it away in a dark place inside her and shied away from thinking of it.

Why she told Garmon, she couldn't fathom, but the relief of speaking of it to someone had created a kind of peace that she had never experienced before. She was melancholy yes, but the unhealed pain of it was eased a fraction by sharing her loss with him.

His fury and his kindness had both stunned and terrified her. Initially his ferocity scared her, but then the idea that someone, anyone, would come to her defence in such a manner, was so foreign to her experience that she had no way of knowing how to react to it.

Could she trust that kind of support? It seemed too good to be true. Her instinct was to run from it, but she couldn't, he would be sending his carriage for her again tonight, to continue their arrangement. If she broke the agreement, he would foreclose on the debt, and she could wind up in debtors' prison and lose the Tavern.

Such a thing was more terrifying than Garmon Lovell defending her. She needed to guard her heart from such a man, he could bring her undone if she wasn't careful. This was a temporary arrangement, not one she could rely on long term. So, no matter how frightening it was to have someone be nice to her, she couldn't run, she must face him and see what the next encounter with this strange, enigmatic and passionate man brought.

CHAPTER 9

*T*wo months ago
Jacob lost more than a month to pain and fever; when he finally emerged from the fog, he was weak as a kitten and could barely rise from the bed. And even then, he was so tired he slept for a good portion of every day. He was unable to lie fully on his back due to the inflammation of the wound and his leg was strapped, preventing him from walking even if he could have got up.

He had cause to be grateful for Maggie's vigilant nursing, and he was too weak to do anything but accept it in any case. He wondered idly what Genevra was making of his absence and how the tavern was faring. He sighed and closed his eyes; he was too tired to care right now. When he was better, he'd go home. Maybe.

GARMON, came himself that evening to collect her. The door of the carriage opened and there he was waiting for her. A flutter in her stomach at the sight of him, *excitement or fear?* He drew her up into the carriage and into his arms.

"I missed you," he said simply, his eyes more green than hazel in the light from the street flambeau, his lips captured hers in a soft, devouring kiss. She sunk into his kiss and did not surface until he broke it to say, "We are nearly there. I am taking you somewhere special tonight."

"Where?" she asked sitting up and peering out the window. *What did he have in mind for tonight?* They had drawn up before an innocuous looking brick two-story building with a triangular pediment.

He smiled and helped her from the carriage. A street light illuminated the pavement. He led her to the door in the centre of the narrow-fronted building. When he knocked, the door was opened by a bent elderly woman, who smiled at them.

"Come in Mr Lovell."

Genevra breathed in the warm steamy air and took in the tiled walls and floor. Lamps on the walls illuminated a room dominated at the rear by an enormous, tiled pool, spanning the entire width of the room, separated from the entry by a waist high balustrade. The light played over the almost still surface of the water, shadow and light.

"There are towels for your use, enjoy." The old woman pocketed the purse he handed across to her, locked the door, shuffled to the stairs and disappeared above.

"What is this place?" asked Genevra amazed to find such a thing in the heart of St Giles.

"This is called Queen Anne's Bath. It's fed by a natural hot spring." He drew her towards the pool. "We have the place to ourselves for two hours." He slid his hands up her arms and bent his head to kiss her. "I thought you might appreciate a hot bath?"

She laughed as his lips grazed her neck and nibbled her ear. "How marvellous, yes what a lovely thing to think of."

"Good, let me undress you." His voice thickened, and she let him unlace her and remove the layers of her clothing. He laid her clothes aside on a bench to keep them off the damp floor and turned to stroke her body, pressing her close against him.

"So beautiful," he murmured. Her body stirred with his proximity; the pleasure they had shared two nights ago reemerging.

She pulled back and reached for his jacket and helped him off with it, in a few moments he was also naked, and he helped her down the steps into the water, which came up to her breasts. The water was deliciously warm and lapped against her skin sensuously. She stretched out and floated.

"This is blissful," she said. "Thank you."

He swam up beside her and reached for her. "You are welcome. I come here regularly, and it seemed the perfect setting for our next encounter." He pulled her into his arms and kissed her damp skin, suckling on her shoulder, his warm tongue lapping at her skin. His hands slid over her back and down to her rump, squeezing, stroking, pulling her closer against his body, his cock, already firm and hot between them. His touch ignited the ready fire in her body, and she pressed close, eager for more of the pleasure he had saturated her in two nights ago. *This man was a drug she couldn't get enough of.*

His tenderness to her last night had got past her defences and she knew herself to be vulnerable to his charm, his seductive lovemaking. Her heart fluttered with apprehension. She needed to shield herself from the allure of his kindness. But it drew her like a moth to flame. Sweet as chocolate. Heady as strong spirits. She needed to remember this was just a business transaction, nothing more and it would end.

The reminder placed a guard around her heart, that vulnerable organ could not take more punishment. She would enjoy what he offered but she would not, could not let herself care.

He lowered her into the water holding her up with one hand under her back while he suckled her breast, licking drops of water off her skin, laving her nipple and making it crinkle up tight. The water lapped around her and between her thighs, caressing her sensitive skin. His other hand ventured lower stroking between her lips and making her buck and gasp, water splashing.

"Steady love," he murmured. "I need to fuck you and I want to know you're ready for me."

She huffed a laugh, and her hand sought him under the water a sense of playful joy in amongst the desire. She brushed his cock with her fingers and then grasped him, grinning in satisfaction when he groaned as she gripped him.

"Sauce for the goose," she murmured.

A finger pushed inside her, making her gasp, and he responded, "Is sauce for the gander."

She stroked him, and he worked his fingers inside her, watching her eyes as he did it, applying his thumb to her bud, she moaned helplessly, her hips rolling. creating waves of water.

He nodded as if satisfied, and withdrew his fingers, moving his hand under her back to pull her upright. She floated weightless with the water, willing to let him do as he wished. She realised with a vague sense of shock that she wasn't afraid of his touch. Hadn't been from the beginning. Instinctively she trusted him not to hurt her. Her heart gave another of those traitorous surges of warmth. *Pleasure for now, that is all,* she reminded herself sternly.

He was undoubtedly strong, she had the evidence under her hands in his biceps and pectorals, but she wasn't concerned he'd use it against her. His lips covered hers again, and she surrendered to his kisses, giving them back in equal measure.

He made a sound in his throat of appreciation and pulled her close against his body. Understanding his intent she wrapped her legs around him, as holding her thighs, he sought the entrance to her body with his cock.

He slid inside her and rocked his hips, and she clung to him, her body suffused with hot desire. He felt so good, deep inside her, the position was different, the luxury of the hot water and its buoyancy gave the whole experience a delicious edge that she would never forget.

"I think," he said, his voice husky. "I could stay inside you forever."

A giggle rose up out of nowhere making her inner muscles spasm and causing him to groan. She smiled enjoying her sense of power to afflict him so, tightening her arms and legs around him, as he began to thrust slowly inside her, his eyes holding hers in a way that she found compelling and intimate.

He seemed to want to delve inside her soul, the way his cock was delving in her body and his next words confirmed it. His voice was husky and low as he drew her face closer to kiss her jaw and neck and then draw back to hold her gaze with his again.

"Look at me Genevra." She obeyed him and lost herself in his hazel-green gaze. "I want to know you, woman. Open to me." His words, a low command, made her heart stutter in her breast and caused a palpable rush of heat and moisture between her legs.

He felt it too, because his response was electric, he thrust deeper inside her, gripping her hips with bruising force, and he flung back his head and groaned.

Lifting one hand to the back of her head, he kissed her, open-mouthed and devouring, as he fucked her hard and deep, holding her to him with his other arm. She clung to him, writhing in his grip, the water lapping around them in hot silken waves, her body consumed with the rising fire his cock stirred in her core. *She was going to come from his thrusting alone!*

She groaned repeatedly with each thrust, as he drove her closer and closer to the precipice, each sound a counterpoint to his grunt of effort. She hit the peak of delicious pleasure, and it exploded in her body, radiating outwards, and moments later she felt the hot rush of his seed deep inside her as he shuddered and groaned his pleasure into her neck, his arm a tight band across her back, his hand clenching her bottom in spasms.

As the waves ebbed and wound down to blissful lassitude, her legs loosened round him, and he moved his arms to hold her to him still, reluctant it seemed to be parted from her body. They stayed that way for endless moments, her head resting on his shoulder, his face buried in her neck.

Finally, he stirred, kissing her neck and loosened his hold on her, letting her legs slip downward until she could take her own weight, and he could slide from her body.

"Each time with you is a revelation," he murmured. He stroked a damp strand of hair from her face and said, "Tell me what you achieved today?"

She pulled back, floating freely, her toes peeking out of the water, using her arms to keep herself afloat. "Let me see," she said contemplating the ceiling. "Took a delivery, sorted out the inventory, sold a great many pots of porter and beer and about half as many meals, placed the order for next week's deliveries and rearranged the cellar. What did you do?"

"Not as productive as you, I fear. I have found the last few days my concentration has been shot to hell. All I can think about -" he reeled her into his arms and kissed her. "Is you." He kissed her again. "And how many ways I can give you pleasure."

Her skin already flushed pink from the water and their lovemaking, flushed further, and a warmth licked around her heart. *Did she really have such power over him?* Thoughts like that were dangerous, but the sensation was addictive, seductive.

"I feel drunk with the pleasure you have given me," she admitted softly. "I was told that you are a harsh and violent man with no compassion. I know that is untrue, for you have shown me nothing but consideration and care. I am giddy with it."

"It is true love, I am brutal, selfish and violent. You saw evidence of my temper last night. I have a shell of a heart, for I've grown up knowing little of the softer emotions. I've had little use for them. But-" he paused surveying her face as if seeking the solution to a puzzle he didn't quite comprehend,

"With you, I am finding that perhaps I have a slither of humanity after all."

She traced his lower lip with her finger and said, "I never thought that I would be grateful to Jacob for anything, but perhaps paradoxically, I am grateful he owed you a debt, or we would never have met. Whatever comes next, I'll never regret this."

She pressed her lips to his in gratitude, and he immediately responded, tightening his hold and deepening the kiss.

HER KISSES WERE a drug he couldn't get enough of and the desire to give her pleasure persisted no matter how often he took her. He was hungry to see her fall apart again. Swinging her round, he lifted her up onto the tiled edge of the pool and spread her legs.

He brought his head in alignment with her sweet, delicious cunny and spreading her wide with his fingers, proceeded to lick and devour her. Her taste was a mixture of the water, her own sticky juices and his musky bitter seed.

He licked inside her and along the length of her lips, worried at her bud of pleasure with his tongue and delighted in her every gasp, moan, jerk and shudder. When he judged she was close, he pulled her back down into the water and swiftly onto his stiffened cock. Pressing her back against the side of the pool he fucked her slowly, watching her face intently. He wanted to see the moment her pleasure peaked and exploded in her eyes.

"Look at me," he said hoarsely when her impossibly blue eyes threatened to close. "Open to me. Let me in," he said, driving himself into her with deliberate hard strokes that made her breasts bounce in the water.

Her skin was flushed, dewed with moisture, her face twisted with the desire he was forcing into her with his cock. With this woman he felt powerful in a way that he never had before. She made him feel greater than himself. More somehow. As if when he was with her, he became someone else, someone with more to offer than the brutal hardness of his past.

She gasped with each thrust, her breath ragged, her body jolting. *He had made her come with his cock alone the first time, could he do it again?* The idea of that made him swell with masculine pride, that she could want him that much. *As much as he wanted her?*

He pulled her away from the side of the pool, holding her in his arms and bending forward, keeping her head above the water he continued to fuck her, her legs streaming behind him. He kept his gaze fixed on hers, watching for the inner fire in her eyes, watching for it to ignite and take flight. He kissed her mouth, fucking her with his tongue in time with his cock.

Lifting his head, holding her gaze again he whispered. "Open to me." Not even quite sure what he meant by it, but wanting something from her, he couldn't name. "Let me inside you," he said his voice a hoarse whisper, a prayer, a plea. It was a ridiculous request when he was already inside her, balls deep, thrusting with relentless strength and power. And yet that physical possession was not enough.

"Come for me!" he said, twisting her body on his. "Clench me!" he demanded.

She obeyed, her inner muscles clamping tight, and he groaned.

"Yes, again!" he pleaded. *He never pleaded for anything. What was she doing to him?*

She repeated the clenching, her breathing ratcheting up and her body shuddering in his hold.

"Again!" he groaned. Clench. Thrust. Clench. Thrust.

"Do it again!" he panted, losing control. She clenched hard, wrenching on him and made a sound between a gasp and a groan. Her hands clutched at him as her inner muscles clamped over and over.

"Gar-mon! her voice was strangled as her body arched, shuddering, and he felt the pulsing intensity of her climax. Like an arc of electricity, her climax triggered his own and he staggered as his knees threatened to buckle with the exquisite pleasure. Hot seed flowed out of him in multiple, intensely pleasurable shots, and he grunted with the force of it.

He panted, the pleasure flowing through his body, loosening his limbs and making him feel light and buoyant.

He let her go, and they floated a moment before he brought her in closer and kissed her damp skin. Her neck, her shoulder, her cheek, her lips.

Had she let him in as he requested? He didn't know. He didn't know what he meant by it. Just that no matter how much he had her, he seemed to want more. The idea should scare the living daylights out of him. But he couldn't seem to muster fear, only desire where she was concerned, and a fierce protective fire, a possessive, all-consuming need to make her his in some indefinable way that yet eluded him.

"Your times up Mr Lovell." The old hag shuffled forward grinning lasciviously at them. No doubt the dirty old girl had been listening to them, perhaps watching from the stairs. The words a reminder that this arrangement with Genevra was only temporary.

"Thank you, Mrs Stevens, if you will give us ten minutes to dress?"

The old lady laughed and nodded, shuffling off.

"Did she see?" asked Genevra in a hushed tone of horror.

"Probably." He smiled at her expression of shock. "I'm sure she's seen worse. After all, we weren't doing anything depraved."

He helped Genevra from the water, towelled her dry and helped her dress. She smiled at him throughout, a glow of happiness to her skin and eyes that made his heart swell in his chest.

He did that, he made her happy. Garmon Lovell, who never made anyone happy.

She helped him dry off and dress and kissed him when she draped his neckcloth round his neck and knotted it in place.

"Thank you, it was marvellous. I shall never forget this."

"We're not done yet love. We have three more nights of our contract to run. I have some more delights in store for you."

She laughed leaning against him as he guided her out of the building and down the steps into the street.

"Anymore and I will not be able to walk in truth."

"Not tonight love, I'll take you home now," he said helping her into the carriage.

CHAPTER 10

"*I*t's time you were thinking of marrying again, Genevra, you can't keep operating the Tavern on your own, it's not seemly," said her stepfather, cutting into his mutton.

Genevra clenched her teeth and counted to ten before she answered. "Thank you for your concern, Sir, but I am doing very well, and it is no burden I assure you."

"Nonsense. You're in serious debt, need I remind you? Why don't you let me appoint a manager to take over the day to day running? You can come back here and help your mother, she will appreciate a hand around the house, won't you Miriam?"

Her mother glanced apologetically at Genevra and mumbled something that could be an affirmative.

Beth, her youngest sister toyed with the food on her plate and surreptitiously fed bits of it to the dog under the table. Genevra noted her pallor with a worried frown and wished she had the means to provide her sister with a much-needed holiday at the seaside, *or perhaps a sojourn in Bath to drink the waters would benefit her? She could stay with Great Aunt Maddie.*

Her stepfather, put down his knife to take a sip of wine and regarded her over the top of the glass. "Genevra if you will not obey me, I may be forced to demand the repayment of your debts in full, immediately. Do I make myself clear."

"Hiram!" protested her mother.

"My dear it's for Genevra's own good. While Jacob's whereabouts were unknown it was reasonable for Genevra to remain at the Tavern, but now that we know he is dead, she should either remarry or return to the family home. It is a scandal for her to be living by herself in a Tavern and hobnobbing with men all day."

"I am not alone!" Genevra interposed. "Mrs Bell stays with me, and during the day Joe and his boys are more than adequate protection."

"My point exactly!" Said Hiram Robinson, with the superior air that never failed to put her all on edge. "The truth is my dear you are not capable of running the Tavern on your own. That is not your fault! No mere female can be expected to shoulder such burdens-"

Genevra, who had heard enough, slammed down her knife and rose. "Mama, I refuse to sit here and listen to this twaddle!" She rounded on Hiram. "I am perfectly capable, and I shall continue to do so!" She turned to gather up her cloak and reticule.

"Genevra please!" said her mother rising from her seat.

"I am sorry, Mama, but I will not be subjected to this nonsense!"

"Genevra, do not speak to your mother like that!" Hiram too had risen from his seat, the only one still at the table was Beth, who was doing her best to pretend the rest of them didn't exist. Genevra flinched internally for her delicate sister, but she was too angry to moderate her behaviour.

"It is best if I leave sir, as I cannot bite my tongue when you insist upon treating me like a helpless ninny! I am no such thing!"

Hiram wiped his forehead with his napkin, his colour considerably heightened. "I make every excuse for womanly megrims my dear, but this is the outside of enough. Your intemperance is all the evidence I need that you are not fit to run a business alone. As I have a considerable stake in your business, I need to ensure that it is profitable. To that end I will be appointing Josiah Neeps to manage the Tavern on my behalf. You can expect him next Monday. Be prepared to turn over the books to him."

"No!" Genevra stared at him in horror. "No, you can't do this!"

"I can and I will!"

"No, no! Please! I will pay you the money I owe you, I promise! I *am* paying it. When have I missed a payment?"

"You have not," he conceded.

"Well then? Do you wish me to pay you back more quickly? I will undertake to increase the monthly sum, pay you weekly if you like?"

"How can you afford to do so?"

Genevra smiled. "We are beginning to turn a profit. I believe I can increase the payments."

Hiram shifted, clearly uncomfortable with this turning of the tables. "Very well. I shall expect a ten percent increase on the monthly repayment."

Genevra suppressed a gasp, doing calculations in her head to figure out how she could meet that demand.

"Very well sir."

"But I warn you, any default will result in a foreclosure. I shall put in my own manager to extract the funds. And-" he added. "I want you to seriously consider the topic of remarriage. While you continue to be unmarried, you remain my responsibility and your current conduct is an embarrassment to the family."

"Yes sir," said Genevra swallowing her wrath.

"And sit down and eat your dinner!" he added resuming his own seat.

Genevra sat and forced down several mouthfuls. She caught Beth's eye and the younger girl grimaced in sympathy.

An hour later Genevra left in a hackney to return to the

Tavern, still fuming and under the anger, severely rattled. Hiram couldn't force her to the altar against her will, but he could foreclose on her. She needed to pay off his debt as fast as possible so that he no longer had leverage over her. It was a timely reminder that allowing any man to have leverage over her was fatal. She swore that once she was clear of these debts: Hiram's and Garmon's, she would never let a man control her destiny again.

She reached the Tavern just as Joe was closing up. Once he and his boys and the bar maids had gone, she finished the last chores of the day and dashed upstairs to change. She was weary after the day's events and the argument with Hiram, and for the first time she was not particularly looking forward to seeing Garmon.

She was exhausted from five nights in a row of broken sleep, to say nothing of the strenuous exercise they had indulged in and the emotional upheaval of it all. Much as she loved how he made her feel, Garmon was demanding, and she was bone deep tired of men controlling her life.

∾

ONE MONTH ago

Jacob rolled over in the bed and winced, his breath catching with the pain radiating out from his wound.

"Are you alright?" came the soft voice beside him.

"Yeah, just catches me if I move suddenly."

"Can I do anything to help?" she rolled towards him, her hands landing on his chest.

He reached for her warm body, she smelled of soap and something earthy that tugged at his cock. His hand found one generous breast through the fabric of her night gown. He squeezed it hard, and she made a noise he took for appreciation. He moved his head to snare her mouth with his and kissed her. She opened her lips to take his tongue and he shifted to roll her under him, using a knee to push her legs apart. But the movement pulled at his wound and made him gasp and curse.

"Fuck!" he dropped his head to the pillow willing the sharp pain to subside.

She stroked his hair. "You're not better yet."

"No, but when I am, I'm going to fuck you so hard you'll scream your pretty tits off!"

She giggled and ran her hand over his shoulders. "I hope so."

He groaned and shifted again, scrabbling to get under her gown, palming her between her legs. He shoved his fingers in her, she was wet and took him easily, better than Genevra, who was always dry and reluctant. Maggie squirmed and panted as he thrust his fingers in her.

"You like it rough, don't you?" he grunted, moving his hips to thrust against her belly. The pain this caused made him howl and curse. "If I could fuck you now I would, but it bloody hurts too much to move like this," he panted. "Get your cunt up here and fuck my cock with your mouth."

"Oh!" she moved to obey him and after a bit of painful rearrangement they found a position that minimised his discomfort. With his fingers inside her and her mouth on his cock, he groaned, this time more pleasure than pain.

He couldn't wait until his body was strong enough to get her under him, his mind roved over the possibilities as her tongue laved and her mouth sucked. She was much better at this than Genevra. All the same, memories of Genevra's tight cunt haunted him as he resisted the urge to thrust into Maggie's mouth to minimise the pain it caused.

Frustration made him growl and grip her bottom tighter, pinching hard. She yelped and he smacked her rump hard. "Fuck me bitch!" he mumbled, licking her haphazardly.

She redoubled her efforts, sliding up and down his cock and he groaned, excitement building. *Fuck yes!* He jabbed her harder with his fingers, all four stretching her, his thumb rubbing her furiously. Genevra hated this, but Maggie seemed to love it.

He fought to keep his hips still, frustration warring with slowly building excitement. *Finally, yes! Fucking yes!* His muscled tensed up as he felt the trigger pulled, and he lost his load in her mouth with a loud groan. "Buggering *fuck* that's good!" he moaned, his muscles going lax in the aftermath of bliss. *No pain now!*

She squirmed and panted, sitting up a bit as she finished herself off with a cry and her cunt squeezed his fingers hard. He smacked her arse lazily. "Good?"

She nodded, panting and moved to slide back down beside him. Subsiding with her head on his shoulder.

"It'll be better when I can fuck you properly," he murmured, sleep over taking him.

CHAPTER 11

$\mathcal{A}$s soon as Genevra stepped into the carriage, Garmon could tell there was something wrong. She looked tired for one, but there was something else too. The glow of happiness she had worn last night was gone. Sensing that crowding her would be unwelcome, instead of taking her in his arms and kissing her as he longed to do, he simply took her hand and said, "What is wrong?"

She smiled but it didn't reach her eyes. "I'm sorry, I am tired. It's been a–a trying day."

He kissed her hand and squeezed it. "Well then, my plan for tonight is perfect."

"What is it?"

He simply smiled. "Wait and see."

She subsided against the squabs and silence fell between them. Not troubled precisely, but not the sort of companionable silence he was becoming accustomed to.

Inside his rooms, he took her cloak and hung it on the coat tree. "Wine or something stronger?" he asked as she prowled towards the fire and held her hands to the blaze. She looked back at him over her shoulder.

"Something stronger?"

He smiled and served her a double shot of single malt whisky. She took it and sipped, closing her eyes, her back to the fire. He could see her gathering herself, and he wondered what had so overset her since last night. The idea that someone had upset her, made his muscles knot up with tension, and he badly wanted to ask, but perversely he wanted her to tell him of her own accord.

She tossed off the rest of the whisky, and he said, "Another?"

She hesitated and then nodded. "Please."

He poured it for her, sipping his own at a more leisurely pace. She drank half of the second glass and set it on the mantelpiece. "Thank you." She turned towards him with a determined smile. "What have you planned for tonight?" The smile didn't quite reach her eyes, but he couldn't stay away from her any longer.

Setting down his glass, he slid his arms round her and kissed her lips softly.

"Come and see." He shepherded her into the bedroom, where soft candles gave a gentle glow to the room, which had been thoroughly warmed by a well stoked fire. Before which, on the floor, was a large sheepskin rug and a pile of pillows, a stack of folded towels, a basin, cloth and pots of scented oils, body scrub and creams.

She turned to look at him one eyebrow raised. "I thought," he said softly, "you might appreciate a massage?"

She bit her lip and glancing from the fire and back at him. "Your imagination is truly phenomenal Garmon. How do you think of such things?"

He smiled and turning her gently, began to unbutton her dress, planting little kisses on her neck and shoulders. "I simply," kiss, "Think of," kiss, "The things," kiss, "I want," kiss, "to do," kiss, "to you." Kiss.

She sighed as he pushed her gown off her shoulders and ran

his hands over her muscles, kneading them gently. She was as tense as steel. She groaned as his fingers bit into her flesh and his cock twitched inside his trousers.

He pushed her gown to her hips and cupped her breasts, squeezing them gently through her chemise. He pinched her nipples, and she gave a little squeak that made him smile and nip her ear. He made short work of her corset and chemise, her garters, stockings and boots. Kneeling behind her, he ran his hands up her legs and kissed her gorgeous round derrière.

"Go lie down. I'll be with your shortly." He nodded to the fire, rising to his feet and ripping off his neckcloth, jacket and waistcoat swiftly. His shirt, boots and breeches rapidly followed, and he fetched their glasses, before joining her by the fire.

He knelt beside her and took a moment to appreciate the sight of her stretched out on her stomach, the red glow of the fire gleaming on her skin as the shadows thrown by the candles danced over the curves and hollows of her luxurious form. She was delicious, a banquet he couldn't wait to sample, yet again. He wasn't growing tired of her. *Would he ever?* She had pillowed her head on her arms, her hair twisted up out of the way of her back and shoulders, and she was regarding him sleepily.

"If I fall asleep on you, please don't be offended." she said.

He smiled and reached for the oil. Straddling her legs, he ran his well-oiled hands from her shoulders to her deliciously rounded bottom. His ball sack rested on her thighs and his cock lengthened and stiffened as his hands ran over her soft pale skin. Like most red heads she had milky white skin, so smooth it reminded him of cream. He squeezed and massaged her shoulders and ran his thumbs down either side of her spine and she moaned softly with pleasure, which made his cock twitch. He ignored it.

With only the crackle of the fire and her occasional moans of appreciation for accompaniment, he worked her skin and muscles to free them of the appreciable stored tension, worrying at what had upset her so and wishing she would confide in him.

Rubbing his thumbs in circles in the indentation above the swell of her buttocks he considered what he could say to entice her to tell him what the matter was, without outright asking. For some reason it was important that she offer the information of her own volition.

He slid his hands under her hips pulling his fingers back across her pelvis and rubbing his thumbs across the swell of her hips.

She groaned at this treatment, and he repeated the action.

"You like that?"

"Hmm."

"You're very tense, I need to do more to relax you, clearly last night's treatment wasn't enough."

She sighed. "That feels wonderful. How did you learn to do this?"

"I was raised in a brothel. The girls taught me how to massage them."

She lost her sleepy demeanour. "How old were you?"

"When I lived at the brothel? Between five and fifteen, I left when Mama died."

"Did you work there?" she asked.

"Yes for the last couple of years." He paused considering what to tell her. "I offered services that some clients were prepared to pay good money for."

"That is terrible," she murmured.

"You do what you must, to stay alive, Genevra," he said gently. "Don't be feeling sorry for me. I make it a policy to regret nothing. It's a waste of time and emotion. What's done is done."

She dropped her head back onto her arms, and he leaned forward and kissed the nape of her neck, murmuring in her ear. "Relax. None of that has anything to do with you or us, here and now. Enjoy."

She blinked and closed her eyes, but not before he saw the moisture in them. Cursing himself for having revealed more of his sordid past than he should, he redoubled his efforts to please her, running his hands the full length of her back and up again. Working at the knots in her shoulders. Gradually he felt her relaxing again and her little moan of appreciation made him smile.

Moving to the side, he spread her legs and knelt between them, leaning forward to knead her buttocks and press his knuckles into the soft flesh, working to release the knots he could feel in her lower back.

He ran his thumbs either side of the spilt in her buttocks and revealed what lay hidden between them. He hadn't ventured there yet with her and wouldn't tonight, but perhaps for their last night together? A pang hit his chest at the thought of this arrangement coming to an end.

He shook it off, he needed to bring this to an end because his business was suffering due to inattention. As much as he hated to admit it, he had spent more time thinking about Genevra, and planning their encounters than he should have. He needed to redirect his energies into his plans to get the hell back and into his network of spies and information that fed his income stream. *He was getting careless. That was dangerous.*

He stroked an oiled finger down the channel between her buttocks and she uttered a noise and wriggled her bottom in response, which made him groan.

"Genevra my darling do you know how erotic that is," he murmured, bending forward and biting one soft round buttock.

"Garmon!" she protested, lifting her bottom in reflex.

He chuckled and sliding his finger lower he pushed her legs further apart with his knees and swirled around her entrance. *So much for relaxing her.*

He brought his finger to his lips and tasted her sticky dew with a soft moan of appreciation. Returning his finger to that place, he pushed inside her, and her hips lifted in response. Reaching for a pillow, he slipped it under her pelvis and worked two fingers inside her, his other hand sliding beneath to stroke her gently.

Her bottom quivered and he huffed a breath. *Fuck she was gorgeous!*

"Garmon!'

"Yes love?" he said sliding his fingers in and out, appreciating each twitch and shiver of her bottom as he did it.

"Is this normal?"

He knew what she meant. "No, it's quite extraordinary in my experience." He bent forward and kissed the nape of her neck. "Which is why I am making the most of it. Come for me, I want to fuck you."

She uttered a sound halfway between a sigh and moan and her bottom shuddered. He rubbed a little faster and thrust his fingers a little deeper and in moments he had her cresting the rise, her bottom trembling, her legs wide and shaking, her inner muscles quaking and clamping on his fingers. *God in heaven he wanted that on his cock!*

Extracting his fingers he leaned forward, sliding his knees back and fitted himself to the shape of her body, seeking and notching the head of his cock to her entrance. He slid inside easily; she was slippery with her own arousal and the oil from his fingers and open and ready from her climax. He lowered his weight onto her back, nuzzling his face into her neck. He loved this position, he loved the angle and the dominance as well as the feel of her under him, pinned and held within the cage of his arms. It was filthy and strangely loving at the same time.

But he felt her tightening up under him. "What's wrong? Don't you like it?" He asked lifting up his weight.

"I feel as if I can't breathe," she said, looking round at him her expression awry.

"You were all right with this position the other night. What's different?"

She shook her head. "I don't know. Tonight, it just feels stifling. I was out of my head that night, perhaps that is why..."

He lifted out and removing the pillow, he slid down beside her on the rug. Running a hand down her side he said, "You're out of sorts tonight. What is it?"

She looked away and he brought her chin round, forced her to look at him. "What is it?"

Her eyes dodged his, and he brought her into his chest. "What is it?" He whispered against her hair, his arms holding her, his hands caressing, her back.

With her face hidden she said, "That position reminds me of something Jacob used to do."

"Ah, I'm sorry love. I'd break every bone in his body if he wasn't already dead."

"He used to pin me down and force me-"

His arms tightened on her, and he ground his teeth. He cradled her head in one hand and kissed her hair. "He can't hurt you any more sweetheart."

"I know, it's silly-"

"It's not! I wish I could erase the damage he did to you..."

"You are." She lifted her head and stroked his face, a slight smile tracing her lips, her eyes glinting with unshed tears. "The pleasure you've given me. It's extraordinary. I'm very grateful."

"I don't want your gratitude," he said roughly, his throat tight.

Her smile grew and she said playfully, "What do you want?"

"I want to be inside you," he said husky voiced with lust and emotions he didn't want to acknowledge. He rolled her onto her back and settled between her legs. "This position all right?"

She nodded, her hair spread around her on the pillow like a blaze of sunlight and flame.

"Good," he said bending to kiss her and sliding inside her at the same time. His cock seemed to know where she was and how to get there with no guidance. *Like a fucking homing pigeon.* He groaned. "You feel so damned good, woman."

SHE SMILED and moved with him as he began to thrust inside her, feeling the pleasurable push and pull, the fullness and the rub of his body against hers, that drew her inexorably towards arousal, towards another peak of pleasure. His eyes looked green tonight, must be a trick of the firelight.

He kept them trained on her as he thrust slow, deep, hard within her, and she found she couldn't look away. *Could he see into her soul, truly?* He had asked her to let him in last night, repeatedly even as he'd moved inside her body and the water lapped around her warm and cushioning, bearing her weight.

He wanted all of her, she could feel the pull of his will, he wanted to delve inside and possess and own her, and it was seductive. A part of her wanted desperately to surrender to that. But she couldn't. She wouldn't. Jacob, and now her stepfather, wanted to control her, own her, make her submit. And as seductive as Garmon's desire for her was, he ultimately wanted the same thing. Her submission, her obedience. And she wouldn't and couldn't give it.

She could give him pleasure though. A pleasure she craved as much as he. They had that. It would have to be enough.

He raised a hand to stroke her hair off her face and kissed her and the pressure of his lips, the insistent exploration of his tongue, the persistent thrusting of his cock inside her, pushed her towards another peak of pleasure, and the heat and warmth, the caring in his touch, drew a response she wasn't prepared for.

She was vulnerable tonight, and he was unravelling her like a ball of twine. She held him tight, they only had two more nights after this one, and she must make the most of it, remember every stroke and touch, thrust and kiss, every exquisite drop of pleasure she could wring from this encounter, for she would never experience anything like this again. *He was right it was extraordinary.*

She clung to him as he pushed her higher, her breath panting and flesh soaking up tingling, swelling pleasure, joy suffusing her body with a lightness and exquisite bliss. She arched her neck, and he kissed it, his teeth grazing her skin and making her whimper.

The knife-edge bliss of impending orgasm swelled, held for a long moment and burst through her body like a dumping wave. In its train she felt the hot rush of his seed within her and held him tightly as he bucked and grunted with his own pleasure. Their bodies moved together in blind need, to wring the last of the wavelets of joy from each other.

He collapsed on her; his breath hot in her ear as he rested his head on the pillow beside hers. Her own body relaxed, her legs flopping loose onto the soft rug and the blissful lethargy letting her drift for a few moments in mindless, sweet forgetfulness.

They must have dozed because at some point he woke and carried her to the bed, tucked her in beside him, and she fell back into a heavy sleep.

When she woke again it was to his lips on her neck and his hands on her body caressing gently.

"Genevra, love." His voice husky and low in her ear as he nuzzled at her neck.

"Hmm." she moved against him, their legs tangling.

"One last fuck before I take you home?" His hand descended spearing her sticky flesh and stirring her in spite of herself. *Hadn't she had enough yet? Seems not and neither had he if the rigid cock poking into her hip was any indication.*

He rolled her over onto her opposite side, bringing her back up against his chest and nuzzling at her neck again. His hands cupped her breast and her mound, his fingers busy rubbing her into arousal. He slid a knee between her legs and pushed his cock inside her. The angle was tight and when he began to move it seemed to rub a place inside her that made her pant and moan.

He held her on him, his fingers teasing her into another rise as his cock played merry exquisite hell with her insides. *What was it about this angle that was so...* her thoughts dissolved in panting, moaning distraction as he sped up his thrusts. He seemed almost frantic to come, his lips on her neck, his breath hot and panting on her skin. His sweat slicked torso rubbing against her back, the hairs slightly scratchy and arousing.

"Fuck Genevra! Come for fuck's sake..." his voice broke on a groan, and she felt him emptying himself into her in hard, hot shots. Three, four of them and several shuddering aftershocks, each with a grunt and a huff of breath. He panted.

"Fuck!" He kissed her shoulder. "Fuck that was good!" He sighed. "You didn't come did you?"

"Not quite," she said with a laugh in her voice, she was quietly pleased by his evident pleasure. "But it felt wonderful, why is this position so..."

"Ah, I'm catching a place inside you that is particularly sensitive, here." He demonstrated with a few thrusts of his still hard cock.

"Ohh!" she shuddered. And he kept doing it, his fingers busy in accompaniment. He moved his other hand to one of her nipples and tweaked it, sending little tendrils of pleasure downwards. The treble assault made her pant and moan, her legs trembling.

"That's it sweetheart," he murmured in her ear, nibbling the lobe and making her shiver.

Held in his arms and tortured in four places, the pleasure built and built, until it hit a wall of suspended pleasure, and she came with sudden, hard force; groaning and shuddering and squirming in his hold, as his fingers cleverly wrung the last thrills of pleasure from her body.

She went lax in his arms, panting. He held her and stroked her gently, bringing her back to earth slowly. "Garmon that was..." words failed her.

"Yes, I know, rear entry is a particular favourite of mine. It feels both filthy and fucking good for both parties if you can get the angle right."

"I've never liked it before." she admitted.

"That's because your oaf a husband was only concerned with his own pleasure. He was a brutal, selfish fuck!"

She giggled. "Yes, you're right." She turned over to face him, her finger tracing a line from his brow to the corner of his mouth. "And you are not. I'm blessed by your passion Garmon. I never knew it could be like this. Thank you."

"Don't thank me." he said low and fierce. "There is nothing to thank me for! A woman should never have to thank a man for making her feel good. It's your right Genevra. It's your fucking right!"

He kissed her fiercely, and she felt a drop of moisture on her cheek. *It must be sweat; the man couldn't be shedding tears over her. Could he?*

He pulled away abruptly and sat up with his back to her. "We had best move quickly, if you're to be home in time."

a **week ago**
    Jacob and Maggie had been sharing a bed for two months now and satisfying each other with a lot of mutual hand and mouth play, but his wound was healed sufficiently he could finally lie fully on his back comfortably and thrust his hips without going through the roof with pain. The strapping had been removed from his leg today as well. He could walk freely at last, and his strength was coming back.

And his cock was active as hell. His lurid fantasies had become obsessive as he contemplated what he was going to do to Maggie when his body would let him. Watching her enter the room from his seat by the fire, with a tray of food for their dinner, he decided tonight was the night.

He smiled at her, and she smiled back. "Hungry?" She set the tray down on the table and his eyes travelled over her body, her generous breasts curving over the top of her bodice, she was like and unlike Genevra. She had Genevra's curves, but she was much more responsive than Genevra. She didn't act like she loathed him for a start. Genevra's cold disdain for him had made him furious with her. A wife was supposed to meet her husband's needs, not the other way around.

He winced internally recalling some of his worst outbursts. But she goaded him, always arguing and talking back. It was her fault he hit her, she would try the patience of a saint, and he was far from that. And on top of that she lost two babies and then proved barren. Altogether she had been a great disappointment as a wife.

Maggie on the other hand liked it rough and hard, she didn't need him to be careful of her, and she took care of herself if his passion took him quicker than it took her to get there. He liked that a lot. Now he was mobile he could fuck her properly and thoroughly, like he'd been promising himself for an age.

"Famished," he said, grabbing her round the waist and dragging her down into his lap. She squealed and laughed as his arm wrapped round her waist and pulled her close for a kiss. "Food can wait," he muttered slewing her round in his lap.

GENEVRA'S DAY was busy as usual, but her peace was considerably cut up by a visit from Josiah Neeps, her stepfather's Manager. The man was built on bullish lines, with high coloured cheeks and a developing paunch. She spotted him from the doorway to the office, but stayed hidden to watch him approach Joe, as he was manning the tap for customers in the public bar when he came in. Joe recounted the conversation to her later, telling her that he recognised his former boss immediately.

Neeps sauntered up to the bar and requested a beer.

"Certainly, Mr Neeps, pot or tankard?"

"Tankard." Neeps cast his pale piggy eyes about and then brought them back to Joe who handed him a frothing tankard.

"That'll be six pence sir."

Neeps handed over the money and took a long pull of the

beer, wiping his mouth. "That's a fine drop of Whittaker's you have there," he said with a friendly smiled.

Joe grunted assent and eyed him suspiciously. "What you doing here, Mr Neeps?"

"Fellow can't have a beer at his local?"

"Certainly, he can but this ain't your local," replied Joe with a frown.

Neeps shrugged. "No need to get your breeches in a twist Joseph, I'm looking for Mrs Tate. She about?"

"What do you want with her?"

"Just a friendly visit." Neep's mild tone didn't fool Joe. Genevra had confided to him something of the threats her step-father had issued, and as Joe told her, he wasn't about to let the likes of Neeps harass or upset her. He was about to tell him she wasn't on the premises, when she emerged from the office.

Neeps seeing her, smiled and headed her way. She took him into the coffee room. A few minutes later Neeps emerged and headed out the door to the street. Genevra came towards the bar to speak with Joe.

"What did he want?" asked Joe quietly.

"He says he came to warn me, because he has a 'soft spot' for me!" Genevra uttered this with a grimace. "In actuality I think he hoped to ingratiate himself with me. I believe Hiram sent him to spy on me, despite his promise not to send him here to take over the books." She thumped a bunch of dirty tankards into a crate to take them out and wash them. "He means to wrest the Tavern from me if he can. I must find a way to stop him!"

"Steady lass," Joe put a hand on her shoulder. "You're paying down the debt, he's got no legal recourse against you while you're meeting the terms of the loan."

She sighed. "I know, but it's tactics like this that he employs to unsettle me."

. . .

FOR THEIR PENULTIMATE NIGHT TOGETHER, Garmon took her to the Theatre Royal in Covent Garden. Entering the box, set on the uppermost tier, Genevra discovered that they had a perfect view of the whole audience below them as well as the stage. The box was deep with curtains on the sides for privacy, the rear part in shadow. It was furnished with a couch big enough for two, upholstered in plush, deep-rose velvet, to match the curtains. He served her sparkling wine and she toasted with him to another evening of pleasure. The theatre hummed with the noise of the audience and the jangling cords of the orchestra tuning up.

The snuffers, began dousing the lights and the opening cords of the performance began, accompanied by the drawing back of the curtain. Genevra loved the theatre and seldom had the opportunity to indulge her passion, so she was looking forward to the performance of Shakespeare's A Mid-Summer Nights Dream with eager anticipation. This was a new semi-operatic production by Frederic Reynolds that had been playing to packed houses since January, she was beyond pleased to finally see it.

She sat entranced through the first half and was happy to stroll in the intermission and stretch her legs. Garmon was a perfect host, attending to her every comfort and keeping her in giggles with his saucy stories of the shenanigans of the cast. She could almost think herself a grand lady being gallanted to the theatre by a noble beau.

Yet there was an edge to him tonight, a tension that spoke of something held tightly in check. Watching his profile as he steered her around a knot of theatre goers in the hallway, she vowed to try to find out what the matter was later, when they were alone.

He had showed her such care and solicitude last night, it behoved her to return the favour.

Returned to the box for the second half of the play, she settled into the couch and prepared to enjoy herself.

Seated beside her he murmured, "Are you quite comfortable?"

"Indeed yes, this couch is spectacularly comfortable," she said wafting her fan slowly. The theatre was warm.

"Good," he said as the curtain rose, his hand holding hers on her knee. She became so absorbed in the performance, it was several minutes before she realised that he had contrived to get his hand up under her skirt and was very lightly brushing over her lips.

She raised her fan and whispered behind it, "What are you doing?"

"It is perfectly obvious what I am doing," he replied quietly. "Keep your eyes on the stage, no one can see."

She waved her fan and stifled a gasp as his fingers traced a line between her lips that set tendrils of fire alight in her body. With the utmost effort, she held herself still, trying not to react to the teasing of his fingers.

She glanced sideways at him, and his gaze was fixed on the stage, but his lips were pursed in a slight smile. The dratted man was enjoying this.

Her cheeks flushed with embarrassment at being fingered in public, but the sheer outrageousness of it, the naughtiness of it, made her wetter than ever, and she swallowed a moan when he pushed a finger lower, seeking access to her body. She sank back against the cushions canting her hips and parting her legs to enable him to push a finger inside her. The front of the box hid what he was doing from anyone's sight even if they could have seen anything in the dimness of the theatre, which was sparsely lit by only a few candles.

She moved lower on the couch, giving him greater access and rolled her hips helplessly as his fingers wrought havoc with her body. Distracted from the performance., she whimpered, and he whispered, "Are you close?"

"Yess!" she hissed back behind her fan.

"Good," he said withdrawing his hand.

She gasped in frustration but any protest she might have

made was silenced when he slid quietly to his knees and lifting her skirt, slipped under her petticoats and set his mouth on her.

The next few moments were suspended, tortuous, bliss, as he brought her off in spectacular fashion with his lips, tongue and fingers.

She stifled the groan that rose in her throat and stiffened, shuddering as the pleasure peaked and broke, trying to keep her breathing as quiet as possible as her hips writhed, pushing her soft, inflamed flesh against his wicked tongue.

She collapsed back against the couch, her body going lax and tried to recover her equilibrium as he withdrew from beneath her skirts and resumed his seat beside her.

"I trust that was satisfactory?" he murmured.

"I will kill you!" she said without heat.

He laughed. "As long as it is the little death, my dear I've no objection."

He captured her hand and placed it over the placket of his trousers, pressing her palm flat against the palpable erection there. She could feel the heat of it through her glove. "You need to do something about that," he said quietly, his eyes still on the stage.

"You want me to stroke you?" she asked, rubbing her hand surreptitiously up and down the shaft through the cloth.

"No, I want you to get up and go to the back of the box, where I am going to fuck you."

"What!" she gasped. "You can't, not here!"

"I can, and I will," his voice had an implacable note, that she had heard occasionally from him before, and it made her shiver.

"Don't be concerned, no one can see us. It is dark enough and there is enough ambient noise to disguise any accidental noises we might emit, in the throes of passion."

"Garmon, you can't mean it?"

"I do. Get up, slowly, and move to the back of the box."

She hesitated and sensing his rising impatience, her body trembled with an echo of alarm.

"Do it!" He said, his voice harsh and low.

She swallowed and rose slowly, edging away from the front of the box into the darkness in the rear. *He was right it was dark back here.*

He joined her a moment later, and before she could say or do anything, he kissed her. A devouring brutal kiss, she could feel the simmering anger in him, it came through in the kiss and the hardness of his hands on her body. Not painful, but firm. It should terrify her. Instead, her body pulsed with desire.

"Bend over and grab that chair," he said quietly.

She turned obediently, not precisely afraid, but something between alarm and thrill sending goosebumps over her skin and wetness to between her legs.

He lifted her skirts, and she heard the faint sounds of rustling cloth. In another moment, his cock was pressed at her entrance and then with a hard thrust and a stifled grunt he was inside her.

He sighed, bending forward over her back he nuzzled her neck and whispered in her ear. "Hold on, this is going to be brutal and quick!"

She gripped the back of the chair and spread her legs further apart to stabilise herself as he drew back and pushed into her hard.

She stared at the stage through a prism of narrowed vision as he pushed into her with repeated hard thrusts, jolting her whole body with the force of it. His cock reaming her inside, made her want to groan it felt so good. *This was really happening. He was fucking her in a theatre full of people while a performance was played out below them.*

Fucking her hard, his hands tight on her hips, her breasts quivering and bouncing in the confines of her bodice with the force of his driving demand within her.

Her flesh clamped and tightened on him as pleasure spiralled upwards, her body so finely tuned by now to his she couldn't resist the siren call of his flesh buried in hers. She quivered and swallowed the cry that rose to her lips, turning it into a muffled grunt in her throat as pleasure spiked and coursed through her like an incoming tide, washing into every part of her body.

He stroked into her again and again, wrapping an arm round her belly, he pulled her tight against him as he plunged deep, burying his head in her neck, breathing hard, through his nose, grunting with the force of his release as it loosed, hot and flooding within her. His arm shook as the last waves beached and ebbed. His hot breath raised goosebumps on her flesh.

His lips traced a kiss on her shoulder, and he murmured, "And that is how you fuck a woman in public." He ran his nose over her skin and kissed her again. "Lends a spice doesn't it, my dear?"

His hand clenched on her belly momentarily, and then he let her go, withdrawing swiftly and dropping her petticoats back into place.

She turned, her knees trembling and clutched the chair behind her for support, her flesh still throbbing from the intensity of the release. He did up the last of his buttons and lifted a curl off her cheek, tucking it behind her ear. With a finger under her chin, he kissed her lips softly and whispered, "Thank you for indulging me."

She let out a breath slowly and let go of the chair gingerly. "You're right, I feel thoroughly fucked," she said softly and smiled wryly.

He smiled back and offered his arm. "Come and watch the rest of the performance."

"WE SHALL HAVE supper in the Piazza" he said an hour later as they left the Theatre. Since the Piazza was in walking distance, he offered her his arm and asked, "Well my dear, did you enjoy the show?"

REVENGE ON THE DEVIL

She smiled, "Yes very much, what I saw of it." Her slightly accusing glare made him grin.

He was not going to apologise for ravishing her in the box, he'd been fantasising about it for days. And the reality did not disappoint. "Thank you for bearing with my rough handling."

She laughed. "That wasn't rough, it was -" she hesitated as if looking for the right word. "Erotic."

His cock twitched at the word." I'm glad you found it so, I did too. That first night we sealed our bargain I said to myself at the conclusion that it was what a fuck was supposed to feel like. It was so pleasurable it made me laugh with sheer joy. I've been in a foul mood all day. You made me feel better tonight."

"I wondered," she said, squeezing his arm and looking up at him with a look that gave him an odd feeling in his chest. *Was that concern he saw in her eyes? For him?* The wound in his shoulder itched.

"What made you angry?"

He hesitated to confide in her, but there was no one else, and he needed to talk to someone.

Before he could say anything, they had arrived at the Piazza, a famous Covent Garden coffeehouse. The building was Gothic in design and adjoined the Piazza Hotel.

Settled at a table and orders placed, the privacy afforded by the high-backed booth in which they sat, and the intimacy of candlelight encouraged confidences.

Twirling his glass of burgundy, he said, "Do you remember Mr Mor?"

"How could I forget? Mr Mor made quite an impression, why?"

"He's disappeared. I can't find any trace of him. My boys have searched high and low and there is no word, no sightings, nothing. He is not in London; I am sure of it."

"You're concerned?"

He nodded. Observing the play of the candlelight on the ruby red liquid in the glass. "I can't imagine that he would have left London of his own volition."

"What is the relationship between you?" she asked sipping her own glass of wine.

"None by blood. He is the son of Irish immigrants. When I met him, he was an orphan who'd been scraping a living as a mudlark and pick pocket for at least three years. He was eight years old when he saved my life." His lips twisted in an ironic smile. "I'd picked a fight I couldn't win and wound up in an alley with a knife wound bleeding out. He staunched the blood, fetched a doctor and nursed me back to health. I was twenty-two. So not quite a son, more like a little brother, I suppose. He's been with me ever since."

Their meal arrived then, and the conversation lapsed until the waitress departed.

"What do you think has happened to him?"

"I don't know. We quarrelled last time we spoke. That is what bothers me most. If he was dead-" he swallowed. "I think I would know, someone would have seen something, he is well known in these parts, and he wouldn't be taken down easily..." he shook his head. "I don't know."

"What is it you fear?" she asked gently.

He raised his eyes from his plate and contemplated her. She was beautiful in any light, but candlelight gave her a luminous quality, her hair glinting like golden treasure, her skin creamy and perfect, her eyes sparkling blue like sapphires, her lips full and kissable.

Anyone else who asked that question would get an abrupt and nasty answer, but Genevra Tate could ask him anything, and he'd be inclined to answer. Possibly truthfully to boot. So, he voiced the fear he'd been fighting acknowledging for days.

"I-" he cleared his suddenly thicken throat. "I fear he has left me." It sounded so pathetic put like that and the pain in his throat made him reach for the wine and gulp it down in an attempt to ease the restriction. He blinked his eyes, trying to bring her into focus as her hand reached out and covered his. He turned his hand under hers and gripped it tight. "Thank you," he said quietly.

He raised her hand and kissed it. They resumed eating, and he poured more wine for himself and topped up her glass. There was a restful quality to Genevra, being in her company made him feel at peace in a way he couldn't ever remember feeling. It occurred to him, not for the first time, that she would make an excellent wife. She certainly deserved a man who would treat her well.

"Do you plan to marry again?" he asked, curious.

"No!" Her eyes widened in alarm and her hands tightened visibly on the cutlery. "No, I do not." Her emphatic reply made him quirk an eyebrow.

"You're very certain about that?"

"Absolutely! Never again." Her mouth set in a mutinous line, and he detected, not for the first time, some steel in her. He didn't disapprove. She would need that if she was to survive in a world of men, which she seemed determined to do. After her experience with Jacob, he didn't blame her.

"If you change your mind, let me know, I'll vet him for you."

She opened her mouth and shut it again. "What does that mean?"

"It's a racing term, used to refer to checking the soundness of a racehorse. There aren't many men of substance that I don't know something about and no one I couldn't find out about in quick order if need be."

"Thank you, but it won't be necessary." She shivered visibly.

"Are you cold?" She had put off her cloak when they sat down to eat.

"No, I just—can we speak of something else? Marriage is not a topic of conversation that I find congenial."

"Of course," he sipped more wine. "How is the Tavern doing?"

"Well. Trade is brisk. I am thinking of acquiring a spirit's licence, but I don't wish to serve Gin, even though it would be profitable. I fear it will attract the wrong clientele."

"What will you serve instead?"

"Brandy, Whisky, Cognac."

"You'll need a reliable source of supply. The best spirits are imported, mostly illegally."

"I know, which is why I was hesitant about it."

"I can help you source a supplier."

"Can you?" She picked up her glass and sipped looking at him over the rim. "Legally?"

"Ask no questions..."

"I'll think about it."

"It is in my interest to help you increase your profits; I'll get my money back faster."

"True, but you have given me six months remember?"

"I'm not likely to forget, Genevra." He took her hand and fondled the fingers. The prospect of this pleasant liaison coming to an end tomorrow night was lowering in the extreme. "I could waive it altogether for-"

"No!" Her response was quick and decisive and if truth be known, a little hurtful.

"I will pay the debt according to the terms set," she said firmly.

"Can't wait to be rid of me?" He asked with an edge to his voice.

She withdrew her hand and flushed. "It's not that."

"Then what is it? I thought you were enjoying yourself?"

"I am." When nothing further was forthcoming, he probed deeper.

"Why?"

She drank off the rest of her wine and set the glass down frowning at the table. Finally, she raised her eyes and said quietly, "I want my independence. I want to stand on my own feet. I don't want to be beholden or controlled. I've had a belly full of it."

"I admire your courage my dear, and I understand why, after what you have been through, but without a man's protection you are vulnerable in the extreme. This world is not kind to unmarried women."

"I know. But I have Joe and his boys to protect me, and I'll figure out the rest myself. I have a brain, I'm not stupid or helpless!"

"I never said you were." he said mildly, "In fact I think you are a highly intelligent and competent woman."

"You do?" She smiled, clearly pleased and his heart lifted. He liked it when she was happy.

He nodded, frowning in thought. "Who is this Joe you mention? You have spoken of him several times."

"He is my tapster. He's a good man. He was a friend of my father's, I've known him most of my life, he worked in the brewery and when Jacob vanished, he left my stepfather to come and work for me. I suppose he is like an uncle to me; his boys are like younger brothers or cousins."

"Why didn't your stepfather intervene with Jacob?"

"Jacob was careful to only hit me in private, so no one knew, and I was too ashamed to tell anyone what he was doing to me."

"Why didn't you leave him after-" he couldn't voice it, just the thought made his blood boil and his stomach sick.

"I was too afraid to. I know it sounds crazy, but I had nowhere to go except back to my parents and my stepfather would have sent me back to him. In fact, he did, the only time I tried to run away. It was only after Jacob disappeared that I began to get my confidence back. The night terrors slowly abated, and I was able to function normally again.

"When he turned up dead, I was elated. The relief. You see I lived in dread he would show up one day and drag me back into purgatory." Watching her face while she recounted this history, was almost more than he could bear. His hands clenched beneath the table, and he fought the urge to punch something.

"Have you finished?" he nodded at her plate.

"Yes."

"Good," he reached across the table between them and pulled her up out of the booth, settled her cloak around her shoulders and walked her out of the coffeehouse, his body thrumming with barely suppressed fury. In the street he hailed a cab and helped her into it. Whereupon he took her in his arms and kissed her until neither of them could breathe. Holding her tight he murmured against her hair. "Never again. You will never suffer like that again. I promise you."

GENEVRA SWALLOWED tears and clung to him, afraid to believe his words. *For how could he honour such a promise?*

CHAPTER 13

Garmon had demanded she be ready by eight tonight and when she stepped up into the carriage, he drew her into his arms and kissed her with urgent heat, tempered by a tenderness that had not been there in their earlier exchanges. She felt it in the caress of his lips, the stroke of his tongue and the touch of his hands. He held her and kissed her as if she were something precious. It filled her heart to overflowing and made it ache. Because tonight, was their last night together.

He broke the kiss and said "We will spend tonight in an hotel, the whole night. I will return you at eight in the morning and not a moment before. We have twelve hours to savour each other, I intend to do so to the fullest capacity."

She swallowed and nodded. Twelve hours. It was more than twice as long as any of their other encounters. He couldn't surely, propose to make love to her for all of that time? She recalled the marathon of their second night together, when he took her to a place of sensitivity and arousal, she had never dreamed was possible. Did he intend a replay of that scenario? Her flesh twitched and throbbed at the notion even as her heart quailed.

Last night he had ravished her in public, like a common,

Covent Garden whore. Yet it was deliciously, illicitly, wicked. She had never known she could be so wanton until Garmon took her on his desk that first night. She had never envisioned the half of what they had done in the last week.

"Keep your head down and your hood up," he said as the carriage drew to a halt. She let him help her down from the carriage and shepherd her up the steps of Grenier's Hotel. The Concierge recognised him and directed him to the stairs with much bowing and scraping. She listened to him order a meal and wine to be delivered to their room, which he had clearly booked earlier. She kept her face hidden and let him lead her up the sweeping staircase to the second floor. Where they were shown into a sumptuous suite of sitting room and bedroom. The Concierge, tipped handsomely for his service, was dismissed, and they were alone.

The room was beautifully and richly appointed with thick Aubusson carpets beneath their feet, luxurious velvet curtains in a deep burgundy with gold tassels and stylish and elegant gilt trimmed chairs and tables and a large very comfortable looking couch drawn up to the fire. Paintings, ornaments and vases of flowers finished the decor and gave it a homely feel, as if this were a private residence rather than a public room for hire. Candelabra gave sufficient light to see while providing the right note of intimacy. The fire had been burning for some time and the room was toasty warm.

"Let me take your cloak," he said standing behind her and unlacing it. Drawing it off her shoulders he took the opportunity to kiss her neck and shoulder, his hand tracing a caress over her arm. Casting the cloak aside over a chair, he pulled her back against him and wrapped his arms around her stomach. "Do you like the room?"

"It's magnificent. I've never seen anything so fine."

"A setting fit for your beauty," he said kissing her neck again.

A knock at the door interrupted further intimacies, and she

went to the fire, placing her back to the room while the waiters brought in their drinks and meal. When all was settled, and the door closed again she came away from the fire to the table laden with a feast. "Good heavens this is enough to feed an army!" she exclaimed her eyes running over the array of dishes before them.

"A very small army love, come, sit and eat, and tell me about your day." He invited.

She sat and let him serve her. Taking a mouthful of the duck she closed her eyes. "Oh, this is exquisite!" She chewed slowly, swallowed, opened her eyes and smiled across the table at him. He was clearly pleased by her pleasure, and so she allowed herself to be pleased by everything. This was their last night, and it should be savoured. The memories would have to last her a lifetime.

For never again would she experience such pleasure as she had in his arms, and indeed she had no intention of allowing herself to engage in this kind of indulgence again. As she intended never to marry nor take a lover in the future, she would not know another man's touch after this. Which was fitting, any other man would surely be a disappointment after Garmon Lovell.

She passed her day under review and debated what to tell him. She resisted the urge to confide in him over her troubles with her stepfather. She needed to deal with the issue herself. To be further beholden to Garmon, would lengthen the time she was hostage to his power over her, and she most emphatically did not want that. As delicious as it was, this liaison must end.

They had been discreet to a point, but if it became public knowledge that she had been disporting herself with Lovell for a week, in this fashion, her reputation would be ruined, and the Tavern could suffer also as a consequence. To say nothing of what her stepfather would do if he got wind of it.

A second, and perhaps even more compelling reason to bring this to an end, was the fascination Lovell exerted over her personally. She had never been truly in love, although she had fancied herself in love with Jacob in the beginning. It became rapidly obvious that she had been duped by his surface charm into an infatuation that died abruptly the first time he hit her.

She was in perilous danger of falling in love with Garmon, and that was fatal. The man had shown her a great deal of consideration, but he was, by his own admission, a hard-hearted man. The brutality of his upbringing left little room for tender emotions, and she was not fool enough to think he had developed them for her in the space of week, no matter how passionate and tender their encounters. At best he was infatuated with her, and it would die a natural death when they stopped seeing each other. At worst he was amusing himself and nothing more. She suspected the latter.

Picking up her wine glass she said lightly, "Business is going well, it was the usual busy day."

GARMON REGARDED her over his own wine glass and pondered whether to call her out on her lie. But decided against it, he really wanted her to confide in him of her own volition. She had clearly been upset the last few days about something, which had prompted him to start gathering information on her stepfather, Hiram Robinson. And what he had learned today had him concerned.

"What about you?" she asked, picking up her fork. "Have you found any trace of Mr Mor?"

He shook his head. "No, unfortunately I have not. Try these, they are delicious," he said offering her some buttered mushrooms. "Have you thought any more about getting a spirits licence?"

"I think it will be a good investment, but I need to clear my debts first before I incur anymore." She tried the mushrooms and nodded. "They are good."

"I'd be happy to help you with the investment."

"No doubt," she said with a smile. "But I prefer to clear my current debts first."

"Even if the investment would enable you to pay them down faster?"

"Would it though?" she frowned at her plate. "I would need to do some sums to work that out, gauge the risk."

"I could do that for you."

She shook her head. "You're very kind, but I prefer to do it myself."

"I'm not kind!" he snapped, unable to hide his irritation. "I am a businessman, and I am offering you business advice, which it is in my best interests to do, since I am one of your chief debtors, but not your only one I fancy?"

She flushed. "That is true. I made no secret of that when we entered into our bargain. I do have another substantial debt that I need to pay."

"Then let me help you!" he pressed, leaning across the table and grasping her hand.

"You are very kind, but I cannot!" she said withdrawing her hand.

"Damn, you're a stubborn woman! Why not?"

"I should have thought, given what you know of my history, my reasons would be obvious!" she said placing her cutlery on her plate and pushing it aside.

"You cannot think I would treat you like he did!"

"I don't! It isn't that."

"Then what?"

She rose from her seat and walked to the fireplace and back clearly very agitated. He watched her, two parts puzzled concern, to one part fury. He wasn't used to not getting his own way and her stubborn refusal to let him help her infuriated him.

"I have told you that I wish to be independent. If I accept your help, I will never be free!" she said coming to a stop before the table. "Don't you see? I'm tired of being controlled and manipulated by men!" her fists clenched in the folds of her skirt.

"I'm not trying to control or manipulate you! I'm trying to help!"

"Yes, that is what you tell yourself, but what happens when I don't do something you want me to do? Or I do something you don't like? You can call in the debt with a snap of your fingers, and I am hostage to what you want!"

"I wouldn't do that-"

"You're asking me to trust you!" she said with a note of despair in her voice that cut him to the quick.

"Yes, I am," his voice low and husky, shook slightly. He realised with a shock that he desperately wanted her to trust him.

"Every man I have ever trusted to look after me has betrayed and hurt me, except my father, and he *died!*" Her voice cracked on the last word, and she turned away, one hand to her mouth and the other to her belly.

He watched her pain helplessly, and for a moment he was five years old and watching his mother cry like her heart was breaking and knowing he could do nothing to ease her hurt. He swallowed the tightness in his throat and rose, going to stand behind her and put a tentative hand on her shoulder.

"Genevra?" his voice husky, he tried to clear his throat of its obstruction. Slipping his arms round her, he drew her back against him and rested his face in her hair. Her glorious, sweet-smelling hair.

And he was supposed to give this up after tonight? He couldn't lose her. He just couldn't. He would have to make her accept his help, but how to do it without pushing her away?

"I'm sorry," she said thickly, wiping her face with her hands. "This was supposed to be a pleasant evening, and I'm ruining it!" She turned within his arms and looked up at him. "Truly I appreciate your offer, but I must politely decline it. Please don't be angry with me." Her eyes swimming in tears and her beseeching expression skewered him through the chest.

"Tell me why you're crying," he said softly.

"I was so angry with Papa for such a long time for dying and leaving me!" she confessed through her tears. "There was no one else to be strong, so it had to be me. Mama was devastated, Mary too timid and Beth too ill. I kept the brewery running after Papa died. Me! A mere woman! My uncle disapproved and tried to take it over, he threatened to take us to court to challenge Papa's will. He refused to accept that a gaggle of women could run a business like that!"

She turned, her fists clenched and glared at him, as if it was his fault.

"So, your mother married again to stop him," he said flatly.

Genevra sighed. "Yes. She meant it for the best, I just wish she had chosen someone other than Hiram Robinson."

"You don't like him," he stated.

"I loathe him. The feeling is mutual. I offend his sensibilities with my frowardness. I am by far too opinionated and independent."

"He's a weak man, he is threatened by you." His lips lifted in a half smile.

"You think so?"

"I'm sure of it."

"You're not threatened by me?" She gave him a sideways look that did something to his chest.

"Do you think I am a weak man?" He spoke softly.

Her lips twisted and she shook her head.

"And I do not think you are a weak woman." He added, bringing her into the circle of his arms. "Jacob was threatened by you too. That's why he hit you. It was his only way of controlling you."

She nodded; her face buried in his shoulder. He tightened his arms round her. "Only a weak man uses his fists on a woman."

Her body relaxed and pressed closer against him. He rested his face in her hair and drew in her scent, gardenia and vanilla.

"I have a niece you know. My half-brother's bastard daughter."

Genevra raised her head to look at him, her expression questioning. *Why was he telling her this?*

"She came to me at age fourteen. She had nowhere else to go because my brother was dead, and his family threw her out of the house. She is a strong woman too." He smiled ruefully. "That is partly my fault. I was hard on her. I set her to work in the hell and taught her how to defend herself. I made sure she was protected as best I could, but I knew she had to know how to fend for herself. She was a bastard like me, and the world isn't kind to us." He laughed but there was bitter edge to it that he couldn't disguise. "I guess she never realised why I was so tough on her, because she betrayed me in the end." *Like Connor has too!* Taunted a voice in his head that made his shoulders twitch, and his hands tighten on her convulsively.

"I'm sorry," she said softly. "How did she betray you?"

"She stole from me." He turned his head aside and coughed, clearing his throat. "Anyone else, I would skin them for that."

"What did she steal?"

"Some jewels to start, but then she helped the Duke of Mowbray take my hell from me. And she shot me."

"Good heavens! Is that the scar you have on your shoulder? I thought it looked like a bullet wound."

He nodded.

"Yes, the damned thing festered and almost killed me."

"Why would she do such a thing?"

"If I tell you that she is the Duchess of Mowbray now, her motives should be pretty clear." He shrugged. "I taught her to take every opportunity offered and turn it to her advantage. I can hardly blame her for learning her lessons well, can I?"

"A Duchess?" Genevra's eyes widened in awe.

REVENGE ON THE DEVIL

"Not bad for a bastard, eh?" In a perverse way he was proud of Diana. She had done well for herself, even if it was at his expense. He had to admire her grit and determination. "He adores her."

"The duke?"

He nodded. "And he's a prick! They used to call him the Devil. He's got flaming red hair and a temper to match. But Diana tamed him, he's a pussycat with her."

Genevra smiled. "How sweet!"

"How nauseating!"

"You're the strangest man," she said with a smile that made him want to kiss her.

"How so?" he asked lowering his head to capture her divine lips.

She dodged, pulling back to look up at him. "You are capable of some of the most romantic gestures I've ever known, and yet when romance is right in front of you, you scorn it."

"My gestures aren't romantic Genevra, they're erotic. There is a difference. I know a lot about the latter and nothing about the former."

"You've never been in love?"

"God no! Lust yes. Love never."

"So that is what this is? Lust?"

He frowned down at her, aware he wandered onto dangerous ground. "I'm not quite sure what this is. Obsession perhaps. Connection certainly. I'm not certain that I know what love is Genevra. I've not had a lot of experience of it." He spoke matter-of-factly. But her eyes teared up anyway. Which was what he was afraid of.

"Don't cry sweetheart. I'm no object of pity nor am I a hero out of romance, in fact I'm more likely to be cast as the villain. Certainly, Diana saw me as such."

She shook her head. "Jacob is a villain. You-" she paused. "I think you loved your mother."

A twinge in his chest made him wince, and he stared down at

her flabbergasted. "How could you possibly know that? I've barely mentioned my mother."

She smiled and traced a finger down his cheek that made his skin tingle. "Do you remember your father at all?"

He shook his head. But then realised that wasn't entirely true. He had a memory of a man with his mother. He was laughing and had his arms round her. It was faint and fleeting, and he'd never known where to place it in his history. But when he learned the truth about who his father was, he'd wondered if the man he remembered was him. "I may have a fragment of memory. I'm not sure."

She nodded as if something made sense. "I think your father loved your mother."

"She said that he did. I never really believed it. I told you I thought Gatwick was my father for years."

"Deep down you knew that wasn't true."

"I *hoped* it wasn't true," he corrected her. "I loathed him so much I strove very hard to be his opposite."

"I think you succeeded," she said softly.

He kissed her, unable to resist any longer the pull of her allure. He was afraid for one heart stopping moment that she would reject him, push him away, but she didn't. After a moment she parted her lips, and slid her arms round his neck, giving back kiss for kiss.

The glory of her lovely curves pressed against his body sent his blood surging and the sense of pleasure and home that she seemed to bring in her wake enveloped him. Which was ridiculous, because he'd never truly had a home in the traditional sense.

He'd had places he lived for a number of years, the brothel, the hell being notable. But a home was something he abstractly associated with a wife and children, not something he had ever experienced or hoped to.

CHAPTER 14

While Genevra resisted Garmon's desire to take over control of her life, she saw no reason to resist his drugging kisses tonight. It was their last night together, she wanted desperately for it to be something special and memorable, as each night had been for the past week. She wanted to be able to take a piece of him with her. To comfort her in the lonely nights ahead. *Having experienced this closeness, this warmth and pleasure, how was she to do without it?*

He drew her down onto that big, comfortable looking couch, and kissed her until they were both breathless and her body was tingling with desire, her nipples taught and the place between her legs full and damp. He bore her back into the cushions so that they lay full length upon the couch, and she expected him to begin ravishing her body. Instead, he tucked her head into his chest and rested his cheek against her hair, his arms holding her close against him.

The fire crackled, the clock on the mantelpiece ticked and his heart beat a steady thud under her ear. She subsided into his embrace and closed her eyes. Suddenly ineffably weary. *She could go to sleep like this, in his arms, warm and safe. So tempting...*

For a moment her heart squeezed with longing and tears pricked her eyes. She swallowed the lump that rose in her throat. *If only she could keep this moment forever, frozen in time.* She nestled her face closer, the cloth of his coat slightly rough against her cheek, his scent, sandalwood and spice in her nostrils. The firm, comforting grip of his arms holding her close. *This was as close to bliss as she was going to get.*

"Genevra?"

"Hmm?"

"I didn't expect this when we signed that contract seven nights ago."

"Neither did I," she admitted, nuzzling her face into his shoulder.

He shifted, so that he could see her face, lifting her chin with his finger. "I don't want this to end, do you?"

"It must." she said.

"Why?"

She shook her head. "We made an agreement. Seven nights in exchange for a stay of execution on the debt my husband incurred."

"I'll absolve you of the debt." Her heart contracted with that thought. *To be rid of the debt? What a relief that would be. But at what cost?*

"In exchange for what?"

"This," he waved between them. "Indefinitely." *Ah, no. Nothing lasted forever. And when she had given him her heart and her soul, he would grow tired of her and cast her off, like old stockings.* Her heart quailed at the thought. *She'd had enough pain to last a lifetime. She couldn't court anymore.*

"Until you grow tired of me?" She kept her voice light. *He would never know how tempted she was.*

"Until we grow tired of each other?" *There! There was the proof, if she ever needed it. He was only amusing himself. He might seem obsessed, but it was a passing fancy.*

She shook her head again. "No." *She would no more be a mistress than a wife. In either role she surrendered control of her life into a man's hands.*

Never again.

"Why not?"

Because you'll break my heart. "Because we made a bargain. It's been a wonderful interlude. Don't ruin it by trying to extend what shouldn't be extended."

This time it was he that stiffened. "You truly mean that?"

She closed her eyes against the prick of tears that threatened. "Yes."

He was still a moment, and she wondered desperately what he would do. *Would he become angry and throw her out? Was their perfect night ruined? Their week of decadent indulgence over?*

"I don't believe you," he said softly. And she felt the press of his lips to the corner of her eye, where a traitorous tear threatened to escape. *Don't do this Garmon. Don't make it harder than it already is.*

"Please, Garmon..." she opened her eyes to see him gazing at her, his eyes glittering green as emeralds in the firelight, his expression hard to read.

"Please what?" he asked leaning in. "What do you want, Genevra?"

"Just to enjoy our last night together. To store up memories." She smiled, wanly, stroking his cheek with a finger. *His skin was smooth, he had shaved for her.* She fought the urge to melt.

"Memories?" He kissed her eyebrow. She sighed.

"It's been a wonderful week." she said arching her neck as his lips skimmed the sensitive skin below her ear. "Let's not pretend it's more than it is." She closed her eyes, and swallowed a moan as his teeth nibbled her earlobe, his hot breath sending shivers over her skin. *God, how was she going to live without this?*

He withdrew and she opened her eyes in alarm. He was standing, removing his coat and neckcloth. In the next instant he stooped and lifted her in his arms. "If it's memories you want, memories you shall have, Mrs Tate."

SHE CLUNG to him as he carried her into the bedchamber and set her on her feet. His heart thudded hard in his chest as his hands came to rest on her waist. Her resolve to make this their last night together only strengthened his determination to find some way to extend their arrangement. But clearly a direct approach was not going to work, so something more subtle was called for. Garmon was not a man to give up easily. When he wanted something, he always got it. And he wanted Genevra Tate.

He shied away from examining too closely what that actually meant. He just knew the prospect of a night without her in his bed, in his arms, left him with a cold, hollow feeling in his belly. It was unpleasant and truth to tell, a bit alarming. *How had this woman, in only seven nights, become so essential to his peace of mind that he could not contemplate being apart from her with anything approaching equanimity?*

Pushing the disturbing thoughts aside, he drew her into his arms and kissed her, his lips skimming hers and then exploring deeper, taking possession with his tongue, his mouth. His hands on her, possessive and owning. *She was his, whether she knew it or not.*

She responded to his kiss, pressing closer, her arms wrapping round him, her hands pushing up under his waistcoat, warm through the fabric of his shirt. Her hands on him were an unexpected comfort. *She wanted him still, despite her refusal to countenance an extension of their liaison.*

Her refusal of his offer to absolve her of the debt, surprised and frustrated him. *Why would she hang onto a debt when she didn't need to? It made no sense. She had enough problems to deal with, without worrying over how she was to pay him back for a debt incurred by a man who had abused and hurt her.*

His feelings on the matter threatened to boil over, but she had asked for memories, and he had promised them. *He must put aside the vexed question of her debt for the moment and give her what she asked for. Plenty of time to address the issue later, when she was more amenable.*

He pulled her closer and focused on the kiss, on the pleasure of her mouth and body pressed to his. There was a rightness to having her in his arms, that went beyond the fevered surge in his blood, the aching hardness she stirred in his cock, the tingling bliss of her lips on his.

Did she feel it too? Perhaps not, if she was so determined to end things?

His lips traced a line down her throat to the hollow at the base between her collar bones. Breathing in her scent, he tried to stem the thoughts dancing in his head, poking him with unwelcome ideas. *Gardenia and vanilla. She was delicious.*

She leaned away from him to give him better access to her throat and bosom, and he grazed one pert nipple with a finger through the fabric of her gown. Her nipples entranced him, so sensitive she jerked and moaned at the lightest touch. He recalled making her come by playing with them and his cock pulsed. *Now there was a memory.*

He reached for the lacing of her dress, and she reached for the buttons on his waistcoat. Her scent wreathed his senses and his cock jumped. He pulled the bow and loosened her bodice; she undid his buttons. He paused a moment in anticipation. Then he pushed her gown off her shoulders, and she pushed his waistcoat off his. He let his arms drop and shook the waistcoat off, impatient to touch her, feel her.

His hands came back to her waist and his lips to hers. Another teasing kiss, deepening to something more. He held her against him, her breasts warm through the fabric of his shirt. He dropped his gaze to the creamy swell of her bosom overflowing the top of her stays, spilling out of her chemise. So beautiful, so tempting his mouth watered. His hands cupped the warm round mounds and kneaded them gently, his fingers finding her nipples and teasing. She gasped and arched her neck, her eyes closing. *Those sensitive nipples again.*

He made short work of removing her stays and pushed her chemise to her waist, where her petticoat cinching in, caught it. Her breasts revealed to his sight were every bit as wonderful as he remembered. *And she wanted him to be content with a memory only, after this?*

She shook her arms free and reached for his shirt to pull it free of his trousers. *Yet she was as frantic to get to him as he was to get to her.*

He helped her pull it off over his head, and she set her hands on his chest, leaning in to nuzzle the hair on his chest with her cheek. *He loved it when she did that, rubbing on him like a cat.* She turned her head and licked his nipple then nipped it with her lips, making him twitch with surprise. *Oh woman!*

She grinned up at him and did the same to the other one. *Her hands on him were warm and right.* He reached for the tie of her petticoat and pulled it free, petticoat and chemise fell to the floor, revealing her naked, except for her stockings. *Venus personified.* His cock lengthened and stiffened to its full upright extent inside his trousers. She tugged at his falls, slipping her fingers through the buttons swiftly. Her fingers grazed him, making him jump and catch his breath, *so sensitive to her touch.* Then she attacked the buttons of the waistband with equal ferocity, and she had his trousers down to his knees. Her impatience made his blood surge.

When she dropped to her knees and took him in her hand, he gasped with surprise and pleasure. She reefed him gently root to tip, and then her mouth engulfed him in wet heat, her lips stretched round his shaft, her tongue sliding against the head and the underside of his cock, making him groan.

"Genevra!"

He hadn't expected this. His body suffused with hot desire as he looked down at her. Her lips moved up and down from the cap to part way down his shaft and back, her tongue working the underside with expert ease. The sensations took his breath, and her eyes danced, as she held his gaze while she did it.

"Minx!" he moaned. "You're enjoying this.

She nodded and kept up the playful sweep of her tongue and the plunge of her mouth to take as much of him as she could.

He closed his eyes a moment to indulge the sensation, the pleasure building in his groin. *It was good. Too good. She'd ruin him for further play, if he didn't stop her.* His breath stuttered on another groan, as he thrust his hips forward into her mouth, once, twice.

Enough! He pulled gently free of her grip, his hands on her head. "Stop sweetheart, I want more of you than a quick spill in your mouth, as delicious as it is."

"Are you sure? I was enjoying that."

"So was I! Too much." He lifted her up and kissed her deeply, relishing the press of her bare form against his half naked body. He pulled back and got rid of his trousers and shoes, then knelt to remove her stockings, kissing the flesh as it was revealed, first one thigh and then the other. Helping her out of her stockings and shoes, he ran his tongue up her inner thigh to the apex and kissed her wiry copper curls, a darker red than the hair on her head.

His tongue speared her lips, and she uttered a soft moan that made him shudder with sharp lust. *Fuck he wanted her. It seemed an age since last night.* A flash of thrusting in her as she bent over the chair, staring out blindly at the stage, seeing nothing in front of him, only feeling her tight wet heat and the building blissful tension in his groin. *He'd been so angry last night and fucking her had fixed his mood, made him happy and relaxed.*

He spread her legs with his knees and her lips with his fingers, he licked her, nuzzling his tongue until she jerked and cried out. Holding her still on his tongue, he ravished her until she was panting and her hips writhing helplessly.

He looked up, breathing hard himself. "Do you feel empty love? You want something to fill you up?" His voice was gravelly with desire. *He desperately wanted to fuck her. Again. Always.*

"Yes," she gasped. "Please, Garmon, fuck me. Take me. I want-" He rose so swiftly at this command that he cut her off, taking her mouth with a brutal kiss. *Yes!* His body reacted to her demand with a hard throb of need. *Fuck yes!*

Sweeping her up into his arms, he tossed her on the bed and clambered on top of her. Pushing her legs apart with his knees he positioned himself and forced his way into her body with one hard brutal thrust. *She must have developed a taste for it last night. And God help him he wanted her that way too!*

"That what you want?" his voice was hoarse, his body convulsed with desire, deeply triggered by her demands.

"Yes! Yes! Please! Oh, God!" She arched under him, and he hammered her to the bed with swift hard strokes. His body reacted to her pleas with uncontrolled passion.

She writhed under him, tearing her pleasure from him, and he gave her all of his. His mouth ravaged hers, his hands held hers above her head, pinned her beneath him as he fucked her hard. The pleasure rose and rose, a tight knot of building desire, forced upwards like a spigot of water in a narrow channel, until his need, his desperate need, long suppressed, burst out of him with a grunting groan and his body fought to give her everything in him, that he had to give. *Everything.*

He felt her reach her own apex with a hoarse cry, and they trembled together at the glorious precipice and tumbled over with an explosive fall, everything pouring out of him with the force of his repeated ejaculations.

He gave her more than his seed, something essential left his chest and flowed into her that he had kept tightly bound and locked away, the flame of himself, deep hidden, and he surrendered it with a groan and a whimper.

The excoriation left him shattered, scoured, emptied out and lighter than air. In the place of darkness, a subtle joy pervaded his body, more than the natural bliss of the aftermath, this lifted his heart and spirit.

He lay on her, as he came back to himself slowly, a peculiar sense of wholeness pervading his soul that filled him with a numinous joy.

Finally, he lifted his head and stroked a lock hair off her face tenderly and kissed her a soft feather-light brush of the lips. He had no words for what had just happened, he didn't understand it. She lay staring up at him, and they held each other's gaze for the longest time. There was pain in her eyes, a shadow he couldn't get past. His heart ached. Her lids lowered first, and he felt a slight shiver pass over his skin.

He opened his mouth to say something, he wasn't sure what, and she shook her head as if shaking off something.

"What?" he asked.

She shook her head again, closing her eyes. "Is that how a fuck is supposed to feel?" She asked.

He grinned recalling his own words that first time on his desk.

"Yes. Mrs Tate that is how a fuck is supposed to feel."

She snorted and giggled. The giggles turned to laughter, and she lay laughing helplessly beside him. He watched her bemused for a few moments, but the laughter was so infectious he was soon joining her, and some little while later, they both lay with tears of laughter streaming from their eyes, hiccoughing and snorting with the last remnants of mindless mirth.

"What -" he stopped and tried again. "What was that about?"

She shook her head. "I don't know!" and she turned her head into the pillow wailing with another round of giggles. "Please, please stop!" she said. "My st-omach hurts!"

"I'm not doing anything," he protested. "It's all you!"

She flopped back on the pillows, taking a few deep breaths in an effort to calm herself. Finally, she said, "Oh that was good?"

"Which, the fuck or the laugh?"

She snorted and swallowed, letting out a breath. "Both, you wretched man!'

"Good, I'm glad you think so. I didn't hurt you, did I?"

She shook her head. "No not a bit. It was very good."

He propped himself up on his arm and looked down at her. "Good. I think we both needed that. Do we get too serious?"

She nodded. "Yes, I think we do."

He smiled and bent down to kiss her. "Would you like some wine?"

"Yes, thank you." He fetched the wine and a cloth to mop up, and they made themselves comfortable amongst the pillows. Absently he noted that the usual tension in his shoulders was gone, his body felt light and relaxed, a hum of something he vaguely recognised as joy pervaded his veins.

"If you were debt free, what would you do?"

"Start my own brewery," she responded with a smile.

"How would you go about that?" he asked, curious.

"I would start with just enough to sell in the tap, and hopefully, if the brew was good enough, we would be selling enough to replace Whittaker's within a year." She took a sip of wine. "Once we had a reputation, I would start to offer it to other public houses and build from there."

"Do you know how much it would cost?"

She nodded. "To the shilling. I know where to source the ingredients, what equipment we would need, how much I would need to invest before showing a profit, how much to charge, how many staff I would need, and how to grow the business. My father taught me well."

"I don't doubt." He drank his wine thoughtfully. "So, all you need is a business partner to provide the investment."

She shook her head. "No. I'll do it myself."

"How?"

"Once I'm clear of the debts I owe, the money I have been paying towards them will go to my brewery investment fund. I would hope to have enough set aside in a year or two to begin buying the equipment and ingredients. Remember, I am going to start slow and small and grow from there."

"But with an investment partner, you wouldn't need to wait that long."

"With an investment partner I wouldn't own the profits. I'd have to pay back the investment before I could grow the business." She took a generous mouthful of wine. "I'd still be in debt. And my investment partner would probably push me to grow faster than I wanted to, because *he*," she paused for emphasis, "would want a greater and faster return on his money."

"You've really thought about this, haven't you?" he said refusing to rise to the obvious bait. *This was an argument best saved for another time.*

"Yes. For years."

He took her glass and put both on the bedside table.

"You're not going to try to convince me?" She asked.

"Not right now, no," he said, taking her in his arms. *Clearly pushing the subject now would end in another argument.* "There are other things I'd rather be doing." And he kissed her. After a bit he moved to her neck and thence to her bosom and specifically her nipples.

"There's a memory," he said raising his head, "I'd like to recreate."

She sighed as he went back to suckling a nipple. "What is that?" She arched her back, pressing into his mouth.

"I think you know," he said, cupping the other breast and pinching the nipple gently.

She moved her legs restlessly. "Hmm, perhaps."

143

"Except this time, you're going to sit on my cock while I play with your ladies."

"I am?" she said breathlessly.

"Mm huh," he said, his mouth occupied with her breast.

"Are you recovered enough already?"

"For that, yes, feel." He moved her hand to his groin, where she stroked his firming cock.

"Ha," she said on an exhalation. "It is always a wonder to me how something so hard can feel so velvety to touch."

He chuckled. "You feel like wet satin."

"Hm, I suppose."

"Come here," he sat up, pulling her across to straddle him. When she was in place, he said, "Guide me into you. If you're ready?"

She nodded and grasped his cock firmly, guiding him to the right place to enter her body. Sinking down on him, she closed her eyes and let out a soft sound of pleasure. He allowed himself a reciprocal groan, she felt so good, tight and hot and so wet.

When she was settled, his hands wandered to her waist and buttocks and back to her breasts, as he increased his suckling of first one breast and then the other. She rode him slowly, her hips rolling, her hands running over his chest and shoulders. She kissed his hair, her hands reaching round to stroke the nape of his neck.

He groaned, the sensation sending shivers down his spine. He redoubled his efforts on her breasts, licking, sucking, biting gently, his hand working the other breast in counterpoint to his mouth. Swapping sides regularly, listening to her breathing and feeling her body clenching and grinding on his. The feelings this aroused in him were exquisite. His cock firm enough for the purpose initially, hardened, pleasure gathering in his groin, and he fought the urge to abandon the breast play to thrust his hips up into her.

She clenched whimpering and rolling her hips faster, her breathing erratic. "Garmon," she moaned.

He suckled harder, tweaked more firmly, his tongue laving her nipples first one then the other in frantic time with the roll of her hips and the cadence of her breath.

She was clenching repeatedly now, and his cock was on fire, the urge to thrust overwhelming. *Come!* He willed her. *Come Genevra, so I can fuck you properly.* His hips twitched upwards, unable to remain completely still, a growl of frustration escaped his throat, his breathing through his nose like a bellows.

She flung her head back, clenching on him fiercely and keened to the canopy, stiffening and shuddering as the orgasm took her. She gasped collapsing forward on him, and he wrapped his arms round her, squeezing her close.

"Good?" he murmured hoarsely.

"Oh yes, very intense, my nipples are so sensitised now."

He huffed a laugh that became a groan, as she shifted on him, clenching again.

"Genevra, I have to–*please.*" He rolled her beneath him and surged into her with a deep firm thrust, groaning with relief at being able to move.

She smiled up at him, stroked his hair off his face and wrapped her arms round him. "Please take what you need," she said softly, rolling her hips up to meet his downward thrust.

Four strokes later he groaned again as the pleasure began to spiral upward, and he rode the wave to its cresting point and over, feeling her swept up with him. He descended with a swoop of explosive pleasure, this time continuing to thrust even past the point of release, as aftershocks continued to wring pleasure from his body for some minutes. He finally came to a stop and lay bathed in a blissful stillness, relaxed and lazily content.

She stroked his back and kissed his hair. He absorbed these gestures of affection into his body like a sponge soaking up water. Peace pervaded his whole being, and he couldn't move. *He never wanted to move again. Never wanted to be separated again.*

GENEVRA LAY LISTENING to her own heartbeat, feeling him relax into her. She hugged him close and closed her eyes, trying not to think what this was, just absorb it into her body as a visceral memory.

They lay, still joined and entwined for an endless period of peace, and she thought that perhaps they both hovered on the margins of sleep, certainly of deep relaxation.

When he finally stirred and lifted his head his expression was so softened, she almost didn't recognise him. All his hard edges seemed blurred, his eyes, greenish hazel regarded her with a light she had never seen before, the usual tension in his jaw and around his eyes was gone. She had never registered that tension before because it was native to his face, without it, he looked much younger. A gentle smile curved his lips, and he raised a hand to stroke a curl off her cheek and cupped her jaw tenderly.

Her heart swelled, and she felt that slippery slope getting closer. Her footing was precarious and the temptation to fling herself over the edge and fly was overwhelming. For a moment she hovered, wanting to dive and swoop and ride the current, but the ever present and insidious fear sent out tendrils and her heart trembled with sudden apprehension. She closed her eyes, blocking out the sight of him, so perilously tempting. She must not surrender. If she surrendered control, she would be lost. At his mercy. Despite how much she yearned to trust him, her experience screamed at her to back away.

"Don't hide from me Genevra," he said softly.

"I must." She swallowed the traitorous tears that threatened.

He sighed, and she felt his lips press against her forehead, warm and tingling. "Memories, sweetheart," he murmured.

"Huh," she huffed, through a clogged throat and squeezed her arms, legs and inner muscled in an involuntary hug.

He groaned softly, burying his face in her neck. "Genie, you'll make me hard again if you do that."

"Really?"

"Hmm." His warm breath puffed against her ear, sending a tingle down her back. "It's a technique the girls used to use to hurry a client along or bring him to full power if he was struggling."

"The girls? Oh, in the brothel?"

"Uhuh."

She clenched again and he moaned.

"I had no idea," she murmured.

"You know I can feel when you're about to climax when I'm inside you," he said.

"You can?"

"Yes, something changes, and I can feel something inside you caress the head of my cock. It's incredibly arousing for me."

"Oh. What happens when I do this?" she clenched again.

"Ahh. Something similar, all along my length. It's most like when you have me in your mouth, and you suck hard."

"Ohh." She clenched again. "What happens if I keep doing it?"

"Find out," he said, nipping her ear.

She laughed. "Alright." This at least was safer than him looking at her with that light of infatuation. That expression that tempted her to throw caution to the winds. She squeezed, remembering his commands to her to squeeze him in Queen Anne's bath. He had begged her then. She smiled with the memory. She rather liked it when he begged.

"GENEVRA!" he groaned as she squeezed and squeezed with rhythmic force. Her arms and legs surrounding him as her inner muscles milked him. In counterpoint to her squeezes, he pulled back and thrust in, pleasure gathering in his groin. He couldn't surely climax again so quickly, but the pleasure was enticing and intense to his sensitised cock, so he kept doing it.

When the climax came it rolled through him a like a wave, her body pulled him though the wavelets of pleasure, extracting every last drop of sensation with the relentless squeeze and release of her flesh surrounding his. The quality was different, not so explosive, but more holistic as his whole body participated. It left him tingling from his scalp to the soles of his feet, his muscles lax and his mind blank.

When his flesh finally softened, he shifted position, disengaging gently and drew her close against him, snuggling into her, his head on her bosom. She held him, her hands stroking his hair and he slipped over the edge into a deep sleep.

GENEVRA LISTENED to his steady breathing and sighed gently. This would be so hard to give up. She rebelled briefly, wondering why she had to give up something so wonderful. But the voice in her head reminded her of the consequences of surrendering control. She closed her eyes against the tears that threatened and swallowed hard. Her hands clenched briefly, and she breathed through it, forcing herself to relax. Weariness flooded her body and she slept.

WHEN SHE WOKE it was just before dawn, judging from the grey light seeping through the curtains, and he was crawling back into bed. Shadowy in the half light, he pulled her close, his skin chilled from being out of bed.

"I didn't mean to wake you," he said softly against her hair.

She tipped her head back. "It's alright. I think that was the best few hours' sleep I've had in a while."

"Yes, I think so too." He smiled. "I was very relaxed."

"Hmm." She rested her head on his chest, listening to the steady beat of his heart.

"Go back to sleep." He tucked her in against him, and she sighed, relaxing.

GARMON HELD her and watched the dawn creep through the curtains. Nothing had ever felt so good as falling asleep in her arms, snuggled into her generous bosom. *Was it some remnant memory from childhood? He was a man grown, not a child. He hadn't been a child for a very long time.* Yet the ache, the longing for the comfort that he had found in her arms, made him shuffle down the bed until he could nuzzle into her body once more with a deep sigh of contentment. In her sleep she accommodated him, letting him rest his head on her bosom and hold her close.

It was full light went he woke again to the feel of her hands stroking his hair. He lay still, savouring the feeling of contentment, afraid that if he moved, she would stop.

Eventually she said softly, "I'll have to go soon. It must be near six o'clock."

"We have an hour yet, before we need to get up. I said eight remember?"

"You did."

"Will you let me love you one more time?"

"Have you anything left?"

He lifted his head, reluctant to leave the pillow of her bosom. "I don't know, but I want to try."

She sighed and stretched, languorous as a cat. "If you want," she said with a lazy smile.

He kissed her bosom, holding both breasts in his hands, drinking in her scent. Cupping them he licked first one nipple then the other and, suckling until he got a reaction, a little grunt and an arching of her back. Satisfied she was awake enough to respond to his attentions, he moved down her body until he could lick between her legs. She was salty and musky, and his tongue sought out her bud and made her squirm.

Applying himself to her pleasure he worked her with his tongue until she was panting and clutching the sheets, her thighs spread wide and trembling. Raising his head to look up over the curve of her belly and the valley between her rising and falling breasts, he said husky voiced, "Will you let me take you from behind? I promise to stop if it's too much."

She looked down at him and nodded. He smiled and kissed her inner thigh, biting the flesh gently with his teeth. Rising to his knees he flipped her onto her stomach, placing a pillow under her belly. He craved this position, and he wanted her to enjoy it, not be afraid of it. She had tolerated it the first time because she was so aroused, she was beyond feeling the fear, but she wasn't in that state now. Could she bear it, or would she stop him?

He nudged her knees further apart and leaned over her back, pushing her hair aside he kissed the nape of her neck and shoulders and kissed his way down her spine. She murmured something, arching her back. He smiled his lips tingling from contact with her smooth skin, his nostrils full of her scent.

He moved lower reaching her tail bone where he kissed and licked the spot then blew on it. She shuddered and made a noise of appreciation and protest. He massaged her bottom gently and then slid his fingers between her cheeks, all the way to her centre where he entered her with two fingers. She was plenty wet enough to take this treatment easily and he worked his fingers in her firmly. With his other hand he sought her nub of pleasure and encouraged her towards release.

She writhed beneath him, panting and moaning in a way that suggested she was enjoying this more than he had hoped. When he judged he had her on the edge he withdrew his fingers gently and sliding his knees back he eased his erect cock in their place.

Holding his weight on his arms and knees he flexed his hips to thrust and withdraw. "Alright?" He asked between pants.

"Hmm," she nodded, squirming under him. "You beast, you're teasing me!"

He laughed and thrust a little harder, a little faster.

"Garmon," she arched up into him, trying to get more of what she needed to come.

He eased his body down a fraction, moving his weight onto his elbows, tracing a pattern on her back with the tip of his tongue and blowing on it.

"Garmon!" she squealed shivering. His plan of distraction was working!

He moved closer, lowering his body onto hers and thrust deeply with his hips. Pushing her closer to release with the movement. She was panting and moaning now, and he judged she was close.

"Tell me if it's too much," he murmured lowering his upper body down until his chest was flush with her back and his head tucked in beside hers on the pillow, his arms caging her either side. *He loved this part, having her so close under him, held by his weight, but would she panic and buck him off?* His hips continued their plundering thrusts, pushing her into the pillow, restricting her movement. Angling his cock to catch the place of pleasure inside her and forcing her body to arc in a rictus of pleasure and pushing her, he hoped the final inch to completion.

She cried out beneath him and bucked, but this wasn't a panicked response, she was coming, he could feel it and his own body responded with a rise of pleasure. *Could he come again? Did he have anything to deliver after their marathon session of love making?*

Feeling the tremors in her body as she tore her pleasure against the pillow, captured and restricted by his weight, his balls pulled tight, and his cock quivered with anticipation. Hot pleasure engulfed him for a final time and his body shuddered through a last release.

The waves of pleasure were not accompanied by the usual

delivery of seed, instead he felt a wave of warm pleasure in his sensitised cock and balls and the muscles behind them spasmed hard, sending tendrils upward over his buttocks to his spine and downwards through his thighs to feet. He gasped, his breathing suspended for a moment as the wash of pleasure eddied through him and left him beached and boneless on her back.

When he could speak, he croaked, "Are you alright?"

"Yes," her voice was muffled by the pillow.

He shifted off her with an effort, rolling sideways and lay getting his heart rate and breath back under control. He turned his head to look at her and clasped her hand. "Alright?"

She nodded. "It was..." she paused and lifted her head to push the hair off her face. "You forced me to come. My body couldn't move the way I wanted it to, and it should have been frightening, but it was erotic instead. You made me climax by stretching my body unnaturally. I think my lower back will be sore later, but it was worth it."

He leaned over and kissed her. "Exactly what I was hoping for."

"Why do you like that position so much?"

"I like the power of it, but also, I love the way it feels from that angle inside you. It is strongly erotic for me to have you under me like that, and the sensations inside are impossible to resist."

She rolled off the pillow onto her back and groaned as she got the kinks out of it.

He glanced at the clock on the mantelpiece and realised with a sinking feeling that their time was over. *While he wanted to find a way to prolong it, he realised that this wasn't the time to do that. While he was determined this wouldn't be their last night together, he was too wise in the ways of women to push the point now.*

THE CARRIAGE DREW up outside the Tavern, and she moved towards the door, but his hand on her arm stayed her.

"If there are consequences, you will tell me?" His tone was more statement than question, and his eyes fixed hers with a stare that was hard to look away from.

She swallowed. "There won't be, but yes if by some miracle there should-" she swallowed again, her throat closing over. She nodded to finish the sentence, and he pulled her close, kissing her hair as she buried her face in his shoulder. For a moment she allowed herself the luxury of enjoying one more hug from this man who made her feel safe. *Was she wrong to refuse his offer of extending their liaison?* Her heart thumped painfully in her chest and her hands clenched tight on the rough fabric of his coat.

"Genevra love..." his voice was husky, and she hugged him back a moment longer before pulling back.

"Thank you, it has been a wonderful week, I will never forget it." She swallowed, blinking. "I must go before someone see's me."

His hand caressed her cheek, and he kissed her lips softly. "I refuse to say goodbye. If you ever need anything-"

"Yes, I know-" she blew out a breath. "Goodbye." She kissed him quickly and turned to the door, scrambling out before he could pull her back and convince her she was wrong.

She stepped away from the carriage as the door closed behind her, and she glanced back to see his face staring at her. It was impossible to make out his expression, but her heart turned over with a sick thump, and she had to restrain her hands from reaching out to call him back as the carriage lurched into motion and headed down the street away from her.

She stood a moment fighting tears.

Straightening her shoulders, she turned to face the Tavern and the rest of her life. *Garmon Lovell had no place in that beyond the settling of the debt between them. She would pay it as quickly as possible to cut the tie and move forward with her plans. She would. She must.*

CHAPTER 15

*J*acob had been working in the tap of the Red Lion for the last month, since he got mobile and fucking Maggie every chance he got. He couldn't get enough of her. Every so often he thought about going home, especially after an argument with Maggie, but the thought of Genevra, cold and hostile waiting for him, deterred him.

Instead, he'd make it up with Maggie, a good fuck always sorted her out. Usually with a thorough spanking. She loved her arse being tanned, made her hot and wet and willing to let him do anything to her. Including taking it up the back passage. Something he'd never managed with any real success with Genevra. The couple of times he'd tried it, she resisted so much he had to punch her, and then she was too hurt to fuck, so it defeated the purpose.

He was, he realised with surprise, happier than he had been in a long while. Maybe he'd never go back.

THE NIGHT after he returned Genevra to the Tavern for the last time, Garmon couldn't sleep. His bed felt vast and empty without her in it, and every time he closed his eyes, phantoms of her teased him. Her scent, her laughter, her skin, her lips, her nipples her delicious cunny... all of them haunted him. He opened his eyes and sat up, ignoring the cockstand between his thighs.

With a growl of frustration, he got up, pulled on his dressing gown, built up the fire and poured himself a drink. Sitting down by the fire he tried to read, but the words all bled together, and his thoughts returned to Genevra, wondering what she was doing, *was she missing him too?*

Her absence was like the ache, he imagined, of a missing limb. He slumped back in the chair, the book slipping from his grasp to the floor as he regarded his stubborn erection. *His cock missed her. That was what it was. Understandable, he was addicted to the pleasure of her body.*

Surrendering to the inevitable he found some oil and took himself in hand, his mind roving over memories and conjuring fantasies until he came abruptly and hard, but not satisfyingly. It felt hollow and base without her. He sighed and reached for the whisky again. He eventually dozed off in the chair and woke, cramped, cold and irritated at dawn.

It was a pattern that persisted. His sleep was poor at best, his temper was frayed. He sent his boys to check on her, and they reported that she was going about her business seemingly quite happily. If she was missing him, she didn't show it. This news worsened his temper and made his men avoid him as much as possible. Only Rooke seem impervious to his foul temper, stoically taking whatever he dished out in unblinking silence.

Apart from missing her like the devil, the other thing that plagued him was the notion that she might be pregnant. He worried over this night and day, wondering, dreading, hoping... he had never desired children, yet the hope persisted. *If she were pregnant, she would have to come back to him. He could have her back in his bed, where she belonged. And he would get a good night's sleep at last.*

If she were, she would surely contact him, she had promised she would. *Was it too early to tell yet?* He became convinced that she was but wouldn't tell him because of the stupid debt.

The following days passed in a fog for Garmon, but the news of Wellington's victory at Waterloo announced on the 21st of June, burst through even his bubble. London was in a state of euphoria. Celebrations of every kind seized the city and went on for days. Most businesses came to a grinding halt, except for the Taverns which did a roaring trade for a week, until Londoners were so hung over they couldn't party anymore.

Garmon's thoughts were never far from Genevra and hoped that the Wellington fever gripping London was bringing her some good fortune. It was having the opposite effect on his business, but strangely he couldn't bring himself to care. He missed her.

Three weeks after their liaison ended, unable to bear it any longer he sent her a note.

GENEVRA RECEIVED the sealed letter delivered by a skinny street urchin while she was serving in the tap. Joe, who was cleaning tables went to shoo him out, but he dodged and came to the tap where Genevra was wiping glasses.

"You Mrs Tate?" he asked.

"I am," she replied gravely, guessing this was one of Garmon's mudlarks.

"Letter for you," he said holding out the folded paper.

"Thank you," she said taking it with a trembling hand, her heart thudding. *What now?* She looked at it and recognised Garmon's seal. She shoved it in her apron and spoke across the boy's head to Joe. "Take him to Mrs Bell and tell her to feed him." she looked down at the boy. "What is your name?"

"Ben, Missus," he said grinning at the prospect of a feed.

Joe looked down at him and up at Genevra. "It will only encourage them you know."

"I know but look at him! Skin and bone."

Joe nodded and shepherded the boy away. Ben looked back at her and smiled. "You're a right one, Mrs Tate!"

She smiled back and turned to a patron wanting a pot of porter.

IT WAS some time before she found an opportunity to read the letter and even then, she was tempted to put it off. She had been doing her best to ignore how much she missed the intimacy and warmth, to say nothing of the pleasure she had experienced in Garmon's arms.

A letter from him brought it all rushing back and threatened to undo her determination to put it behind her, a wonderful memory yes, but that was all it was, or could be. *Any further contact with the man would destroy her self-control. And she could not afford that. She could not allow him to inveigle his way back into her life. Despite all his protestations to the contrary, she knew he wanted to control her, he wanted her there for his convenience, his pleasure. She would not surrender her independence to a man ever again. It brought too much pain in its wake.*

With that thought uppermost, she broke the seal on the letter and read it with a heart beating faster than it should. She sat down slowly when she reached the end of the short missive and stared at the wall of her office blindly for a moment or two.

Mrs Tate,

I write to absolve you of your husband's debt to me. Upon reflection on the matter, it seems to me unacceptable to hold you accountable for a debt you did not incur nor would have had any way of preventing. In

*particular, consideration of his treatment of you, makes it uncon-
scionable that I hold you responsible for it.*

Please consider the debt paid in full.

Yours faithfully

Garmon Lovell

She reread the letter three times. *To be free of the debt...* the thought was unbearably tempting. *But what happens next? What does he demand in return?* A man of Garmon Lovell's temperament did not give anything without an expectation of something back. And she knew in her heart what that thing would be. He had made it clear on their last night together. *He wanted their liaison to continue. Until he grew tired of her...*

No! Her heart clenched. *She would not be so used and tossed aside. The cost to her heart and reputation were too high, no matter the temptation. She would not let him get that close. No man was getting close to her again. She wouldn't, couldn't allow it.*

She sat down at her desk, drew a piece of paper towards her, dipped her pen in the ink pot and began to write.

GARMON RECEIVED her letter by the hand of the boy who had delivered it. His hand unaccountably shook when he opened it and read the short missive, his heart thudding heavily in his chest.

Dear Mr Lovell,

thank you for your kind offer, but I cannot accept it.

Sincerely

Genevra Tate

Garmon ground his teeth and scrunched the paper in his fist. He threw it across the room. "Stubborn wench!"

He had waited and waited to hear from her, and not a word. His spies told him she was well and going about her daily activities as if nothing were wrong. While he suffered from broken sleep and a relentless aching desire for her that nothing would satisfy. She was driving him mad. And the thought that she might - despite her conviction to the contrary–be carrying his child haunted him. *Surely, she would tell him if she was? She had promised... and the stubborn little wretch wouldn't even accept his waiver of her debt.*

He got up and paced the room a moment, considering his options. Finally, he picked up the screwed-up paper, dropped it in the fireplace where it flared and burnt to ashes in moments. Opening his drawer, he drew out Jacob Tate's IOU, carefully tore it into pieces, put them in an envelope and penned her name to the front of it. He called the boy back in and sent him off to deliver the packet.

An hour later, he received the envelope back, along with a purse.

He opened the envelope and found that she had glued the pieces to another sheet to restore the IOU and added a note.

The debt still stands. Here is the first instalment. Twenty guineas.
Genevra Tate

He opened the purse and counted the contents. Twenty guineas. It spoke volumes for the boy's loyalty that he had carried that sum and not stolen it.

He looked up and beckoned him forward.

"Did you know what you carried boy?"

"Aye Mr Lovell." He wiped his perpetually dripping nose with a grubby sleeve.

"Yet you brought it straight to me. Why?"

The lad regarded him solemnly for a moment. "I'd rather die than steal from you Mr Lovell."

"Good God." Garmon sat back in his seat, floored for a moment. *Another Connor?* "Your honesty and loyalty shall be well rewarded boy."

The boy looked at his grubby feet and added, "'sides Mrs Tate's a good lady, dinna want her to get in trouble."

"Ah. Good lad." He rose and went to the door where he found Mr Rooke standing sentinel. "Rooke, I want you to see this lad -" he stopped. "What is your name boy?"

"Ben, sir."

"Ben. Rooke you are to see him cleaned and outfitted as befits a young gentleman. See also that he has suitable lodgings and three meals a day at my expense."

Ben watched this with eyes big as saucers. "That true Mr Lovell? You not having a lend o' me?"

"It's true Ben. From this day forward you will be my personal courier. You will report here for work each morning at seven. Are we clear? You will be paid well for your services, but I expect absolute loyalty and honesty."

"Aye Mr Lovell." Ben grinned widely, then he fell to his knees sized Garmon's hand and kissed it. "You can rely on me Mr Lovell. Thankee."

"Go with Mr Rooke, he will see you looked after."

Ben eyed Rooke a bit apprehensively. Which was understandable. Rooke was big and dark and menacing.

Rooke regarded the boy impassively and said in a deep gravelly voice, "come along and don't dawdle."

Ben left with him and Garmon sat down to review Genevra's riposte. *The woman was infuriating. Should he return the money or-*

He tapped the desk with his fingers while options flitted through his mind. A smile curved his lips, and he picked up the purse and put it in the drawer, his mind made up.

FOUR DAYS later Genevra was in the cellar doing a stock take ahead of the monthly delivery, the Wellington celebrations had depleted their stores, when she heard footfalls on the cellar steps.

"Is that you Joe?" she said, not looking round from her ledger where she was recording the count of wine bottles. "Would you move these barrels for me, it's-"

"I'd be happy to."

The voice sent a thrill down her spine, and she whipped around, a hand going to her hair in a fruitless attempt to push the falling curls back into the sagging bun on the nap of her neck.

He was handsome as ever in a blue coat, elegantly tied cravat, grey satin waistcoat and fawn breeches above shiny black boots. *God, how she had missed him!*

"Garmon! What are you doing here?"

He took a step towards her, his eyes a glittering green in the dim light from the lamp beside her. She noted that the cellar door was shut, blocking any outside light. *He had shut them in, how had she not heard the door closing? What did he intend-*

"You want some barrels moved?" He stepped closer and shrugged off his jacket, hanging it on a convenient hook on the end of the wine rack shelf and rolling up his shirt sleeves.

Flustered, she attempted to slow her racing pulse and assume a calm demeanour. *What was he here for? How did he find her in the cellar?*

She swallowed and smoothed down her grubby apron, which covered most of the grey worsted skirt of her work dress. She was not at her best, with her hair falling round her face, sweat on her brow and a dull, dowdy gown that was too tight across the bodice.

"Yes, if you could move those two in the corner over there and stack them? We have a delivery due tomorrow."

He nodded and picked up one of the heavy kegs easily and moved it to where she indicated then put the second one on top of the first.

"Anything else need moving?" he asked turning back towards her. His rolled-up sleeves revealed his muscular forearms. She couldn't take her eyes off them. She had always had a weakness for male forearms, especially ones covered in hair, and Garmon's were fine examples, generously dusted with curly brown hair. She remembered well what it felt like to touch them and rub her cheek against them.

A rush of heat washed through her body and all the aching longing she had been trying to ignore for the past three weeks came flooding back.

"That is all, thank you," she managed round a constricted throat and dry mouth. "W-what are you doing here?" she asked again.

He stepped closer and caught her hand. "I came to see you of course."

She shook her head. "Why?"

His eyes took on a quizzical gleam. "You are a stubborn woman, Genevra Tate. I've never had anyone refuse to accept a debt being waived before."

Her heart thudded and she stiffened. "I told you-"

"I know," his voice dropped, and he cupped her face with his other hand, still keeping a grip on her hand with the other. "I know what you told me, your letters made your position very clear. Despite that, I had to see you. You promised you would tell me if-"

She shook her head. "My courses came two weeks ago, you have nothing to concern yourself with, I am fine."

He nodded, but the flicker of, *was that disappointment in his eyes?* gave her a shock. She had shed tears at the time and tried not to think why, except that it was confirmation of her barren state. *If she had not conceived after the number of times, he had released inside her, she was never going to.* But in truth it was a relief, for she didn't want anything tying her to Garmon Lovell beyond the debt, which she would settle as soon as possible. *So, it was a good thing.*

He held her gaze with his as he lowered his head and whispered, "I've missed you."

She dropped the ledger from nerveless fingers, her skin

tingling from his touch. *She should step back, push him away, tell him no...*

Then his lips captured hers, and she felt her body melting as her eyes closed. He let go of her hand to sweep an arm round her waist and pull her tight against his body as he deepened the kiss. Her mouth and body responded despite her mind screaming at her to pull away, to stop.

His lips and tongue reduced her to a panting puddle of need. He broke the kiss and murmured, "I think you have missed me too."

She gulped and tried to step back, but his arm held her captive against his chest. She gazed up at him helplessly. "Garmon you can't seduce me into doing what you want!"

"Can't I?" he traced the curve of her cheek with one finger, poking a wayward curl behind her ear. "I want you Genevra, and you want me, I can feel it! Why are you fighting this? It's inevitable." His voice, low and liquid, turned her insides to hot aching need. *He was right...*

He bent his head and kissed her again. A consuming kiss that swept away her scruples on a tide of want and desire. Her arms came up round his neck, her hands tangling in his hair, her body flush against his. She could feel the hardness of him, hot and insistent against her belly.

His hands slid down her body, one to cup a breast the other her bottom, kneading and caressing through the fabric of her gown. She hadn't bothered with a corset, her gown being tight enough across the bodice to keep her ample breasts confined. But his nearness and his touch made her nipples hard and achy, forcing them to poke through the fabric. His fingers found one and pinched gently, dragging a moan from her throat.

The hand on her bottom, pressed her closer against him and her traitorous hips rolled. Fire licked between her legs, her weak flesh, swollen and slick just from his kisses, a devouring reminder of all the pleasure they had shared.

Gasping for breath she pulled back from his kiss. "Garmon-"

"Don't think my darling, just feel!" His voice hoarse his eyes molten, he claimed her mouth in another knee-weakening, breathtaking kiss. His lower hand scrabbled at her skirts and found her flesh. Her knees gave way at the sharp pleasure his fingers wrought, and she clutched at his shoulders to stop herself from falling, her face buried in his shirt. He abandoned her breast to circle her waist and keep her upright. "I've got you," he murmured.

"Garmon please-" Her hands dug into the fabric of his waist-coat and shirt as she leaned into his touch.

"You are so wet..." he groaned. "Your body betrays you!" he panted. "Let me inside you. You want it as much as I do," he said, hoarse and low.

His words and fingers drove a desperate moan from her and taking that as consent, he walked her backwards until her bottom hit the bench.

Lifting her slightly so that the bench took her weight, he kneed her legs open and pushed her skirts up, undoing his falls with a shaking hand. He was so hard it hurt, he hadn't had a full night's sleep since she left his bed and his body had refused to be satisfied with his hand. *Nothing would satiate this hunger but her.*

He found the entrance to her body and pulled her onto his cock with a hard jerk. The shocking pleasure of being buried in her tight heat took his breath and he held still a moment his face nuzzled in her neck. "Genevra!" her name was a groan and a prayer.

Her legs came up round his hips, cinching him inside her, and her hands dug into his shoulders. Her hips rolled and his moved in response, he found her mouth blindly and lost himself in the pleasure of holding her, of being inside her after what felt like an age of only remembering and imagining.

For long moments the pleasure consumed his every faculty, nothing existed outside of her, she was his whole world as he drove towards the pinnacle of release, and she kept up with him, as hungry for it as he was.

When she cried out, he lost the last vestiges of his control and took her the last mile with savage, violent force. The avalanche of pleasure took him in a blinding wave and beached him hard on her body, his knees weakened, his body trembling with aftershocks.

He was vaguely aware of making noises, possibly of cursing.

He clutched her tight, as if she were the only thing that would keep him from drowning. When he came to enough to become aware of her as a separate entity from himself, he realised with a shock that his throat ached and there were tears on his cheeks.

She stared up at him dazed, and he kissed her lips and her cheeks and cradled her close, something warm and foreign in his chest, filling it to bursting point. *Whatever it was about her, he needed this woman.*

Her response was unequivocal, he had been right that she wouldn't be able to resist once he kissed her. Whatever scruples she had were swept away in the flood of desire that consumed them both.

"You see," he murmured against her hair. "Inevitable." He disengaged their bodies carefully and her feet dropped to the floor. She pushed him gently away and stood letting her skirts fall to her ankles while he rebuttoned his falls and rolled his sleeves down before reaching for his jacket. By the time he had put it back on she was standing with her back to him, her hand on the wine rack, as if to steady herself.

He approached her, put his hands on her arms about to reassure her that everything would be fine when she said, "this changes nothing Garmon. I shouldn't have–this was a mistake! Please go."

"Genevra-" shock tightened his throat.

"You will have your next payment tomorrow."

"Gen-" his voice softened, cajoling, she couldn't mean this.

"I told you that you can't seduce me into doing what you want! I won't be manipulated!" She shrugged off his hands and turned, her eyes bright, her colour high, her expression determined.

"That wasn't -" *she had it all wrong he wasn't trying to manipulate her!*

"You said you wanted me, and I don't doubt that. But what happens when you're tired of me?"

"I would never abandon you. I told you I would look after you." *God, didn't she understand how much he needed her?*

"I don't *want* you to look after me! I don't want-" her voice cracked. She swallowed and put up a hand to stop him when he moved towards her. "Don't. Just go." When he didn't move, she shouted, "Go!"

His heart contracted with a stab sharp enough to make him recoil. Her words scalded him, the soft part of him that she had opened up, closed over and anger surged to mask the pain. "You'll regret this, Genevra Tate!"

SHE FLINCHED from the look in his eyes and a frisson of fear ran up her spine. *This! This was the reason she couldn't trust him. If she pushed him hard enough the real Garmon was revealed. The hard man, the ruthless, brutal killer. His sweet words were just that, words to entice her into surrender. She would not surrender.*

"I'll make you sorry you refused me woman!" The threat reverberated round the cellar and made her knees go weak with fear.

He turned and ran up the steps, slamming the cellar door behind him and in the silence a chill settled into her bones and her heart. She stumbled to a cask and sat down heavily, her knees giving out her stomach quaking. *Had she made an enemy of the most powerful man in London?*

Fear curdled her stomach, but something much more painful pushed through the fear and made her throat ache as she tried and failed to hold back the tears. Curling round the pain she bent double and cried, jagged sobs, the like of which she had sworn she would never cry again. *Not over a man. Not ever again.*

She let the flood out and finding a handkerchief in her pocket she wiped her face, blew her nose and straightened, determination in every line of her body. She picked up the ledger, straightened the crumpled pages and resumed her inventory.

CHAPTER 16

Genevra paid her instalments to Garmon religiously, but that meant she had to reduce her repayments to her stepfather and one week she defaulted altogether, unable to pay both. Which brought Mr Neeps down on her, trying to nose out what was happening. Which made her so angry she sent a note round to her mother declining to attend the weekly family dinner. *If she tried to sit down at the same table with Hiram she would throw her dinner in his face!*

That prompted a visit from Hiram himself the next day. He came into the Tavern when she was out the back with Mrs Bell, and Joe sent one his boys to find her. Informed that Mr Robinson wished to speak with her, she took a few moments to compose herself and then marched into the tap room where she found him propping up the bar talking to Joe and sipping a pot of porter.

"You wished to see me?" she said, her arms crossed under her breasts.

Hiram turned and ran his eyes up and down her form, which made her flush, since her hair was coming out of its bun again and her apron was stained with grape juice from the mishap in the kitchen.

"Genevra. Are you well?" His tone implied she couldn't be.

"Yes Hiram, I am perfectly well, are Mama and Beth well?"

"I am happy to report that they are. I came to see what was transpiring here, given the events of the last few weeks. Perhaps we can speak somewhere a little more private?"

She bared her teeth and swept behind the bar to the office at the back. He followed and took a seat across the desk from her. She didn't miss the way he looked around and eyed the pile of papers on the desk. She resisted the urge to sweep them up out of his sight. Mostly bills.

"Genevra, it pains me to have to do this-"

"Then don't do it." She smiled. A fixed smile, more grimace than grin.

"It's really for your own good-"

She slammed her fist onto the desk and leaned over it towards him. "Don't! Don't give me that line. You're here for your own good, not mine!"

His thin mouth pursed in an ugly line. "You have defaulted on your loan Genevra, you know the consequences of that. Mr Neeps will be assuming control of the Tavern from tomorrow morning."

"Over my dead body! If that man so much as pokes his nose into the building tomorrow Joe's boys will throw him into the street!"

He sighed. "Genevra if your boys lay a finger on him, they will be charged with assault and appear before the Magistrate."

Genevra ground her teeth. "I will pay the amount owing to you right now and the next instalment by the end of the week. Will that satisfy you?"

"You have the money?"

"I will find it. Anything to keep Neeps out of here."

Hiram breathed out audibly through his nose before rising and putting his hat back on his head. "You have until Friday to pay both amounts. But if you fail to pay any future instalments on time I will take over the running of this establishment *myself*. And I will issue you with a warrant to vacate the premises. A woman alone cannot be allowed to continue to run an establishment like this. It is obscene. Your reputation is in tatters, and it is impacting your sisters' prospects. Have you thought about that?" He turned and headed for the door.

He was halfway across the taproom before she caught up with him. In a low voice she said, "My reputation is fine! And Beth is in no danger from me. I wouldn't do anything to harm her, and you know it!"

"I must find a husband for her as soon as possible, before your behaviour makes it impossible to do so." He nodded to Joe and exited through the front door. Leaving Genevra fuming.

~

WHEN GARMON STORMED out of the Tavern after his argument with Genevra he maintained his temper tantrum for the better part of a week before he could no longer deny that the ache of missing her was greater than the pain of her rejection. He had to find a way to get her back into his bed. He couldn't sleep without her.

Her surrender in his arms, was ample proof that she felt the same degree of attraction to him that he felt towards her. He simply had to get her alone and seduce her, again, but this time it would be on his turf, and she couldn't be allowed to reject him again.

The problem was Genevra wasn't a recalcitrant debtor that he needed to persuade to pay up. His usual methods of getting his own way wouldn't work in this instance. He needed another way to get her willing and wholehearted agreement to resuming their liaison. He had to somehow get her to admit that she wanted it as much as he did. And that he represented no threat to her independence. That was the clincher. *The stubborn darling was deter-*

mined to stand on her own feet and arced up at the slightest suggestion of masculine interference or control. How to get her to do what he wanted without her realising it?

He composed a dozen letters and consigned them to the fire unsent. He came up with and discarded a dozen ideas for her surrender and abandoned each one in turn. He was paralysed by a kind of internal conflict he had never experienced before. Normally he was ruthless in the execution of his plans, paying no mind to the impact of his strategy on the victim, beyond the requirement to get their cooperation. But in this case he kept thinking of her and what she would feel or how she would react and every time he found himself dissuaded from going through with his plot. He was discovering he had some scruples after all. *It was decidedly uncomfortable.*

His boys kept him fully informed of her activities and when she sustained a visit from her stepfather - one which his informant made clear had upset her—he was tempted to stop dithering and just go to see her and find out what was going on, and how he could help. His other instinct was to pay Robinson a visit, but again he was stayed by the notion that Genevra wouldn't like that. He resolved instead to go and see her himself, he couldn't bear this separation any longer, he was going mad with frustration.

He was on the verge of leaving to do so when Ben came in grinning.

"Mornin' Mr Lovell sir!" he said executing an enthusiastic bow. Garmon hid the smile this provoked, it was impossible to be grumpy with Ben around.

"What's news Ben?"

"Well!" said Ben portentously, clearly enjoying himself. "Word on the street is the Missus—that is Mrs Tate, is lookin' to set up gamin' nights at the Tavern to earn a bit more rhino, attract more custom and such. Thought you'd want to know that."

"I do, thank you, Ben." He frowned a moment and then waved

Ben to a chair. "Sit down a minute, I have a couple of commissions for you."

He sat down and penned an instruction which he handed to Ben along with a small purse.

"Take this paper and the purse to the printer downstairs, Mr Maybury and then find the mudlarks and get them to spread the word about the Globe Tavern. It's the best place to go for a great night's entertainment. Good food, booze and fun. Got it?

"Yes Mr Lovell sir."

"Good work Ben, tomorrow you and the team will deliver leaflets all over about the good times to be had at the Globe Tavern, understood? We are going to make it the place to go."

Ben grinned and nodded. "Yes we will, sir."

Garmon grinned back and the ache in his chest that had been plaguing him since he parted from Genevra eased a bit. He desperately wanted to go and see her, but fear that his reception would not be warm, made him hesitate again. It would be better to wait a little longer, see this plan come to fruition, and visit her when she had cleared her debts. She couldn't keep him at arm's length then. And he could make her a present of the debt money once he had her back in his bed where she belonged.

He poured himself a drink as Ben let himself out of the office and contemplated what a reunion with Genevra would be like. He ignored the whisper that said, *why don't you go now?* And the reply in his heart that said *Because I'm afraid she'll show me the door again, and I don't think I can bear it.*

GENEVRA SHOUTED in Joe's ear over the hubbub in the tap room, the whole place was packed, every room they had, pressed into accommodating the surge of customers wanting to come in and join the fun. "Can you send one of the boys to the cellar for another cask? This one is nearly empty!"

Joe nodded and sent his eldest on the errand. Genevra grinned. "This seems like it was a good idea, I wasn't expecting such a response though. How did the word get out so fast? Poor Mrs Bell is run off her feet in the kitchen."

AT THE END of the night Genevra toted up the take and was very pleased. At this rate she would be entirely debt free in under four months! She stashed the money in the safe, locked it and pouring herself a drink put her feet up on the desk and contemplated life without debts. It was a pleasant prospect.

She sipped her whisky and her thoughts inevitably wandered to Garmon. Wondering what he was doing. *Was he well? Did he miss her?* She had been afraid he would exact some kind of vengeance on her after the way she threw him out, but she had heard nothing from him at all. The silence was almost more unsettling than if he had done something.

She finished her whisky and rose with sigh. Her body ached and she was tired. That was why she felt out of sorts. She washed up her glass, snuffed the candles and lamps and climbed the stairs to bed. She would not think about how nice it would be to sink into Garmon's arms and sleep.

CHAPTER 17

Genevra pushed damp curls off her sweaty brow with a sudsy hand and suppressed the cough trying to rise in her throat. Her body ached, but there was too much to do to go and lie down, as much as she longed to. Joe and both his boys had succumbed to the fever that was raging through the city, and she had been running the tavern with just herself and the girls for a week. It was no wonder she was tired and achy, with all the lifting and hauling she'd had to do in Joe's and his boy's absence. Even Mrs Bell had had to take a turn in the tap, and her boy Neil had done his best, but he was only twelve and not at this full strength yet.

She lost her battle to suppress the cough with the next breath and fell into a coughing fit that left her chest aching, her throat raw and her eyes and nose streaming. Mopping up with a handkerchief, she returned to washing glasses and pewter mugs, trying to ignore the throbbing in her feet and her aching limbs.

"Mrs Tate?" It was Annie, one of the barmaids.

She turned. "Mrs Whittaker's here to see you. I put her in the parlour at the back."

"Mama?" *Good heavens what would bring Mama out, on a night*

like this? It was bucketing down outside. What had Hiram done now?
Drying her hands on her apron, she nodded to Annie. "Thank
you." She hurried out of the scullery and along the corridor to the
private parlour, her personal sitting room, which she hardly ever
had a chance to sit in. Entering she found her mother sitting on
the edge of a chair swaddled in a heavy cloak with a muddy hem
and soaked shoulders.

"Mama? What is it?"

"Genevra!" her mother rose, her expression distraught and
hugged her. "I had to come, its Beth! She's run away, and I can't
find her anywhere!"

"Run away?" Genevra's heart thudded and her stomach turned
over in alarm. "Why?"

Her mother dabbed at her face. "It's your father. He got it into
his head that since you wouldn't marry Mr Neeps, Bethany
should. I've never known Beth to be so obdurate. She refused
utterly to even entertain the idea and when Hiram insisted, she
said she would die rather than marry him. He locked her in her
room, and I thought she would settle down after a rest, but when
I went to check on her, she wasn't there!"

"When was this?" Genevra's mind raced with possibilities.

"She hasn't come to you?" her mother interrupted, catching
her hands. "I was sure she would do that. You would tell me if she
was here?"

"Yes of course! I wish she *had* come to me. Perhaps Mary?"

Her mother shook her head. "I went there first. Mary was
horrified."

Genevra sniffed, her wretched nose was running, and her skin
was on fire, her head foggy. *Think! Where would she go?* "When did
she leave the house, do you know?"

"Sometime between four, and half past eight, that was when I
went to check on her. I don't know how she could have got out of
the house without anyone seeing her. Oh, where could she be?"

"Does Hiram know you're here?"

"No, he thinks I am lying down with a headache."

"You had best go home before he discovers you have left the house too! Does he know she is missing?"

"No! I was afraid of what he would do if he found out. I was positive she would have come to one of you girls, but if she hasn't, oh lord where could she be?"

"Do you know if she took anything with her?"

"A cloak and stout boots. She took your old valise, the one with the rose pattern embossed on the leather, she always liked it remember?"

Genevra nodded. "Did she have any money?"

"Only her pin money, a couple of pounds perhaps?"

"You must go home Mama and try not to worry. She may come home on her own when she realises what a foolish thing this is to do. But if not, never fear I shall find her."

"Do you have any idea where she might be?"

"She didn't leave a note I gather?"

Her mother shook her head.

"I suspect she may have some notion of catching the stage-coach to Bath."

"Bath? Great Aunt Maddie?"

Genevra nodded. Her father's spinster Aunt, Madeline Whit-taker, had never approved of mama's marriage to Hiram Robin-son. The old lady was formidable, but never left Bath, where she had retired for the sake of her health. If Beth was seeking someone to protect her from Hiram, Great Aunt Maddie was the most likely candidate.

"The nearest stagecoach for Bath leaves from The George and Blue Boar in Holborn, but I'm not sure of the times. Rest assured Mama, I will find her even if I have to go all the way to Bath to retrieve her!" She swallowed a cough and hugged her mother. "Go home before horrible Hiram realises you are gone, or he will think you have run away too!"

Having seen her mother off the premises and into a cab,

she asked Annie to lock up for her. She went upstairs, put on her thickest cloak and stoutest boots, grabbed the miniature she had of her sister and her purse and hailed a cab for Holborn. Huddled in her cloak, she shivered, her skin hot despite the chill and her heart skipping with worry for her little sister. She could murder Hiram for driving Beth into such a desperate act, but that would come later, first of all she had to find Beth.

She asked the driver to wait for her when they arrived at the George, but he demanded his payment and drove off as soon as she paid it. With a tired shrug, she traipsed into the Inn which took up three sides of an open courtyard, occupied by several carriages and horses. No sign of the stagecoach, which meant it either wasn't due for a while or it had already departed. She couldn't remember if this was a morning, afternoon or night-time service.

"Sorry ma'am you've missed it by several hours, leaves at 4:00 pm sharp does the stage," the man behind the counter informed her.

4.00 pm. Then Beth had also surely missed it, Mama said she was locked in her room at four. That was if her surmise was correct, and Beth had come here seeking the coach. She showed the man Beth's likeness and asked if he had seen her.

He took the little miniature and turned it towards the light. After a minute or two he said. "Aye I think there was a young miss seeking the coach that might be her."

"What happened to her?"

"Why you asking?" he squinted at her passing the miniature back.

"She's, my sister!" she said impatiently, trying to suppress a shudder and stop her teeth from chattering.

"Ah well, she ain't here. I told her she'd missed the coach by more than two hours and the next one wouldn't be by until tomorrow at four. She looked like she was going to cry, so I offered her a room, but when I told her the price, she said it was too expensive, and she left."

Genevra's heart sank and for a moment she thought she might cry too. She felt wretched. Her head was swimming, her legs felt weak, and shivers wracked her frame. She opened her mouth to ask a question and fell into a coughing fit instead. Alarm lit up the man's face as she coughed helplessly into her gloved hands.

"Eh, you've got the fever! You'd best be going ma'am we don't want any sickness here!" he said backing away and covering his face with his handkerchief.

When she could speak, she said hoarsely. "Is there a stage-coach in London that leaves at night?"

"Only the Royal Mail, it would've left from the Swan with Two Necks in Lad Lane at 7:30 pm."

"Did you tell my sister about it? Would she have gone there?"

He spread his hands. "I don't know. She didn't ask, I didn't tell. She just left."

Genevra sighed. "Thank you for your help," *such as it was.* She left the George and debated what to do next. If her sister had arrived here around six, she would have had ample time to get to the Swan with Two Necks and catch the Mail Coach for Bath. *If there were seats available. If she knew about it. The question was, did she?* Genevra shuddered convulsively and pulled her damp cloak around her more tightly. *Or did she seek lodging for the night in some cheap hotel near here?*

Oh Bethy, where are you?

She left the hotel courtyard, emerging onto High Holborn and looked for a cab, but there were none in sight. Not that there was a lot of visibility, it was raining hard, and it was dark, the flam-beaux all extinguished by the rain. Pulling her hood up, she stepped out into the street and set off towards the Swan. She had to find out if Beth had got on the mail coach or not.

Half an hour later she staggered into the Swan and asked if a young woman answering to her sister's description had boarded the Royal Mail. The young man she addressed initially looked at her as if she was mad and disclaimed all knowledge of any young women boarding the mail. But as it turned out, after further questioning, he wasn't there when the mail arrived. After significant prompting and the supply of coin, he was moved to find someone who *was* there at that time and could provide accurate testimony. By this time Genevra was soaked through and shivering so badly she could barely speak for the chattering of her teeth. Her head was pounding, and she ached all over.

Her second informant proved frustratingly vague but with the supply of more coin eventually said that no he had not seen a young lady of Beth's description board the mail. Genevra wasn't sure if she was relieved or devastated by this news. *Beth was still somewhere in London. But where? Was she safe? Was she lost? Had someone taken advantage of her? Hurt her?*

Her mind spun with nightmare possibilities as she stepped out into the rain once more and stood swaying in the freezing wind. She was so cold by now she couldn't feel her feet or her fingers or even her nose. She turned in a desperate hope of finding a cab and spotted one on the other side of the street. The jarvey was heading home and took some persuading to turn around, but the promise of sufficient coin persuaded him, and Genevra climbed wearily into the cab and collapsed on the seat, a wet puddle forming at her feet.

IT WAS after midnight when a furious banging on his door woke Garmon. He had been sleeping a little better since he was able to help Genevra, unbeknownst to her, through promoting the Tavern and increasing its custom.

Rising he pulled on a banyan and opened the door, a demand to know what was so damned important it couldn't wait till morning, on his lips. He didn't utter it, for standing bedraggled and shivering on his doorstep was Genevra. Straight out of his dreams to his door. He had imagined many scenarios where he saw her again, but none like this.

The sight of her, soaked through and shaking with cold, made his stomach clench, *what in the hell happened to send her to him like this?*

"Good God woman what are you doing–come in!" He noticed Ben hovering in the background. The lad acted as his porter by night and his courier by day, he must have let her in. He pulled her over the threshold and nodded to Ben, "Wait I may need you."

He shut the door and drew her to the fire only half listening to her babbled words, which were mostly unintelligible due to the chattering of her teeth. His first concern was to get her warm and dry.

"Here take this off," he removed her cloak and flung it aside, pushing her into a chair by the banked fire. Ignoring her babble, he poked the coals up to a flame and added more fuel, then went to find some towels to dry her off.

Returning he was brought up short by her shouting at him, "You must help me!"

"Of course, I'll help you." He finally brought his full attention to her face. Her cheeks were a hectic red, and the anguish in her eyes, made his heart stutter.

"You have to find her!"

"Find who?" he said wrapping a towel round her shoulders and using the other to dry her hair. He just wanted to hug her, but she needed to be dry first. He'd seen many women carried off by an untreated chill.

"Bethy!" she sobbed. "My sis-sister B-Bethany! She's r-run away, she's l-lost in L-London. She's sick! If she's out in this w-weather she c-could die! P-please you h-have to h-help me find her!" Her voice cracked.

"Of course I'll help you." He grasped her fluttering hands

trying to calm her. "Sit down and tell me slowly how this came about, and I'll help you."

He pushed her gently into a chair and gave her a glass with a generous splash of whisky.

She took it and sipped the amber liquid, wiping her cheeks with her other hand.

"Hiram the horrible is trying to force her into marriage with his Manager Neeps, the man is forty-five if he's a day and Beth is seventeen! It's obscene!" she coughed into her hand helplessly for a few moments, unable to go on.

"Take it slowly," he said grimly. "Sip the whisky." *Neeps for a young girl, it didn't bear thinking of. He would definitely be having a word with Mr Robinson in the near future and the older man wasn't going to like it!*

Subsiding weakling back in her chair, she closed her eyes a moment, and he stroked her hand. He felt helpless to do more, a rising tide of frustrated anger directed at Robinson for causing Genevra so much anguish.

Rousing herself she went on, "Mama told me that she went up to her room at 4:30, and she was gone by after 8:30. Mama came to see me then at the Tavern, after she had checked with Mary, my eldest sister. She was sure Beth would have come to one of us.

"I believe Beth's aim was to board the stagecoach for Bath to seek refuge with our Great Aunt Maddie. But she missed the stage by several hours and she wasn't staying at the inn where it leaves from.

"I then went to see if she caught the mail coach, but she d-didn't." A convulsive shudder ran through her whole body and more tears ran down her cheeks. "She's lost in London, some-where! She is small and innocent and sweet-tempered, trusting! Anything could ha- happen to her!"

"Tell me what she looks like."

"I have her likeness, here" she dug in her reticule and produced a miniature passing it to him. He glanced at it while listening to her description. "She isn't above five feet tall, slender build, small breasts, her hair is guinea gold and curly, her eyes light blue, her complexion cream and roses. She is very pretty. And hasn't a clue how to defend her-herself." She broke down in sobs again. "Please, please help me find her."

"Absolutely. All my resources will be devoted to this. We will find her, Genevra. I have a large network and a reliable team. My men and boys will find her." He rose went to his desk and wrote a short note and popped it along with Beth's likeness into an envelope, went back to the door and called Ben in. Instructing him to go to Mr Rooke with the note and do whatever he told him to do. "Mrs Tate's sister is missing, you must find her. Do not come back here until you find her, you understand? Recruit the mudlarks and do as Mr Rooke tells you."

"Aye Mr Lovell. Don't you worry Mrs Tate, we'll find her." Ben assured her, his thin face full of concern.

She was lying back in the chair exhausted by her ordeal. She opened her eyes and smiled at Ben wanly.

Garmon closed the door on Ben and went back to Genevra. Her skin was white, almost blue, except for the two red flags on her cheeks. Touching her brow, he felt the heat radiating off her, despite the deep shudders still wracking her body. "How long have you been sick?" he asked harshly, his heart thudding with worry.

"I s-started feeling tired and achy earlier today." she stopped as a coughing fit took her breath.

A shudder of fear ran over his skin, *it was worse than he thought.* He swept her up in his arms and took her into the bedchamber where he proceeded to strip her out of her wet clothes and bundle her into one of his shirts. He shoved her under the covers and fetched a hot brick for her feet, which were frozen. He had seen many women die of fever from various causes in the brothel, and Genevra's condition chilled him to the bone with fear.

"Never mind your sister taking ill, it's like to be you carried off by an inflammation of the lungs!" he said roughly, stroking the hair off her face.

"I th-thought I could find her myself. But I don't know where she is. You will find her, promise me?"

"Mr Rooke and Ben will find her. I am staying here to look after you. I'll have the doctor to you shortly. Now rest and sleep if you can."

"I can't. I should be looking for Beth. She's only seventeen! She isn't fit to be alone in London at night, anything could happen to her."

And probably has already, he thought grimly. Instead of voicing his thoughts he said calmly, "She has probably gone to a cheaper hotel to spend the night. She will be fine, and Mr Rooke will find her. Rest. I shan't leave you."

Her feverish eyes closed, and she seemed to settle for a little, while he made her some lemon tea with a generous dollop of honey. Sitting her up so that she could drink without choking, he wrapped one arm round her and helped her hold the mug. She took a few sips and rested her head on his shoulder. "I didn't know where else to turn for help."

"Coming to me was the right thing to do. I just wish you had come to me immediately you learned she was missing instead of running all over London making yourself ill!" He scolded gently.

"I'm sorry," she murmured, lachrymose. It was a mark of how ill she was that she was so meek. *Very unlike the Genevra he knew.*

Settling her down in the covers again he watched her drift off to sleep, her face so pale surrounded by the lovely halo of her copper hair. Assured she was sleeping, he left to fetch the doctor who lived three doors down.

Returning with that gentleman some ten minutes later, he waited while the man examined her. Genevra was barely conscious while he did so, her fever having advanced to the next stage. She was burning up and didn't seem to know who Garmon was when he tried to calm her.

The doctor prescribed a paregoric draught and some laudanum. He was grave when he listened to her wheezing breath and Garmon explained about her cough. His pronouncement that the fever was well advanced and could prove fatal, left Garmon rattled to the core.

Alone with his patient once more, he built up the fire, made more tea, and left it to cool in a jug. He then sponged her face and hands to cool them and fed her sips of the tea when he could.

She slept fitfully, and he dozed in between her restless movements and muttered cries.

Daylight found her still hot to touch and barely conscious. He spent the day glued to her side, too afraid to leave her. The only time he did, for no more than a few minutes, he returned to find her out of bed and walking unsteadily towards the doorway.

"Genevra!"

"Must find Beth!" she muttered, her eyes glassy, her skin flushed and burning to touch. She shivered convulsively, her teeth chattering. "So cold!" She moaned.

Grabbing her round the waist he led her back to bed and tucked her in, ignoring her protests. He held her hands tight and tried to soothe her, but she didn't seem to hear him.

He poured her another dose of the paregoric draught and forced it down her throat. Which made her cough and her eyes stream. But it settled her down and she fell into another fitful sleep.

Her temperature began to climb as the daylight faded, and he kept vigil by her bedside, listening to her laboured breaths and anxiously sponging her hot dry skin.

. . .

GENEVRA WAS SO HOT, her chest and limbs ached. Raging thirst parched her throat. She flung out a hand blindly. *There was something she was supposed to be doing. What was it?*

Beth! Beth was missing!

"Must find her!" she muttered, trying to force her heavy lids open, make her aching limbs obey her. "Bethy! Where are you?" her voice croaked, her throat felt raw.

"Beth is safe," a deep familiar voice reassured her. A cool dry hand held hers and squeezed it. "Do you hear me Genevra? Beth is safe."

"Ah-!" she tried to reply but a coughing fit took her breath. *It hurt!*

Shivers convulsed her body. Someone offered her a drink, she swallowed the cool lemony liquid greedily. Lowered back onto the pillows, she blinked up at the face leaning over hers. *Garmon?*

She smiled. "Garmon-" it came out a broken whisper.

"I'm here Gennie, I won't leave you. Rest." He stroked her face with a soothing damp cloth.

She closed her eyes, exhaustion claiming her. *Safe. Garmon.*

GARMON'S HEART clenched from that brief moment of recognition. It was precious, for as the night wore on her temperature continued to climb until she was so hot to touch, he feared for her reason.

She was delirious now and didn't know him, his repeated attempts to bring her back to herself her failed. She continuously flung off the covers and her skin was dry and burning. Her eyes glassy with fever, blind to her surroundings.

Her throat was too raw for her to do more than croak and cough, but among the unintelligible sounds he caught fragments that made his blood run cold.

"Jacob! Don't!"

185

"Jacob isn't here Gennie, he can't hurt you," he responded trying tuck the covers round her again.

"Must hide…"

"Oh Genie…" he murmured brokenly, blinking back tears as the desperate note in her voice.

"Hurts!…" this last a whimper that caught his heart and squeezed it.

"What hurts, sweetheart?" he asked wiping her febrile skin with the wet cloth.

The wet cloth came away hot to touch. It didn't seem to be enough to keep her temperature down. He touched her flushed skin convinced she was getting hotter.

He had heard that such severe fever could permanently addle the brain. In desperation, he filled the hip bath with cold water and picking her up he lowered her into the water.

She cried out, shivering convulsively and flailed about, splashing him generously with the water.

He poured cupfuls of water over her head, a cloth on her brow to stop the water running into her eyes. She gasped lying back in his arms in the tub, shuddering and crying. He held her in the water until it brought her temperature down and her skin felt cooler to touch.

Towelling her dry, he put her back into bed and sat holding her hand, willing her body to fight the infection. Her temperature began to climb again and he kept up the wet cloths on her forehead, arms and torso.

Her breathing became erratic, and his heart stuttered with fear each time it failed. His nerves were worn to a shred with desperate fear as the clock on the mantle ticked slowly forward.

In the dark of the night at its lowest ebb, he sat in silent vigil taking each breath with her, willing her to live. A life without Genevra in it was unthinkable. Disjointed prayers fell from his lips in a torrent. He had never prayed in his life and he had no idea how to go about it, the words were a jumble of exhortations and begging, bargaining and swearing.

"God, please don't take her from me." The whispered plea a broken rasp of desperation.

Time stood still and nothing in his life before this moment mattered, only that she continue to breathe.

She breathed and he breathed with her. Time dragged and his head swam with fatigue, his eyes closing. He fought them open time and again.

Desperate anguish tugged at his heart. "Gennie. Don't leave me!"

And then, with the first grey light of predawn, he saw it. Her skin bloomed with sweat and her breathing evened out. Tears of relief at this sign of the fever breaking, rolled down his cheeks and he gripped her hand and kissed it with feverish hope. "Gennie, Gennie, love! My strong girl. You can do this!" He stroked her brow with the damp cloth and watched her slip into a deeper calmer sleep.

"Genevra, my love," he whispered, sniffing. His vision blurred and he gulped, breathing out. "Thank you Lord," he muttered.

Full daylight found him face down on the coverlet. Lifting his head, he could see her brow was still dewed with sweat, but she was sleeping peacefully. Tears gathered in his eyes again as he watched her sleep. *So close. To come so close to losing her.* The true horror of it sank slowly into his bones and made him shudder. Tears stung his eyes. *He could not lose her. Not again. Not ever.*

He had fought the temptation to go and see her, again and again. Each time he resolved to do so, something held him back. He realised now it was fear of her rejection again. It had cut so deep without him realising it, masked initially by his anger and later by concentrating on his strategy of winning her back. Then to have her turn up on his doorstep in the middle of the night half out of her head with worry and fever. All considerations except helping her fled his mind. *She was in trouble and needed him. That was all that mattered.*

the truth broke over him like a wave. He loved her! Genevra Tate was more precious to him than his own life. He would give anything to save her one moments pain or anguish. he blinked tears from his eyes as his throat closed, aching and lowered his head to the bed holding her hand in both of his. His tears fell silently on her palm. Gratitude that she had been spared filled his heart and he whispered. "I love you Gennie, nothing and no-one will hurt you again. I promise." It was was an impossible promise to keep but he would do his damnedest to make it true.

She slept on oblivious of his epiphany and he kept watch over her, smiling through tears of joy and relief.

CHAPTER 18

Genevra woke to the sensation of soft sheets on her sensitive skin and a raging thirst. Her lids were sticky, and her nose blocked, her chest felt tight. She blinked and the light made her shut her eyes quickly against the pain that seared them. *Where was she? What happened?*

She opened her eyes cautiously, squinting and looked around the room. It took her a moment to recognise it, she had never been here in daylight before. *What was she doing in Garmon's bedchamber?*

She took an incautious breath and was seized with a coughing fit. Even as she fought for breath, fragmented memories of the night before filtered through. *Beth!* She pushed back the covers, trying to sit up and swing her feet around to stand up.

Garmon appeared in the doorway with a tray in his hands and seeing her trying to get up he spoke sharply. "Genevra stay where you are, you are in no fit state to get up!"

She waved at him trying to catch her breath and mouthed "Beth!" it came out more of a wheeze than anything else.

"Beth is safe, you have no need to worry, now lie down!" He set the tray on a table and came to the bedside, pushing her gently back against the pillows which were banked up to lift her upper body at an angle. Smoothing the covers back into place, he reached for a cup and offered it to her. "Here, this will sooth your throat."

She drank the lemon and honey water and sank back against the pillows exhausted. Swallowing, she gazed at him, a thousand questions on her tongue. She asked the most pressing of them. "Where is she?" her voice was raspy.

"Mr Rooke has her."

"Rooke?"

"My lieutenant. Don't worry, she is in good hands."

"Is she well?" her voice cracked.

He nodded. "There is nothing for you to worry about."

She wanted to ask more about Mr Rooke, but she was too weary to push the point and nodded, closing her eyes.

He sat on the bed and took her hand. "Sleep my dear, recruit your strength, you're not out of the woods yet."

"Thank you," she murmured and slipped over the edge into sleep.

GARMON WATCHED HER SLEEP, a half-smile curving his lips. Typical of Genevra that all her thoughts would be of someone other than herself. He raised her hand to his lips and kissed it, a warm feeling welling up in his chest and filling it to bursting. She was, he hoped, through the worst of it, but she could still relapse. He would do everything in his power to prevent that.

His heart warmed to the thought that in her most desperate hour she had turned to him for help. *Perhaps his cause wasn't so hopeless after all?*

He forced his mind away from Genevra for a moment to consider her sister. Mr Rooke had sent a message via Ben during the night to advise him that he had recovered Miss Whittaker. She was currently sleeping off her ordeal, Rooke did not provide details, which made Garmon's skin prickle with alarm. *What had transpired? Had Rooke recovered her before any damage was done?*

The second problem was what to do with her? By rights she should be returned to her parents. She was underage, but returning her to Robinson's care went against the grain with him and would be the last thing that Genevra would want.

The best thing would be to transfer her to the tavern under Genevra's care, but until Genevra was restored to health, he had no intention of letting her out of his sight. There was only one option. Rooke would have to keep Bethany safe until Genevra was well enough, and he could help her enforce her claim to take care of Bethany.

He drafted a note to Rooke to that effect, with the rider that he trusted the man to take care of the girl and to take no liberties with her, or he would cut off his balls and feed them to him.

He received a curt note back: *No harm shall come to Miss Whittaker under my care.*

Garmon smiled, Mr Rooke was offended.

When she woke some hours later, her first words were: "The Tavern!"

"Don't worry I have sent men round to guard it until either Joe or yourself are ready to reopen it."

"You think of everything!" she sighed with a smile, her eyes drifting shut. She opened them again and said, "How is Beth? Where is she?"

"Safe and well. My men are guarding her too, until you are well enough to assume responsibility for her."

She nodded and yawned, which turned into a cough. He had gone to the apothecary for a cough serum for her while she slept, and he helped her sit up and take some of it now.

"You make a very good nurse, sir. How did you learn such skills?"

His lips twisted in a half smile. "In the brothel of course. I nursed a lot of the girls through their illnesses. Some recovered, others did not."

She squeezed his hand. "Thank you. I don't know how to repay you for this."

"Do not mention payment in relation to this." He held her hand tight, his voice rough with emotion. "I confronted the idea of losing you last night. It was–untenable."

"Was I so close to death?" Her eyes widened in shock.

"According to the doctor, yes." And his own witness.

She sighed and said drowsily, "I am more in your debt than ever…"

He kissed her hand and watched her fall asleep again. He was bone weary himself, having had almost no sleep for forty-eight hours. He removed his shoes and stretched out on the other side of the bed beside her.

He woke sometime later to a darkened room, only the glow of the coals giving enough light to see by. She was restless and had flung off the covers. Sitting up with alarm he checked her skin; she was hot again. But not so hot as last night, yet.

He rose and fetched the bowl of water and cloth and resumed his bathing of her face and hands, wrapping the cloth round her wrists to lower the temperature of the blood that flowed there.

He sent one of his men for some food, reluctant to leave her while her temperature was spiking.

He fed her chicken broth and sponged her down, helped her to the chamber pot when she needed it and watched over her as she tossed and turned, lost in fever dreams. Offering her honey and lemon water and the cough serum when thirst and the wretched cough plagued her sleep. It wasn't as fraught a night as the one before, but he got little sleep and did not count the cost. His whole focus was on her and ensuring her comfort and recovery.

He had plenty of time to contemplate what he would do when she was recovered enough to listen to him. He rehearsed a dozen

different approaches and reasoned arguments to gain her cooperation and consent. One thing he was adamant about she could
not be left to carry these burdens alone, she could not fight her
stepfather over custody of Beth. The man had the law on his side.
Only another man could challenge his authority and hope to win.
And only one circumstance would give him the power to do so.
As her husband he could do it, but would she have him?

Genevra woke with the dawn, fragmentary memories of the
past thirty-six hours flitting through her mind. Her head was
clearer, the pounding headache had receded, and she was no
longer wracked with pain and shivers, she just felt light and
weak. Her chest still felt tight, and her breathing was impeded by
a slight wheeze.

Garmon was stretched out beside her on the bed, curled
towards her on his side, his head pillowed on his arm. She
watched him sleeping for several minutes, her heart so full it
threatened to break open and spill the infection of love through
her whole body.

The shock of it took her breath away. Panic followed swiftly.
She couldn't love him. She must not love him. Yet how could she help it?

*Whatever possessed a grown man to turn nursemaid for an adult
woman?*

She sighed, the warm feeling flooding her chest. If she gave
into that she would be lost. *You're lost already girl, whispered a traitorous voice in her head. You have been for weeks.*

She shied away from the thought, her heart quailing. *No more
pain remember?* She forced her mind away from that to Beth. He
had promised her Beth was safe and well, but she really couldn't
lie here any longer. *She needed to get back to the tavern and Beth.
And away from the temptation that was Garmon Lovell.* She pushed
the bedclothes down and struggled to a sitting position. Putting a
hand to her head, she waited for the room to stop revolving.

"What do you think you're doing?"

"Getting up," she said opening her eyes cautiously. The darkness had receded, and the world steadied.

He was already off the bed and around to her side to offer her his support. Helping her to the screen he said, "I hope you are not entertaining any foolish notions of going anywhere yet? You're not strong enough."

"I need to get back to the tavern and take care of Beth," she said, emerging slowly. She wore one of his shirts, and it came to halfway down her thighs. Her legs felt horribly wobbly and her head, light, so it was a secret relief when he scooped her up and deposited her back in bed.

"Not today," he said firmly. "You need food for one thing, you've barely eaten in two days.

Sinking back against the banked pillows she regarded him wanly. As much as she hated to admit it, he was right. Her stomach growled as if to confirm it, and she laughed, which made him smile.

The laugh turned to a cough, and it was a few minutes before she could say anything. Collapsing back onto the pillows exhausted by the coughing fit, she nodded. "Very well, you win. Feed me, I'm famished."

He grinned. "Coming right up ma'am. Stay put while I fetch a meal." He pulled on boots and coat and was gone.

Ten minutes later he was back with soft crusty bread, still warm from the oven, soft cheese, and a pot of hot chocolate and one of coffee. To this he added butter, olives, dates, honey, milk, sugar and salt from his own stores. Surveying this largess spread out on a tray over her knees she smiled ruefully. "Thank you, are you going to help me with this?"

"Of course," he shed his coat and sat down on the bed, offering her a plate upon which to pile her selection of goodies. "Coffee or chocolate? Or would you prefer tea?"

"Oh Chocolate! I haven't had such a treat in a long time," she said round a mouthful of bread and cheese. "Umm, this is so delicious, thank you."

He shook his head preparing her a cup of the hot bitter chocolate. "Do you want sugar?"

She nodded. Taking the sweetened cup from him, she savoured the rich flavour with her eyes closed. "I have never been so spoiled in my life as with you," she said quietly, setting the cup in its saucer carefully. "Why?"

"Why, what?" he said, chewing a date and spitting out the pit.

Instead of answering his question, which she took to be an evasion, she said, "I was warned against you, you know. Your reputation is-"

"Horrific. I've spent considerable effort over the years to make it so." He pulled another piece of bread from the loaf and slathered it with butter, cheese and honey. "I've seldom had to kill directly in recent years, I've had other men to do that for me, but that doesn't absolve me of the responsibility." His eyes caught and held hers, and she flinched inwardly. His words were harsh, and the flat look behind his eyes, told her that he spoke the truth.

She ought to be horrified, terrified to be here with him, but it was impossible when he treated her with such kindness. *Such tenderness even.* How to reconcile the two sides of his personality? The one she knew existed but seldom saw any evidence of and the one before her now, that went to extraordinary lengths for her comfort and protection?

Was it all some ploy just to gain power over her? Was he so driven by the need to control her that he would do all of this just to lull her into a false sense of security, before springing a trap on her? It seemed a ridiculous premise.

Or was it possible that this hard-hearted man actually cared for her? Both seemed equally impossible. And yet...

She swallowed another mouthful of chocolate. Her heart yearned for that to be the case. That he genuinely cared for her. *If that were so...* The prospect was both tempting and terrifying.

. . .

AFTER BREAKFAST she slept and he attended to correspondence, Ben having arrived with a bundle of papers for his attention. He was not going to his office, so it more or less came to him.

Rooke was managing the mudlarks and his other ventures on his behalf, ably assisted by Burridge and Fenwick. Rooke had stepped into the gap left by Connor's defection, but the wound still rubbed him raw and at least once a day he found himself wondering what happened. All his efforts to find any trace of Connor had so far failed, but the mystery pricked at him like an unhealed wound.

His other unfinished business, the matter of Mowbray and the gaming hell, likewise had faltered. No one was interested in a bounty on a duke, too risky. Mowbray had very effectively created a protective barrier around himself that Garmon was having trouble breaking down. He needed someone desperate, with nothing left to lose to take the bait he was holding out. Admittedly, Mowbray wasn't his highest priority lately.

He looked across the room to the bed where his priority lay sleeping. Genevra. Her hair was a tangle of light copper on the pillow and her face still a little pale, but her beauty to him was luminous. His obsession with her was showing no signs of abating. On the contrary it was worse than before. She was the most stubborn, infuriating woman he had ever met, and yet he couldn't contemplate a world in which she didn't exist. It was unthinkable, untenable.

He was not a man given to prayer. Raised as he had been, he'd seen little evidence of the mercy of God, but his desperate prayers in the early hours of yesterday morning had been answered. She had been spared. Not, he thought, because of any favour from the Almighty towards him, but because God favoured her. *Surely, she deserved some good fortune after the hand she had been dealt? Could he be her good fortune? Would she let him?*

He understood her reluctance, her wariness, after what she had suffered, to surrender herself to a man of his reputation. He had to earn her trust. He had to persuade her to let him look after her, protect her and her sister. He had to let her know he *could* protect her, that he would do anything to keep her safe. He could not hide what he was from her, she needed to know the worst of him and know that no matter what happened he would never turn that side of himself on her. He would only exercise it in her defence.

She stirred as if conscious of his scrutiny and her eyes opened. She smiled sleepily at him, and he rose moving towards the bed, towards her, as if drawn on a string. Her power over him was irresistible and the worst of it was he was so besotted he didn't care. Nothing mattered but her comfort. Sitting down on the bed he took her hand and kissed it.

"Can I fetch you anything?" he asked returning her smile. It was a delight to see her so much restored. He never wanted to see her so ill again.

She cleared her throat. "Perhaps a drink? I seem to be thirsty all the time."

He nodded and reached for the jug of lemon and honey water he had kept topped up. Pouring her another glass, he helped her sit up and take it from him.

"Thank you," she said sipping the drink and regarding him over the rim of the glass. "Why are you doing this?" She waved towards the table he had set up as a temporary desk. "You obviously have work to do that my presence is interrupting. You never do anything without a reason, an–agenda. I know this much about you. What is your motive for dropping everything to nurse me?"

His heart skipped with panic. *She had given him an opening; was he brave enough to take it?* He had thought to delay this, wait for a more opportune time, until she was recovered, yet when would be a better time? Once she was well, she would leave him to go back to the tavern, and he would have lost his opportunity.

He took a breath trying to steady his pulse. He wasn't afraid of many things, but he was suddenly afraid of her reaction to what he would say. *Could he say it the right way? Not to frighten her off? To persuade her...* he gave himself a mental shake. He had to say something, he had been thinking too hard and too long.

"If I tell you the truth, will you believe me?"

She rested the glass in her lap, cupped in her hands. "If it's the truth, yes."

He took the glass from her gently and moved a little closer on the bed to take both her hands in his. Fixing her gaze with his, he said slowly and carefully, "My only motive is to ensure your comfort, health and safety. I have discovered in the last forty-eight hours that nothing matters more to me than your happiness and well-being." He stopped, swallowing a sudden lump in his throat. "Genevra I can't pretend to be a good man. I'm not. I've done things that would truly horrify and repulse you if you knew about them. All I can promise you is that I will do anything to protect you, because you matter more to me than anyone on this earth."

Her hands stirred in his grip, and he tightened his, afraid she meant to pull away. "Please let me finish." He searched her face for a clue as to her feelings, but her expression was strangely blank, as if she had retreated behind a screen.

With a thudding heart he took another breath and plunged on, a sick feeling of dread in his stomach. *He was committed to this course now, but he was very much afraid that the answer he was going to get was not what he wanted to hear.*

"I never believed in love, not the romantic sort anyway." His lips twisted. "I've plenty of experience of physical passion, and I thought that was principally what we had, an extraordinary degree of it admittedly, but just a physical connection that would eventually burn itself out.

"You were very right to be wary of me for that reason. But facing the real prospect that you might die in my arms, and I could do nothing to prevent it..." He stopped, his throat closing over, a cold shiver running up his spine at the thought. "That convinced me that this, whatever it is between us, is much more than a physical attraction."

She bit her bottom lip, and her fingers squeezed his slightly, but still she said nothing. Encouraged he went on. "It was only with the dawn that I fully realised what this meant." He paused and took a breath.

"I love you, Genevra." Her hands jerked and her lips parted on a gasp, her skin flushed. He tightened his grip and ploughed on before she could say anything. "I love you with all my heart, soul and spirit. I love your strength, your intelligence, your kindness and compassion, your passion and yes, your infuriatingly stubborn independent spirit."

He swallowed the lump that threatened to choke him.

"I want you to be my wife, I want the right to protect you from all harm and to ensure, to the best of my ability, your safety and happiness. Will you please give me that right, Genevra?"

He stopped and listened to his heart beating hard in ears, his eyes straining for some sign of what she would say. She had kept his gaze until the last, when her eyes had dropped to their linked hands. It was then he saw the tears on her cheeks. His heart cracked.

"Ah no! Don't cry love. Please I can bear anything but that!" he let go of her hands to pull her against his chest and nuzzle into her hair.

She collapsed against him and wept, and he held her close and murmured nonsense, rubbing her back. "Please love, don't cry. I shouldn't have said anything while you're so weak. But you asked and I wanted to tell you..."

. . .

GENEVRA GASPED ON A SOB, her hands clutching his shirt, her heart so full it felt like it would burst. She tried to speak, but it came out a jumbled mess of sobs and broken words.

"What was that love? I can't hear you," he said pulling away a little to look at her face.

She swallowed and wiped her face, trying to stem the flow. "I said, w-was afraid to l-love you. But I can't h-help it." She sobbed some more.

"Help what? Be afraid?" he asked, his hand cupping her face. "I know sweetheart, you have good reason. I understand that." He swallowed. "How can I convince you not to be afraid of me? That I'm not Jacob Tate, that I would never-"

"No!" she shook her head. "I meant l-loving you!" she said on a sobbing rush.

"Oh." He blinked hard and hugged her tight. "Does that mean-? Will you marry me, Genevra?"

"Y-yes!" She said flinging her arms round his neck and hugging him, a rush of relief coursing through her body. The surge of love filling her heart was terrifying and exhilarating at the same time. "I've been in l-love with you for w-weeks," she confessed. "I just wouldn't admit it, even to myself!"

"That's my stubborn girl," he said with such a look of love her heart melted all over again. His face had softened from its usually harsh lines, his eyes mellowed to a warm hazel. "Can I kiss you?" His voice hoarse and low, sent a thrill through her body and rush of heat that had nothing to do with the fever.

"Of course," she said softly. It felt so wonderful to allow herself to feel all the emotions she had been suppressing, the softness, the warmth, the melting longing. His lips were gentle, the kiss searing and loving at once, his arms held her tight as he deepened the kiss and made her head spin.

Breaking the kiss he said, breathing quickly, "that will have to be enough for now, you're in no fit state to be ravished."

"I don't know, I'm lying down, I can't fall any further," she said drunkenly.

He groaned and kissed her again, bearing her back into the pillows.

After a bit he raised his head and said with a smile that melted her bones, "You have made me the happiest man in the world you know. We will be married just as soon as you are well enough."

She nodded, tracing his cheek and jaw line with a finger. "I swore I would never marry again, but I didn't bargain on you."

"You will not regret it, I promise." He kissed her hand and her wrist and then her mouth again, as if he couldn't get enough of her. "I'm ravenous for you, I want to eat you all up!" He said, nibbling on her neck.

She giggled, and he raised his head to look at her. "I didn't mean-who am I kidding? Of course, I did." his eyes darkened, and he licked her neck and kissed it. "You taste delicious, slightly salty and sweet."

"I need a bath," she said arching her neck for his attention.

"I'll give you a tongue bath," he said with a wicked smile.

"That should sound icky, but it doesn't," she said on a sigh.

"No," he said sitting up. "You're not well enough for all this yet, I'll fill up the bath for you."

"Who said I'm not well enough?" she said reaching for him. "After all I just have to lie here, don't I?"

"Genevra-!" She tugged him down, and he gave in with very little resistance.

"If you start to cough-" he said burying his face in her breasts.

"I won't" she said softly.

HE WANTED TO TAKE HER, ravish her, love her. But he wouldn't. He would wait. Wait for their wedding night, save all the feelings and passion up for a special joining that would mark the beginning of a new life for both of them.

Instead, he stroked her and kissed her and licked her to the edge and over while he came in his trousers, so aroused by the erotic delight of her surrender. Then he held her while she fell asleep in his arms, and he let tears of happiness roll silently down his cheeks into her hair.

When she woke a little while later the first words out of her mouth were "Mama. I must tell Mama that Beth is safe. She must be out of her mind with worry." She sat up her eyes fever bright and two flags in her cheeks.

Cursing himself for causing her to relapse, he said soothingly, "I will let her know, you need to rest and not agitate yourself."

"But I must tell Mama-"

"I will do it, you're in no fit state to get out of bed, and I am not subjecting you to an interview with your stepfather. Stay put. Ben will come and sit with you while I'm gone."

"But Mama doesn't even know you-"

"I have no qualms about introducing myself to her as her future son-in-law." He kissed her hand. "Trust me, hm?"

She sighed and nodded. "I'm so wretchedly weak, or I wouldn't let you do this without me!"

He smiled and kissed her forehead. "You stay here and rest, I'll be back before you know it and I'll tell you all about it."

CHAPTER 19

*L*eaving Ben to keep an eye on Genevra, Garmon washed and dressed to pay a visit to his prospective mother-in-law.

Ushered into her presence he found a small, slightly rounded, middle-aged woman with curly brown hair going grey, dressed with propriety and taste in a lace cap and dark blue morning gown. She was employed in some embroidery, which she abandoned upon his entrance, rising in agitation.

"Mr Lovell? You have some news of my Beth?"

He had provided the housekeeper, who opened the door to him with his name and the message that he had news of Beth in order to gain admittance. He bowed and came towards her. "I do Mrs Robinson, let me assure you she is safe and well."

"We thought she must have gone to Bath. Hiram has gone there to bring her home. When I didn't hear from Genevra, I was sick with worry." She wiped tears from her face with a fine lawn handkerchief.

"Mrs Tate has been unwell, which is why you didn't hear from her."

"We thought she must have gone to Bath too, when the

Tavern was closed up and those men would tell us nothing when we went there. We have been so worried. Where are my girls Mr Lovell, and how do you come to be mixed up in this?"

"Please sit down Mrs Robinson and I will attempt to explain."

She nodded and resumed her seat on the couch. He took his place beside her and said, "Firstly I should tell you that your daughter Genevra has done me the honour of accepting my proposal of marriage, which I hope is sufficient explanation of why I am, er 'mixed up in this'."

"Genevra marry? But she was adamant she would not!" Mrs Robinson's pale blue eyes blinked at him myopically.

"Yes, I know," he said with feeling. "It has taken all my powers of persuasion to convince her to have me, but I have finally been successful in that endeavour. I must tell you Mrs Robinson that I love your daughter with all my heart, and she has finally admitted to returning my regard."

Her tired expression was chased away by a smile, and she patted his hand. "I am very pleased to hear it Mr Lovell. My poor Genevra deserves some happiness."

"I am aware." He nodded gravely. "You can rest assured her heart is safe with me. It is my sole ambition to ensure her comfort and wellbeing for the rest of her life.

"And what is your profession Mr Lovell?"

"I am an entrepreneur. I dabble in all manner of business ventures, but I can assure you that I have the means to keep your daughter in all the comfort she could desire."

"Will you continue with the Tavern or sell it?" she asked with what he suspected was a whisper of hope.

"Genevra desires to continue running the business. In fact, it was a condition of her acceptance. Your daughter is stubbornly independent Mrs Robinson."

"Yes, that is my Genevra." She smiled again, her eyes tearing up.

"It is her dream to own and run her own brewery. I want her to have her dreams fulfilled."

She nodded and heaved a sigh. "To see one's children happily established is the greatest wish of any parent's heart, Mr Lovell." She dabbed at her eyes again. As if recollecting the purpose of his visit, she straightened and fixed him with an anxious stare. "And what of my Bethany?"

"As I said, she is safe and well. I am sorry if this pains you Mrs Robinson, but it is her desire and Genevra's, that she make her home with us in the future."

"Oh but-"

"You will be aware of the circumstances that drove her from this house. I have promised your daughters that Miss Whittaker will not be subjected to that kind of pressure again."

Mrs Robinson's face crumpled. "Mr Robinson means well! He and Genevra have never got on, but Beth is usually quite biddable. I was stunned by her reaction to Hiram's plan for her to marry Mr Neeps." She wiped her face. "I admit I could not like the match, but Mr Robinson was most set on it and when he gets an idea in his head it is as hard to dissuade him as it is Genevra." She sighed. "As long as Beth is safe, and I can visit her..."

"Yes, you will be welcome to visit her of course, perhaps on Tuesday? And to attend the wedding. It is to be held on Friday."

"So soon?"

Garmon smiled. "Neither of us want to wait and there is no reason to."

After supplying her with the details of the wedding, he took his leave and returned to reassure Genevra that her mother's mind had been set at rest.

LYING beside her on the bed with her head on his shoulder he kissed her hair and asked a question that had been plaguing him for months with no answer. "Where did you get your colouring from? I thought it must have been you mother, but she was a blonde like your sister."

"Yes both Beth and Mary take after mama, I got my red hair and blue eyes from papa." She said." Why do you ask?"

"Because when I first saw you I thought you looked familiar but haven't been able to work out why. It's your eyes, I swear I've seen them somewhere before."

"Really? How strange. Papa always said he got his looks from his mother. Great Aunt Maddie is papa's mother's sister, but she doesn't have that colouring either." She shook her head. "I've never thought about it. I just took it for granted that papa and I were alike." she smiled tearily. "I still miss him."

He kissed her hair and stroked her arm. He envied her the bond with her family. *That sense of belonging somewhere to someone...*

～

THE FOLLOWING day he took Genevra home to the Tavern and Mr Rooke brought Beth there mid-morning to be reunited with her sister.

Watching the two sisters greet each other it was easy to see the affection between them. Garmon knew a stab of envy to have that kind of family feeling.

Leaving the girls to their chatter he drew Mr Rooke aside for a word.

"I haven't told Mrs Tate of the circumstances in which you found her sister. It would distress her and if as you have assured me there was no damage done-?"

"None sir, I arrived just in time, any later and-" Mr Rooke shuddered visibly, his expression very grim.

"We will take steps to ensure other young women are not so endangered, such depravity will not stand."

"You can count on it sir. What did you have in mind specifically?"

~

"ROBINSON IS BACK," said Garmon, poking his head into the parlour two days later, where Genevra and Beth were having breakfast. He came in and shut the door. "I expect he will come here shortly, what do you want to do?"

Beth looked up apprehensively from her plate of toast. "Do you think he will force me to go back with him?"

"Just let him try!" said Genevra.

"Don't be concerned Miss Whittaker, Mr Rooke and I will ensure that doesn't happen."

Beth flushed. "Mr Rooke? Is he coming here?"

Garmon nodded. "I've sent for him."

Beth looked down at her plate but the smile on her lips gave Genevra pause. She really needed to pay more attention to Beth, she had been so busy with wedding preparations and catching up on tasks neglected during her illness that she had spent very little time with her sister. Beth had been in Mr Rooke's care during Genevra's illness, what exactly happened between them to cause Beth to look like that at the mere mention of his name?

A few minutes later Mr Rooke arrived and after a short colloquy, Beth was bundled upstairs and locked in her room for her own security and Garmon and Mr Rooke took up a position in the tap along with Genevra. The Tavern remained closed to customers. Shortly after 8:00 o'clock, Hiram stormed into the Tavern, looking less than his usual pristine self.

"Where is my daughter?"

"I'm here papa," said Genevra sweetly emerging from behind the bar.

"Not you, Bethany! What have you done with her?" Hiram's flushed face got even redder, his wispy hair was all on end, his suit was rumpled, and he looked exhausted. Not surprising since he had journeyed all the way to Bath and back in five days. "That girl is my responsibility, and she will return to our roof immediately! I don't know what you were thinking Genevra to aid and abet her in this madness -!"

"She stays here, Hiram," said Genevra, her voice hardening. "You can threaten and browbeat Mama and Beth, but you can't do so to me!" She crossed her arms and glared at him.

"Miss Whittaker will be making her home with us," said Garmon quietly. It was the tone that caused shivers down spines in the those that knew his reputation. Hiram was oblivious.

"And who in damnation are you?"

"I am the man who is going to marry your daughter, Mrs Tate." Genevra moved to his side and placed her hand on his arm.

"Lovell, is it?" Hiram sniffed. "Miriam mentioned your name. I see you lack the manners to apply to me as her father for permission to address her."

"She's of age and doesn't need your consent."

"But Beth is not. Whatever you choose to do Genevra, I'll not let you ruin your sister! Consorting with thieves and low-lifes. Don't think I haven't heard of you, Lovell for I have, and none of it good!"

"I'm glad you've heard of me Robinson; I won't have to explain to you what will happen to you if you don't accede to our wishes in this matter. I repeat, Miss Whittaker will make her home with us, and you will give up all attempts to marry her to unsuitable persons!"

Hiram went from red to white at this threat and swallowed. "I'll not be threatened! You won't get away with this. I'll go to the magistrate! I have the law on my side!"

"Try it," said Garmon. Genevra's heart thudded with pride and a slight thrill of fear. She had agreed to let Garmon intimidate Hiram, but she didn't want him actually hurt.

Silence followed this for a moment as Hiram visibly struggled with himself. "You haven't heard the last of this matter! I will not be manipulated by the likes of you Garmon Lovell!" He turned to Genevra. "Do you know what kind of man you're marrying?"

Genevra smiled up at Garmon. "Yes, papa I do. I love him and he loves me." She looked round at Hiram with a smile. "May I remind you that you were eager for me to remarry? You should be pleased."

"It's to be hoped he can keep you in line! A more froward girl I never met!" He huffed and mopped his brow with a handkerchief. "When is this accursed wedding?"

"Friday, and you're not invited!" snapped Genevra.

"Forgive me my, love," said Garmon, "But I did issue an invitation to your mother when I spoke with her."

Genevra glowered at Hiram. "Mama is welcome, he is not!"

Hiram blinked, his face blanching even further and for a moment she wondered if that was hurt she saw in his eyes, *but surely not. The man hated her as much as she hated him. Nonetheless, he swayed where he stood and reached out to grab the back of a chair. No doubt the rigours of his journey catching up with him.* A momentary stab of guilt shot through her. *He wasn't a young man, had he overtaxed himself?*

Mr Rooke took a step towards him, but Hiram waved him off, seeming to recover, he straightened his back and made them a stiff bow.

"Very well. You may treat me as you choose, but I'll not have you upset your mother. I will not repeat your cruel words to her, for they would cut her to the quick. Good day." And he stalked from the room, his shoulders drawn back stiffly.

Genevra sagged when he closed the door with a snap behind him, she was shaking. Garmon turned and enveloped her in hug. She clung to him a moment as she blinked tears from her eyes.

CHAPTER 20

*F*or all the multiple ways Garmon had made love to Genevra already, tonight was different. Tonight, he would love her with his body, his heart and his soul, because tonight, she was his wife.

He couldn't quite believe it. He had never thought he would marry, never thought he would meet someone like Genevra, who made him feel more than himself. Never thought that a woman so strong and brave and beautiful, inside and out, as Genevra, existed.

Mrs Lovell. It would take some getting used to, and unaccountably he was nervous about their first night as husband and wife.

The wedding had gone off smoothly, the ceremony held at St Giles in the Fields Church followed by a wedding breakfast at the Tavern, after which he had swept her off in his carriage for a night at Mivart's Hotel. His choice of hotel was deliberately different than the night they had spent together at Grenier's.

Mivart's was an exclusive up-market hotel patronised by the haute ton. Fortunately, money was the entrée to most things and Mivart's was no different. Mind, if he had been a loud, vulgar sort, no amount of money would have secured him a suite, but his years on the continent under the tutelage of the Chevalier de la Salle, had provided him with the requisite skills to ape the appearance of a gentleman, in dress, manners and speech.

Mr Robinson made his excuses and did not attend as per Genevra's request, but her mother came and her eldest sister with her husband, which was a comfort to Genevra. Mary was a slender frail looking woman with her mother's brown hair and pale blue eyes, her husband, a slightly pompous clergyman sliding quickly into middle age.

Garmon was supported through the ceremony by Mr Rooke and the enterprising Ben, but he missed Connor with a peculiar ache of the heart. He very much feared that something fatal had happened to Connor, because he could not believe that he would forsake him so thoroughly. Following that fear, he had charged the mud larks with finding Connor's body, abandoned in an alley or coughed up by the Thames, like Jacob Tate. So far nothing.

Genevra was stunning in the deep blue satin gown she chose as her wedding dress, with blue cornflowers in her hair, the colour of her eyes. Adorned by a set of matching sapphires round her neck, his wedding gift to her, she was a sight to behold. She was supported by her sister, Miss Bethany Whittaker, recovered from her own ordeal in London's streets and tastefully turned out in pale blue silk. She was a pretty girl, but her honey blonde hair and light blue eyes, were a pale imitation of Genevra's bold colouring, as was her slight figure, that lacked Genevra's luscious curves and height.

Genevra was a bold strong woman, and this was proclaimed in every inch of her being, and he loved her so much it almost hurt just to look at her. The thought that he could have lost her so recently to the fever, turned him into a quivering mess. If anyone so much as hurt a hair of her head, he would murder them. Fortunately for the health of London's population no one seemed inclined to do so and they left their inebriated guests to continue their revelry at his expense at the Globe, while his carriage took them to Mivarts.

Alone in their suite he poured her a glass of champagne and offered her a toast.

"To a long and happy marriage, my love."

She nodded, her eyes bright, and whispered huskily, "To a long and happy marriage." They drank, but he didn't miss the slight shiver that made her body quiver, and he put their glasses down and pulled her into his arms.

"Ghosts still bothering you sweetheart?" She snuggled into him and sighed.

"Sorry I shouldn't bring the mood down."

"But?"

"I just -" she stopped, and he waited with a heart thumping hard for what she would say. *God don't let her be regretting this already.*

"I never thought I would marry again. I didn't think I could bear to after -" she swallowed and wiped her eyes. "And then you." She looked up at him and smiled through her tears. "You're difficult to say no to!"

He grinned and kissed her. "I think I told you once I always get what I want, eventually," he kissed her again. "And I wanted you more than I've ever wanted anything in my life."

"I still can't quite believe it," she said after another lingering kiss.

"I can't either," he admitted, stroking a lock of her lovely hair off her face. "You are so beautiful. You looked magnificent today, but you know you're beautiful to me in your oldest gown with your hair in a mess."

She smiled, "and when I'm sick as a dog or out on my feet with fatigue?"

"Yes, all of that," he squeezed her close. "You will always be beautiful to me, I love you Genevra, I will never stop loving you."

She hugged him tight, burying her face in chest. "Thank you. I don't know what I've done to deserve -"

"I don't know what I've done to deserve you!" He cut her off roughly. "And as for deserving- " he swallowed. "Genevra the pain you have suffered- no one should suffer like that. And in spite of it all, there you are running a business all on your own and worrying about your little sister and your staff and thinking about everyone else but yourself!"

"Garmon," she sighed.

"Yes love?"

"I love you."

He smiled and kissed her again. And went on kissing her. After a bit he said husky voiced, "I know it's the middle of the day, but do you think we might go to bed? I want to make love to my wife."

She nodded with a smile and even after everything they had already done, a slight flush to her cheeks. They undressed each other slowly, between kisses and caresses and appreciative murmurs, until they were both naked, and he lifted and carried her into the bedroom and set her down gently on the bed. It was warm enough not to have to worry about covers, and he joined her on the bed.

Starting with her neck, he worked his way slowly down her body, spending a lot of time on each voluptuous breast. *God, how he loved her breasts, their full roundness and heft in his palm, those luscious, full, dark-rose nipples, their responsiveness to his touch.*

All these were a heady aphrodisiac to him, but most of all was the way he felt about her. The intensity of his feelings lent a spice to the whole experience, the fact that he now knew she returned his feelings...he never knew it was possible to feel this level of comfortable warmth coupled with intense eroticism.

Since the moment he first kissed her, he had felt an intense desire for her body, but it was her heart and soul he now sought to encompass within himself. Her pleasure had been his paramount desire, now he wanted her to feel not only pleasure but love and comfort and above all safety. To know she was loved and protected.

Moving down her belly to the core of her pleasure, he used his tongue to lave her, his fingers to stroke and push inside her, making her moan and move in restless desire, to arch and mewl and beg. When he judged she was at the very precipice, on the very edge of going over, he swiftly changed position to enter her body with his straining cock.

Caging her with his arms, his eyes locked with hers, he slid inside her and joined their bodies as one. Moving inside her slowly, holding her gaze with his own, he felt as if his soul was bared to her, nothing to hide and nothing to come between them. Her arms and legs wrapped around his body, drew him closer as her breathing lifted along with his. Her pale skin flushed with her arousal, her pupils blown, her lips full from the punishment of his mouth, her warm, soft body beneath him, responsive and giving at the same time.

He ploughed her with increasing urgency, the pleasure rising and tightening. It felt so good it took his breath and suffused his senses with an overload of tingling, overwhelming pleasure. *How could it get any better?*

Her cry of delight, quickened his pleasure and he groaned, thrusting faster and deeper, he lost control when he felt her inner muscles squeezing and fluttering on his cock. She groaned deeply as she tossed her head and arched her back, gripping him tight in her release.

Plundering her body with the final strokes of his own crisis, he bellowed her name, loosing his seed in violent jerks of his body, grunting with the force of it. The intensity took him by surprise, the build-up had been so gentle, but the way his release tore through his body and left him boneless in its wake, was anything but gentle. He shuddered with remaining aftershocks, little rills of pleasure ebbing through his body.

Whether he possessed her body and soul or not, she certainly possessed his. He buried his face in her neck and pulled her close, his throat too tight to speak. She wrapped her arms round him and kissed his hair.

"I love you Garmon," she murmured. He shuddered, battling the sudden rush of tears. Where they came from, he didn't know, but some well inside him seemed to have opened up, and he didn't have the strength or will to shove the lid back on it.

He curled into her and cried like a baby. He couldn't remember the last time he had cried. Not like this, jagged sobs that shook his body. He had occasionally experienced the odd wetness in the eyes perhaps or tightness in the throat, but nothing like this.

He cried for his mother and his younger self. A young man wound tight as a drum and furious at life, hiding hurt behind anger. *And so lonely.* It hit him in this sudden attack of feeling how lonely he had been, without realising it.

The tears abated slowly, and he muttered an apology.

"Don't!" she said softly but firmly. "Don't you dare apologise to me for this. You have held me when I cried a half dozen times, I swear. Do you want to tell me what it was about?"

He rolled onto his back, sniffing and wiping his face. "I don't think I realised until now how much I missed out on growing up as I did."

"You were robbed of your childhood, Garmon. You never had a proper family."

He smiled wryly. "I had the girls in the brothel, it was like having a half dozen mothers, aunts or sisters."

"It's not the same," she said quietly.

He groped for her hand and squeezed it. "You're right, but I didn't know that. I made the best of what I had."

"You did and it made you strong, but hard." She rolled to face him, propping her head on one arm. "I marvelled at the softness in you, the gentleness you showed towards me. Where did that come from?"

He shrugged. "The girls I suppose. For all their rough ways and difficult circumstances, they looked out for each other. I learned to take care of them through making their lives easier, and it won me the occasional bit of appreciation and affection. I don't think I fully realised how starved of that I was until you."

She nodded and swallowed. Reaching out, she stroked his face and then leaned over and kissed him. "You have a new family now. We're not perfect. Hiram and I don't get on, but mama and Beth and Mary are sweet. Her husband is a good man, even if he is a bit of a know-it-all."

"I miss Connor, it's eating me up, not knowing what happened to him. He was like a son or a younger brother. It felt like such a betrayal when he left. But the longer it goes on, the more convinced I am that something has happened to him."

"You've found no trace of him?"

"None. It's as if he vanished into thin air. I can't believe he would have left me with no word like this. Even if he was angry with me, and he was... I can't shake the feeling that something has happened to prevent him contacting me." He let out a breath. "At least I hope so, because the alternative doesn't bear thinking of."

He rolled towards her. "Enough maudlin thoughts, this is supposed to be a time for happiness and pleasure." he kissed her. "And you have given me great pleasure so far my lady."

"More could be arranged," she murmured, her hand gliding down his stomach to his stirring cock. Palming his sticky member, she slid down the bed and when her tongue licked him, he jerked, his cock firming in her hand. In moments her hot mouth had him hard again. And shortly after, groaning with the pleasure of her tongue, mouth and hand.

"Genevra," he protested, but she held up a hand staving him off.

"My turn," she said releasing his cock briefly from her delicious mouth. "You have nearly killed me with pleasure before, my turn to drive you crazy."

He subsided into the pillows, closing his eyes and let her. Her mouth and hands drove him relentlessly higher, until he was a panting, quivering mess, his hips thrusting and groaning for release. Which she refused to give him, teasing him to the brink and stopping over and over.

The last time he was so close to coming he felt the ripples beginning, the wash of pleasure through his body heralding the point of no return, and then she squeezed the base of his cock hard and stopped it dead.

He groaned in frustration. "Genevra, you're killing me please, I need to come!" He sat up on his elbows and glared down at his red quivering cock. She grinned and sat up, straddling his legs, her quim on full display which made him groan again and his cock bob and dance.

"Alright. I suppose you have earned your reward," she said shuffling up the bed on her knees and lining up his cock with her cunny, fed him inside her, and slid down until she was fully seated. Then leaning forward with her hands on his chest. "But you can't come until I do," she grinned down at him wickedly.

"I'm going to die," he said fatalistically. "I take no responsibility for what happens next," he added, moaning as she moved on him.

She moved faster and moaned, closing her eyes. "You feel so big and deep inside me," she panted her breasts jouncing with the movement. He grasped them, squeezing and massaging, tweaking her nipples, watching her face with greedy delight. She was lost in her pleasure, and he forgot his own in absorbing hers.

He kept up the twiddling of her nipples, knowing how much that aroused her, using spit on his fingers to aid the slippery sensation. When she moved a hand to pleasure herself, a jolt of lust went through him at the sight. His balls felt tight, he couldn't last much longer. That burning ache behind his ball-sack was getting worse and his cock was on fire. His hips bucked and he said hoarsely, "Come Genevra, please I can't hold-"

And she came with a cry and stiffening of her whole body, her head flung back and her inner muscles quivering and throbbing on his cock. His body surged up, the lightening ignited, and searing pleasure rushed from his balls up his cock and spilled out in hot spurts that made his muscles cramp and made him grunt and groan with the intensity–yet again.

She collapsed on him panting, and he jerked with aftershocks until he was still and relaxed beneath her. Wrapping his arms round her, he sighed and murmured, "thank you, Mrs Lovell."

She nodded and slipped off him bonelessly, curling into his side.

They drifted off to sleep in each other's arms, and he thought muzzily he had never been happier.

CHAPTER 21

$\mathcal{T}$wo days after the wedding, Garmon was working late in his office in St Giles, and just contemplating packing up to go home to Genevra at the Tavern, when Ben popped in with a letter for him.

"Who is this from, Ben?" he asked turning the letter over.

"Mr Rooke, sir. He said to give it to you at 7:00 o'clock, which it is, just gone."

"I see. You didn't think to give it to me before then?" He frowned at Ben and the boy had the grace to flush.

"Mr Rooke said not to sir." Ben bit his lip and looked at his shiny boots.

"Who pays your wages Ben?"

"You do sir," said Ben looking miserable. "Mr Rooke said as how he'd take the blame sir, and the letter explains everything."

"I see." Garmon regarded Ben in silence for a moment and then broke the seal on the letter. Spreading the sheet out, he read with gathering wrath. By the time he got to the end of the letter he wasn't sure what he was feeling.

"May I go sir?" asked Ben tentatively. "On account of I gotta feed the kittens."

"Kittens?" Garmon looked up distracted.

"Mr Rooke's kittens," said Ben, as if that explained everything. He waved Ben away, returning back to the letter.

Folding the letter, he put it in his pocket and prepared to leave to go home.

∼

HAVING SEEN Beth off on her 'errand', Genevra kept herself busy in the tap waiting nervously for Garmon to appear. *He had sent a note earlier to say he would be late. It was after seven, how late, was late? It would be dark in another hour.*

She had been pleasantly surprised at how easily Garmon fitted into her life at the Globe. He split his time between the Tavern and his business in St Giles, but he left the running of the Tavern to her and Joe.

This had been a fraught topic between them, and she had been afraid he would try to take over. But so far there had been no signs of that. He had agreed easily to moving into the Tavern with her, as she wanted to continue to run the place herself. He seemed inclined to grant her every wish and she took some shameless advantage of that, revelling in having a man's love without his controlling hand on her every move and thought.

He appeared shortly after half past seven and found her in the office working on the accounts. He came in, shut the door and rounded the desk to pull her up into his arms for a kiss.

"I missed you," he murmured.

With her arms round his neck she said," I missed you too."

"How's trade?"

"Steady all day," she said.

He sat down in the desk chair and pulled her down into his lap. "I received an interesting letter from Mr Rooke this evening. You want to tell me about it?"

"He and Bethany are in love, isn't it wonderful?"

"Is it?"

"Certainly it is," Genevra sat up and regarded him. "He's taken her to his father, so he can marry them. His father is a Vicar."

"Yes, he explained that. A fact I was hitherto unaware of." He frowned. "How much did he divulge to you about-?"

"Everything. It is the best thing that could have happened to Bethany. She has been moping around here looking miserable for days. I knew something was wrong, but the silly darling wouldn't tell me. It was very clear to me Mr Rooke's feelings are fully reciprocated, and I am delighted to tell you that he is head over heels in love with my darling Beth.

"I am very confident he will care for as she should be cared for. He is a good man. But surely you know that already? Or is there something I should know?"

Garmon shook his head. Rooke *was* a good man, loyal, honest, hardworking. And a more ruthless enforcer he had never employed. But Genevra didn't need to know about that side of his dealings with Mr Rooke, he was quite sure Bethany would see no evidence of the man who had terrorised London's underground for five years in Garmon's name.

"There is one thing Mr Rooke seems to have overlooked in his preparations. He appears to have omitted to obtain a marriage license."

"Oh, does he need one?"

"If he wishes to be married immediately rather than wait the mandatory three weeks for the banns to be read. I obtained one for us, which was why we could be married so quickly."

"Oh dear! What can we do?"

"I'll obtain one, and we can take it to them, it's only about four hours to Pinner."

"What a splendid idea! I do adore you Mr Lovell!" She said giving him a hug and a kiss. Some little while later she said, "Do you think we could take mama with us? She would hate to miss Bethany's wedding."

"We could, but how do we avoid telling your stepfather?"

Genevra bit her lip. "I've been feeling a bit guilty about Hiram. I think I may have hurt him over my refusal to let him attend my wedding and Beth was always his favourite. That is why I was so surprised that he wanted to shove her into marriage with Josiah the horrendous."

"Then we will go to see them in the morning to inform them of Beth's impending marriage and offer them a lift in our carriage, shall we?"

"I love you!" she said in such a gratifying way that it was sometime before either of them said anything.

Reluctantly he broke the kiss and said, "I had best be going before it gets too late to be paying calls on the bishop, his excellency keeps early hours."

CHAPTER 22

Genevra had never known such happiness as she experienced in the weeks following her wedding to Garmon. Her second marriage was nothing like her first and as the days bled into weeks, she began to realise just how very bad her first marriage had been and the damage it had done to her.

She had begun her foray into brewing with her first small batch of beer, brewed up in the converted kennel at the back of the Tavern. The beer offered at a discounted price in the tap, went so quickly she was working on a second batch twice the size when Garmon came into the brew house and shut the door behind him.

She glanced over her shoulder at him as he came up and put his arms round her from behind. Holding her against his front he peered over her shoulder at the kettle full of wort. "How is it coming along?"

"Good, it's about ready to add the hops. You're early, I wasn't expecting you for hours."

"I missed my wife," he said nuzzling her neck.

She sighed moving to accommodate his wandering lips. "I missed you too," she murmured.

"Good," he said reaching for the front of her gown and loosening the laces on her bodice.

"Garmon, anyone could come in!"

"Let them," he growled, nipping her ear just as his hand found its way into her bodice and cupped a breast, squeezing the nipple. "I want you, now."

She uttered a stifled moan as one hand continued to torture a nipple and the other reached lower to hoick up her skirts, exposing her quim to his fingers. Spearing her flesh, he groaned. "And you want me too because you're wet!" he said sliding his finger through her lips. "Bend over and grasp the edge of the kettle."

"Garmon!"

"Do it!" he said pushing her down and lifting the back of her skirts. Cool air wafted over her exposed bottom, and he nudged her legs further apart and plunged two fingers inside her, using a third to push forward and graze her bud. She panted and moaned at this treatment, while the rustle of cloth told her he was undoing his falls with his other hand.

In the next moment he pulled his fingers free of her and then his cock was lodged at the entrance and thrust inside with a hard shove, accompanied by a grunt and a sigh.

"Fuck!" he muttered. "I've been thinking about you all morning." He thrust again, jarring her and forcing her to grip the kettle rim tighter to hold her balance. "I couldn't concentrate for thinking about your tight, wet, cunny!" with each word he thrust hard, and she whimpered, pushing back on him, caught up in the sudden surge of lust.

He leaned over her back and nipped her neck where it joined her shoulder and cupped a breast again, fondling and pinching the nipple. He wrapped his other arm round her belly and continued thrusting harder and faster, pinching that nipple mercilessly.

The flesh between her legs throbbed, and she moaned helplessly, pushing back on him, desperate for more. He adjusted his angle slightly, forcing the head of his cock against the place inside her that drove her crazy, provoking a groan from her with each thrust.

"God, I love you!" he panted. "Come Gennie, please! Oh, fuck!" His groans joined hers as he jolted her hard, holding her on his cock, and she felt the hot rush of his seed as he grunted loudly. The spark of it set her own flesh alight and a flood of throbbing pleasure coursed through her body, making her moan with relief.

She sagged in his arms as her legs gave out, and she clung onto the kettle, the cold metal digging into her hands, her arms trembling as she sobbed or breath.

He kissed her neck and murmured. "That is better. God, I needed that. Needed you!" He squeezed her tight against him, his nose buried in her neck. "I'm addicted to you."

Sudden tears stung her eyes at the desperate note in his voice. To inspire such need frightened her. *What if he grew tired of her?* The old fear whispered in her head. She tried to squash it, but it niggled and persisted. He withdrew from her body, and she straightened letting her skirts fall back into place as she felt his seed seeping down her legs. He rebuttoned his falls and she tidied her bodice. She bent over to hide the action of wiping her eyes and then turned to him with a smile.

"I need to get back to adding the hops now, are you going back to the office?"

"I thought I'd stay and have luncheon. Is there anything I can do to help?"

"No, I have it all under control," she said quickly.

He caught her hand and kissed it. "I can be useful you know."

"I know, I just-"

"Want to do it yourself."

"Yes." She searched his face. "You do understand?"

He nodded smiling ruefully. "Will you at least come and eat with me?"

"Yes, I can do that," she linked her arm in his, and they went back into the tavern to partake of Mrs Bell's excellent fish stew.

~

SOME WEEKS later

Genevra was halfway up a ladder, putting jars of preserves on the top shelf in the pantry when she suddenly felt dizzy. Spots formed in front of her eyes and her vision darkened round the edges. She clutched the shelf as a wave of nausea washed over her, weakening her knees, her vision darkened, and she felt herself falling.

She cried out as she fell and knew no more until she woke stretched out on her bed with Mrs Bell bathing her face with a damp cloth. Joe hovered anxiously in the background.

"What happened?" she asked muzzily.

"You fainted love. Joe brought you up here and the doctors been sent for."

She moved on the bed and cried out as a sharp pain struck her shoulder.

"Looks like you hurt your shoulder when you fell. Would you like a sip of water?"

"Yes, thank you." She took the water and lay back. "Has Mr Lovell been informed?"

"Aye," said Joe. "Sent one of the lads to him straight. The other went for the doc."

She nodded. "Thank you, Joe, who's minding the tap?"

"Annie, but I'll get back down there now, if you're feeling better?"

She smiled wanly and nodded; her stomach was still uneasy. It must have been something she ate.

Joe left and she said to Mrs Bell, "I'm alright, you can get back to the kitchen, the lunch crowd will be here soon. I'll just lie here and wait for the doctor."

"You sure, dearie?"

"Yes, thank you."

"You're still very pale dear. The bowl's there if you need it." She nodded to a bowl on the bedside table and got up.

Genevra closed her eyes and concentrated on soothing her roiling stomach. She must have dozed because she woke when the door opened and blinked at Dr Borden as he came towards the bed. He was a middle-aged man with a slight paunch and greying hair at his temples. He wore a pair of wire rimmed glasses on the end of his slightly hooked nose.

"So, what's all this about falling off ladders Mrs Lovell?"

"I fainted," she said and proceeded to explain what happened. He listened carefully and then examined her.

"Your shoulder's bruised but no permanent damage done, I think. But you're quite pale. Have you been eating enough red meat?"

She swallowed at the mention of meat and closed her eyes.

"You're feeling nauseated?" he noted.

She nodded.

"When was your last monthly flow, Mrs Lovell?"

She opened her eyes and stared at him. "I don't know. I've lost track, about five or six weeks maybe? I-" she stopped. "Sometimes they're late, but-"

"Not usually this late?" he prompted.

"No. I hadn't thought about it."

"Are your breasts sore? Fatigue, hunger?"

She nodded. Her heart thudding.

"I think it is likely that you are with child Mrs Lovell."

"But the doctor said I couldn't. That after the last miscarriage-"

"We doctors are not infallible Mrs Lovell. Sometimes we get things wrong."

"But the damage- he said I was ripped inside, that I wouldn't-" she stopped her voice wholly suspended by tears.

"There, there, Mrs Lovell," he said patting her arm. "It's perfectly normal to be emotional in situations like these, is you husband here?"

"Yes," Garmon stepped into the room and shut the door, going straight to the bedside.

"What happened doctor?" he seized Genevra's hand his face pale with worry.

"Your wife grew faint and fell off a ladder Mr Lovell. She has bruised her shoulder but nothing serious. I have just concluded that the cause of her fainting spell is that Mrs Lovell is with child."

GARMON'S HEAD spun and for a moment he thought *he* might faint. "You're sure doctor?"

"Not one hundred percent certain, but the symptoms are all there. Time will tell, but it seems likely, yes." he transferred his attention back to Genevra. "I suggest you rest for the remainder of the day, take some honey water to recruit your strength and eat when you feel able to."

She nodded and wiped her eyes. "Garmon?"

"Yes love," he squeezed her hand and kissed her forehead. "I'll just see the doctor out, and I'll be right back, don't get out of bed, promise me?"

"I don't think I could," she admitted with a fractured smile.

"Good girl, I'll be right back."

He held the door for the doctor and escorted him downstairs.

"If I might have a word with you?" he said opening the parlour door and inviting him in.

He waved the doctor to a seat and said, "Are you aware of my wife's medical history?"

"She mentioned something about a miscarriage?"

Garmon swallowed. "She has suffered two, brought on by the violence of her previous husband towards her. The last one -" he stopped and tried to master his emotions. "The last one tore her inside, according to the doctor. There was a lot of blood, and she almost died. Needless to say, the infant did not survive. The doctor told her she would never conceive again." He dashed his hand across his eyes and sniffed. "If she is indeed pregnant, can you tell me the odds of her carrying this child to term?"

The doctor shook his head. "I cannot. It is in God's hands. I can only report what I see, she appears to be gravid, judging from the symptoms. I would suggest that she rest and eat as well as the sickness allows. Usually, the nausea abates within a few weeks. I recommend ginger and mint tea and small frequent meals. She should watch for pain in the pelvic area, or the lower back and any bleeding what-so-ever and immediately rest if that should occur. Otherwise, there is not a lot we can do."

Garmon nodded. "Thank you doctor. I appreciate your plain speaking."

The doctor nodded and went to rise but Garmon stayed him. "I have one more question," he flushed faintly. "It concerns marital relations. Should I desist-? Will it harm the child?"

"No, provided it is not overly vigorous, and you do not apply undue pressure to the abdomen." The doctor flushed and his eyes slid sideways for a moment. "I have observed that women frequently become quite ah, demanding in that regard in the second trimester. It seems the presence of the child stimulates the female body parts and makes them considerably more sensitive to ah arousal. It is advisable on a number of fronts to ah satisfy the needs of your wife in that condition." He cleared his throat.

"You have learned this from-"

"Both professional and personal experience Mr Lovell. My wife and I have four children and I have attended many ladies in a gravid state during my thirty years as a practising physician." he was quite flushed by this stage and Garmon took pity on the man. Smiling he grasped and shook his hand.

"Thank you doctor I am most grateful for the advice. I will heed it."

Garmon saw the doctor off the premises and headed for the stairs to return to Genevra's side. His emotions were all over the place, divided equally between elation and fear. Carrying a child was a risky endeavour at any time, with Genevra's history the risks were increased fourfold. *If he had realised that she stood even a small chance of falling pregnant, would he have taken precautions to prevent it? But she had been adamant that she couldn't conceive.*

He paused with his hand on the door handle searching for some equilibrium and failing to find it. He pushed the door open and stepped into the room shutting it behind him. She had her eyes closed. Her face was less pale, that was a good thing, but there were tear tracks on her cheeks. He trod over the bed and sat down gently on the edge.

She opened her eyes and stared up at him, her deep blue eyes pools of pain and hope.

"Garmon?" She groped for his hand.

"Yes sweetheart, I'm here. We will get through this together, whatever happens." He gathered her up in his arms and held her while she wept, his own tears running down his cheeks.

"I'm happy and terrified at once," she confessed.

"Me too," he admitted with a smile.

She raised her hand and wiped at his tears. "The prospect pleases you?"

"Of becoming a father?" Warmth flooded his chest and a smile he couldn't suppress broke out on his face. "Yes, I am pleased, so very pleased. I never thought I would be. But having a child with you will be the most wonderful gift I could ever imagine." He swallowed, he wouldn't speak of the risks to her and the child. They would face that if it happened. For now, they would hold fast to hope.

"The doctor said you are to rest and eat well." He repeated all the doctor's advice, and she nodded. He didn't mention the bit about marital relations, he would wait and observe what his wife wanted. What she needed.

"I think I will transfer my office to here for the next few months," he said. "I don't think I can bear to be apart from you and I will worry ceaseless about you taking risks if I'm not here to look after you."

She lay back on the pillows and regarded him with a slight frown. "You're going to drive me mad, aren't you?"

He smiled and kissed her gently. "I'm going to look after you and our child." he laid a hand gently on her belly and she covered it with her own.

"I suppose I'll just have to get used to it?"

"You will." He said and kissed her again.

In Richmond

Jacob rolled off the body under him with a grunt and lay getting his breath back, sweat congealing on his skin.

"Fetch me a drink," he said shoving Maggie towards the edge of the bed. She threw him a sour look, which he ignored, she was in a mood again, and he was getting sick of it. The sex was still good but everything else had soured.

He missed Genevra, time to go home. Hopefully any hue and cry over his brother's body, had died down. He'd been away more than long enough.

"Here!" the woman thrust a tankard at him, sloshing some of the liquid onto his chest.

"Fuck, you're a clumsy bitch!" he said, rearing up and smacking her across the face. She stumbled backwards and the tankard went flying. Disgusted, he hauled himself to his feet and went to wash at the basin. When he was done, he pulled on his clothes and headed for the door of her room at the Tavern.

"Where are you going?"

He stopped near the door. Half turned to look back at her. She was leaning on the table nursing a bruised cheek.

"Home," he said simply and walked out.

CHAPTER 23

Genevra spent the next six weeks being coddled by Garmon as the fatigue and nausea were terrible. But miraculously it vanished one day and after a few days of being able to eat without vomiting she was feeling so much better she insisted that Garmon let her return to working in the tavern.

A visit to her parents for dinner at which both her sisters and their husbands were present, provided the perfect setting for the announcement of her pregnancy. She hadn't wanted to say anything too early for fear that something would go wrong. But she was feeling so much better now that she felt confident of sharing the good news.

She waited until the dessert was served and a lull in the conversation enabled her to say, "Garmon and I have some news." Garmon took her hand under the table and squeezed it, while she smiled round the table.

Mama, who had picked up her spoon put it down and fixed her with an enquiring look. Hiram, in the act of spooning extra custard on his generous slice of apple pie, said, "the tavern doing better now you have a man to run things?"

Genevra bit her lip, determined to ignore Hiram's needling. She would not allow him to spoil her surprise. "We are expecting a baby."

Stunned silence greeted this announcement for a moment and then everyone was talking at once, tears, congratulations and hugs were exchanged and for the first time Hiram looked at Garmon with approval and Genevra with pride. Garmon had his hand wrung and received several pats on the back from the other men. Hiram broke out the best brandy and there were smiles and flushed faces all round.

THE WEATHER WAS GETTING cold now as the year headed rapidly towards winter and Garmon bundled Genevra into a blanket when they got into their carriage to head home.

Wrapping an arm round, her, he said," that went well, don't you think?"

"Yes, better than I expected. Hiram behaved himself."

"You know I think he is fond of you girls despite what you think."

"He just has an odd way of showing it!" said Genevra tartly, obviously still not convinced. She ran a hand up his thigh and leaned into his shoulder. Garmon glanced down at her as her hand continued to rub his thigh, causing his cock to thicken and heat behind his falls. The last few weeks Genevra had been too ill to want to do anything much except sleep when they went to bed, and he'd been in the habit to tending to his own needs manually in private, unwilling to bother her with his desire for her, which had abated not one whit.

She turned her head into his shoulder as her hand reached higher and cupped him boldly, provoking a groan from him.

"Genevra!" She lifted her head and grinned at him slightly flushed. "Do you think we might-?"

"God yes," he said, kissing her. "If you're feeling well enough?"

he added, running a hand across her ribs and up to cup one large breast. Always generous, her breasts had become quite huge with the baby and her nipples exquisitely sensitive as he proved just now by brushing one very lightly with his fingers and getting a moan in return.

"I've been thinking about it for days," she admitted, kissing him back with fervour. Heat flared in his groin and pleasure wreathed through his body, his mind already on logistics and how to make the best of this opportunity without hurting her or the child.

The carriage arrived at the tavern, and he sent her upstairs to get ready while he helped Joe, and the boys tidy up. Racing up the stairs after locking up, he found her snuggled under the covers, her hair spread out on the pillows a glorious halo round her head. The fire in the grate had only just begun to take the chill off the air, and he undressed rapidly, crawling under the covers and pulling her into his arms with a convulsive shiver.

"I loathe winter," he muttered burying his face in her neck. "You smell delicious."

She wriggled closer and murmured, "you do too." He found her mouth and fell into a deep kiss, his body lighting up with desire, it had been so long since he'd been inside her, his hunger was sharp and demanding.

Her hands ran all over him, and she straddled his thigh, pressing and rubbing herself on him with increasing urgency, making little noises of pleasure and demand that set fire to his blood. He was panting and shaking with wanting her when he broke the kiss, as frantic for her as she was for him.

"Turn round love and I'll spoon you," he said husky with passion," it's better for the babe." Reluctantly she turned within his arms, and he reached down to stroke her sticky flesh and draw a long moan from her.

"Please Garmon, I need you!" She pushed her bottom back

into him, and he moved to find the right angle, reaching lower to guide himself into place.

Sliding inside, he groaned as tight heat enveloped him and gasped as she wriggled and pushed back on him.

His fingers slid between her folds giving her what she needed, as his hips reflexively thrust and his other hand brushed her nipples very gently, if a little haphazardly.

It was a heated rush to the finish line for them both as she clenched and shook, moaning her release, and he lost any control he'd had, which wasn't much and grasping her hip thrust wildly to bring himself off with a ravaging rush of pleasure that took his breath and made him groan loudly into her neck.

Not his best effort, he thought muzzily through the waves of intense pleasure, his cock loosing his seed in hard pulsing shots.

He huffed and panted, "sorry I couldn't hold back."

She sighed, "no matter, that was wonderful." She moved on him, and he gasped as she clenched.

"But not enough," he murmured, stroking her gently with his fingers, swirling and bringing her rapidly to the peak again. After the sixth time, she stayed his hand with a panting moan.

"Enough, that is enough."

"For now," he said nuzzling her neck and letting himself slip out of her. She turned and snuggled into him.

"You want a cloth to clean up?"

She shook her head, "Sleep..." she murmured.

He smiled and kissed her mussed up hair. Listening to her breathing level out, he didn't think it was possible to be any happier. He offered up a prayer of gratitude and entreaty to keep her and the child safe. That worry was never far from his mind, though he tried not to dwell on it.

~

JACOB GOT wind of the price being offered for the duke's ransom when he got off the boat from Richmond and headed to the nearest Tavern for a drink. He was still two days from home on foot, unless he could cage a lift, or some form of transport, and with no coin to trade he was hopeful of finding a way to pick up a little easy cash. He didn't expect to stumble across such an opportunity as this. The furtive conversation he overheard, made his ears prick and his heartbeat faster. Going home could wait, this opportunity seemed too good to pass up. He approached the table where the conversation was taking place and introduced himself.

CHAPTER 24

The Duchess of Mowbray was eating breakfast at Seven Oaks the country seat of the Earl of Stanton, with her hosts, the Earl and Countess, her sister-in-law, when their conversation was interrupted by the entrance of the Stanton's very correct butler, Porth, bearing a silver salver on which rested a plain envelop.

"Excuse the interruption my Lord, but this has just arrived for the Duchess of Mowbray." He offered the silver tray to Diana with a bow.

"Thank you, Porth," said Diana picking it up with a frown. "How did this arrive?"

"By courier your Grace."

"From?" she asked turning the envelope over, looking for a clue as to its contents.

"London, I believe," said Porth. Turning to the Earl he said, "is everything satisfactory with the meal, my Lord?"

"Yes, thank you," murmured the Earl looking up from his newspaper.

Porth bowed and left the room, closing the door quietly behind him.

"It must be from Anthony, but why he would write to me when he will be here later today..." Diana opened the envelope with a sudden prickle of presentiment and spread open the single sheet.

The writing was black and bold, but the letters were ill formed and the spelling incorrect. It was definitely not from Anthony. She read the text with starting eyes her heart thudding heavily in her breast, a hand stealing to her throat in horror.

WE HAVE THE DUKE. BRING THE TITLE DEEDS FOR LOVELS TO THE PRINTERS SHOP IN MONMOTH CORT AT 8 PM SHARP OR HE WILL DIE

"My dear what is it?" asked the countess alarmed by her manner.

Diana lowered the sheet and said woodenly, "Someone has kidnapped Anthony, and they are holding him to ransom."

"Good heavens!" said the countess faintly.

"Show me the note," said the Earl holding out his hand. He read it swiftly and looked up, "Who-?"

"I know who!" said Diana in a choked voice, rising from her seat, her body stiff with fury. "My Uncle, Garmon Lovell!"

She paced away from the table towards the window, dashing the tears on her cheeks away with an impatient hand. "How could he?" She swallowed the lump in her throat, a pain in her chest that threatened to stop her breath.

"But he warned me!" She turned, her hands in fists. "I will kill him myself for this! How dare he!"

The Earl rose and went to her. "My dear I will leave at once for London and alert the constabulary. This will not stand. A peer of the realm, a duke no less, to be kidnaped and held to ransom? The perpetrators are mad if they think they can get away with this!"

"What if they hurt Anthony?" said his sister who had obtained the letter and read it.

"I imagine they have hurt him already to have taken him prisoner. They must have tricked him somehow and overcome him...," said Diana.

"There must have been a few of them, Anthony would not be easy to take down," said the Earl heading towards the door. "I will order a horse -"

"Make it two!" snapped Diana, "and ask Porth if that courier is still here."

At the Earl's look she added impatiently. "I'm not waiting meekly here while you ride off to be noble my Lord. He's my husband, and he's been kidnapped by *my* uncle. I'm bloody well coming! Just give me time to change, this requires breeches!" on which she opened the door and ran up the stairs.

JUST OVER THIRTY minutes later Diana and Stanton set off for London; it would take them six hours hard riding to get there, but the roads were clear, the weather had been cold but fine for several weeks. The courier had gone by the time Stanton sent the servants looking for him and no trace was found of him.

GARMON WAS ABOUT to sit down to dinner with his wife and the Rookes who were visiting London for a spell, when a commotion in the tap drew him out of the parlour and towards the tap room, followed by Sebastian.

"Garmon! Where are you, come out, you son of a bitch!"

Diana, dressed in breeches, boots, shirt and a cloak stood in the middle of the tap room a pistol in her hand and a look of wild fury on her face.

"Diana, what -?" he stopped dead as she raised the pistol, cocked it and took aim at him. The customers in the tap began edging for the door, slipping out one by one and legging it. The staff, Joe and Annie, stayed behind the bar.

"Where is he?" she said, her voice hoarse.

Behind her, a gentleman by the cut of his dress, with fair hair and medium build stepped forward, "Diana, you can't shoot him!"

"I can and I will!" she said glaring at Garmon. Through clenched teeth, she said, "Where is he, you arsehole!"

"Where is who?" said Garmon. He felt Genevra come up behind him and panic made him sharp. "Go back to the parlour Genevra!"

Genevra ignored him. "Who is she?"

"My niece! Now go -"

"I'm running out of patience Garmon, tell me where my husband is, or I *will* shoot you and I won't miss!"

"Mowbray? I've no idea. What is this about Diana?"

"Don't lie to me!"

"I'm not lying. I've been here all day; I have no idea what you are talking about. Can you please lower that gun, so we can speak rationally. If your husband is missing, I'll help you find him."

The gentleman behind Diana, spoke clearly and calmly. "We received a ransom note for the duke at breakfast this morning. I'm Stanton, by the way, I don't think we've met, although I've heard of you."

Garmon nodded to him. "Thank you." He transferred his attention back to Diana. "And you think this ransom note came from me?"

"Who else would it come from? It demands the title deeds for Lovells in return for the duke's safety."

"Fuck!" Garmon closed his eyes. He had forgotten about the order he put out months ago on the duke, *someone must have taken it up? But who?*

"You do know something!"

"I do, but I swear to you Diana, I had no idea this was happening. I admit I did put out a bounty on the duke months ago, and I forgot to rescind it. But I have had nothing to do with this plot."

"You bastard!" tears of rage spilled down her cheeks.

"I'm sorry. I really am." He swallowed, trying to think. "I can fix this, show me the note. I promise I can fix it, trust me!"

"Why the hell should I?" she

"No reason, except I think I'm the only one who can get him back for you. Show me the note."

She uncocked the pistol, and dug in a pocket, producing a piece of folded paper. She pointed the pistol at the floor and waited while he read it.

"Fuck! How could I have missed this?" *Not paying attention.* "Ben!"

"Yes Mr Lovell," said Ben popping up from behind the bar.

"Assemble the mudlarks." He glanced over his shoulder. "Seb, I know you don't work for me in this capacity anymore, but can I call on you in this instance?"

Sebastian Rooke nodded. "You can."

"Good man." He turned back to Diana and Stanton. "Come into the coffee room, we need a plan of attack."

"You will help us?" Diana glared at him suspiciously.

"Of course, this is my fault." He turned around and found both Genevra and Beth. He slid his arm round his wife's thickened waist. "Go back to the parlour love, this is not something you need to be involved in."

Genevra put a hand on her hip and gave him a look he knew only too well. With a sigh he drew her apart and gave her a rapid summary of the situation and its background. "So, you see it's my fault. I have to help Diana get the duke back, as much as I loathe the man, I can't let this stand."

She nodded thoughtfully and stroked his cheek. "You've changed."

"I have? If I have, it's due to you." He kissed her gently, pushing a wayward lock behind her ear. "At one time I was obsessed with getting the hell back. Getting revenge on Mowbray. But once I met you, suddenly it didn't matter half so much, and now I couldn't care less. You and our child are the only things that matter to me."

She smiled and kissed him. "Go help Diana recover her duke, Beth and I will be fine here. But don't get shot, or I'll have to kill you!"

He smiled at the joke and kissed her. "I won't, I promise."

She waited until Beth had taken leave of her husband and the two women returned to the parlour. Garmon led Diana and Stanton into the coffee room, followed by Sebastian.

Seb shut the door and leaned on it, his arms crossed over his massive chest. Garmon took a seat at the table and waved Stanton and Diana to sit also.

"Who has Anthony, do you know?" asked Diana laying her pistol on the table.

"I don't. I didn't even know this was happening." Garmon frowned, tapping his chin with his joined fists. "Whoever they are, they got wind of my bounty for the capture and extortion of the duke. It was a bounty I issued months ago. I'd forgotten about it." He looked at Seb. "Have you heard anything Seb?"

The big man shook his head. "But I've been in Pinner, out of the network."

Garmon nodded. And if Ben had heard anything he would have told him. As if summoned by his thoughts a knock at the door heralded the return of Ben, who burst in panting. "Mudlarks on alert Mr Lovell, what do you need us to do?"

"In a moment Ben. Diana will you trust me?"

She frowned at him, and he could see her internal battle. He reached out a hand and covered hers with his, squeezing it. "I'll get him back for you, I promise. I understand now how much he means to you."

Diana swallowed visibly, her eyes glistening. She spoke softly and low. "He means everything to me."

He nodded, "I know. I owe you an apology, I never understood before, but now," he took a breath to clear his suddenly clogged throat. "If someone threatened Genevra I'd kill him."

Diana nodded, "Very well. Do you have a plan?"

"Yes, we don't just want to recover the duke unharmed, we want to get these curs off the streets permanently, you agree?"

"Yes," she grimaced her fist clenching.

"Good. Ben?"

Ben, who had been hovering near the fire keeping warm, straightened, "Yes Mr Lovell sir!"

"Take a message to the Magistrate for me." He rose and went to the desk in the corner and unlocking the drawer took out paper, quill and ink. He scribbled a quick note, sanded, folded and sealed it. Handing it to Ben the boy left the room and Garmon brought another piece of paper to the table with the ink and pen. Setting them down he drew a rough map.

"This is Monmouth Court, the print shop is here, it has two entrances, front and rear." He marked them on the map. "We need to surprise these devils and get them to confess their crime in front of the magistrate. This is what I suggest we do..."

JACOB PACED THE ROOM RESTLESSLY, casting a worried eye towards the clock on the mantle over the fireplace. The duke lay trussed and gagged, tied to the heavy iron base of the printing press that dominated the room. The printer, similarly, bound and gagged, lay in a crumpled heap in the corner, neatly felled by a blow to the jaw from which he had not yet recovered. Jacob's compatriots, Joss a thickset man with tattoos and a broken nose, and Hal a tall, skinny fellow with several teeth missing, sprawled in the two available wooden chairs. Lead letters strewed the floor from the tussle to overcome the printer.

It lacked but a few minutes to eight o'clock, the time of reconning was here and Jacobs nerves pulled tight with anticipation. *Would the duchess be on time? Would she come at all?*

The duke rolled over, his hands above his head and said casually, "you won't get away with this you know."

Joss got up from his seat leaned over the duke, "Shut up your Grace, or I'll shut your mouth for you."

"My wife will put your balls in a vise and squeeze them till they pop!" He made a popping noise with his mouth to underline his point.

Joss reached towards him, but that didn't deter the duke who smirked and added, "In fact, I've no doubt she'll use this device to which you have tied me, I can't wait to see it." Joss grabbed the duke's fine coat and hauled him up, his Grace's unfashionably long red hair hung down as his head lolled back, his arms pulled back at an unnatural angle behind him. Joss shook him, the biceps on his arms flexing.

"I said shut up!"

The clock struck eight and Jacob strained to hear a sound from the street. "Shut him up!" he snarled going towards the curtain that covered the entrance to the front of the shop.

"With pleasure," grinned Joss and kicked the duke in the ribs with his boot. The duke made an oof sound and curled round the blow.

Jacob lifted the curtain and paused as the shop door opened with a tinkle and two men stepped in. *Not the duchess, but perhaps these were her messengers? Or late customers?*

"The printery is closed gentlemen, can I help you?" asked Jacob, putting on his best publican accent.

"You're not Mayberry, where is he?" asked the first of the gentlemen, he was above medium height and build, with brown hair, just flecked with grey, in his forties Jacob surmised. The man behind him was much bigger and had dark hair and a swarthy chin in need of a shave.

245

"Mr Mayberry had to go home, he left me to lock up. Are you a customer sir?"

"No, his landlord, names Lovell."

"Mr Lovell!" Jacob grinned. "That's fortuitous sir, we may have something you want."

"Aye" what would that be?" Lovell stepped closer to the counter and the man behind him flanked him one step behind and to his left.

Jacob lifted the curtain, "step this way sir and see for yourself.

Lovell stepped through followed by the black-haired giant and Jacob followed letting the curtain drop behind him, his heart thudding with anticipation.

Lovell grinned at sight of the duke, who was curled up with his eyes closed. Seemed that Joss had given him a good belting for his insolence.

"Mowbray!" Lovell said with satisfaction. He turned to Jacob. "My informants were correct; you do have him!"

The duke's eyes opened at the sound of his name, and he squinted at Lovell, his mouth thinning. "Come to gloat have you Lovell?" he said.

Lovell ignored him, taking in Joss and Hal as well as Jacob he grinned. "Well done gentlemen, you have done the seemingly impossible. Now it only remains for me to get my property back-"

"That is in a way to being accomplished sir, "Jacob interrupted him. "We are in momentary expectation of the duchess arriving with the title deeds for Lovell's gaming hell. That is what you wanted, isn't it sir?"

"It is indeed!" Lovell nodded and Jacob's fingers tingled with suppressed excitement.

"I am doubly impressed. Your reward will be significant if you can pull this off," Lovell said with relish.

"Lovell you bastard!" growled the duke from the floor. "Have you no conscience?"

Lovell turned his gaze on the duke and said coldly, "None at all. I thought you knew that about me?"

The duke pulled at his bonds and tried to sit up panting, his face as red as his hair. "Damn it Lovell, call off your dogs. I'll play you for the deeds again. Best of three. I can't be fairer than that. Just leave Diana out of it!"

Lovell appeared to consider this offer for a moment and Jacob tensed, fearing that his reward was to be snatch away before he had even grasped it.

"I don't think so Mowbray. I want my hell back, and I've no mind to risk it on the turn of a card when I have a certainty within my grasp."

"Blast and damn you, I should have run you through when I had the chance!" swore the duke, his colour alarming.

Lovell turned away. "Gag him, he talks too much. When are you expecting the duchess?"

"Any moment now sir." Jacob said with a smile.

Lovell nodded, "Mr Rooke and I will wait in the backroom. It won't do for the duchess to catch sight of me, she will likely want to shoot me. Better if you handle the negotiation."

"Aye sir."

"Lovell!" bellowed the duke.

"I told you to gag him!" Lovell snapped. Jacob waved at the other two who sprang into action and wrestled the duke into submission, tying a gag round his mouth.

"Word of warning, if you kill him, you'll hang. He's a duke and even my power won't save you. But the duchess doesn't need to know that, make her think you'll go the whole way, and you'll get what you want. Understand?"

"Yes Mr Lovell, clear as daylight." Jacob rubbed his hands.

DIANA SHUFFLED the documents in her sweaty hands, pushing them into the inside pocket of her jacket and wiped her palms on her breeches. She touched the pistol thrust through her belt comfortingly and glanced over her shoulder at Stanton, standing with her in the shadows across the street from the printery. It seemed like an age since Garmon and Rooke had entered the shop.

Stanton nodded and put his watch away. The ten-minute wait was up.

With a deep breath she crossed the street, Stanton on her heels and pushed open the door. A bell tinkled, announcing their arrival and a man appeared through a curtain, he was of medium height and broad through the shoulders, mid-thirties and handsome enough.

"May I help you sir-" as his eyes registered that Diana was in fact a woman, he corrected himself. "Madam." His gaze gleamed in sudden appreciation of her legs and crotch revealed by the tight-fitting breeches. Diana ignored the salacious look and marched up to the counter.

"I've come for the duke, where is he?"

"Your Grace?"

The man's uncertain tone irritated her, and she snapped. "Yes, where is my husband?"

The man's expression hardened, and he said, "You have what we asked for?"

"You'll not see it until I see my husband." She swallowed, she was supposed to act nervous, but in truth there was little acting required. Her nerves were stretched to breaking point. She could not relax until she saw Anthony and knew he was safe and unharmed. She gritted her teeth. "Where is he?"

The man smiled and held up the curtain, "This way your Grace." He glanced at Stanton, who had said nothing, remaining impassive, yet slightly threatening behind her. His presence was more comforting than she expected. She was grateful not to have to face this alone.

She stepped into the room and her gaze fell on the body curled below the printing press, his flaming hair half covered his face, and his hands were bound above his head pulling his arms into an uncomfortable position of strain, binding him to the iron foot of the press. His feet were bound also, and his knees bent up as if to protect his stomach. Her heart lurched and thudded hard with distress.

"Anthony!" she moved towards him but found her way blocked by a beefy man with tattoos visible on his neck and forearms. Anthony turned his head at the sound of her voice, and she could see he was gagged. He made a muffled sound in his throat and her gut clenched with pain and fury at the way he was being treated.

"Release him at once!" she turned on the man who had shown her into the room as he seemed to be their leader and spokesperson. The third man was a skinny sort with missing teeth. *Could she and Stanton take all three out?*

"Certainly, if you give me what I want,' said the man with a smile that made her skin crawl.

"Not until you release him!" She advanced on him, her hand snaking towards the pistol in her belt. In her peripheral vision Stanton straightened and his hands slid towards his pockets. He had two pistols and she had one. *She was going off script, but damn it she wouldn't stand for Anthony to be treated this way. How much damage had they inflicted on him?*

"I wouldn't do that your Grace," the man said, nodding towards the duke. She followed the direction of his gaze and halted the direction of her hand. The skinny fellow had a knife at Anthony's throat. She put out a hand to stay any potential action by Stanton and dropped her other hand to her side.

"Good girl," the man said with another of those smiles that made her skin crawl. "Now the papers your Grace, if you please." He held out his hand.

Anthony tried to say something, but it was just a jumble of

sounds. She glanced at him and tried to convey reassurance. *This would all be over in a few moments. She hoped.*

With every show of reluctance, she reached into the pocket of her jacket and drew out the papers. She stretched out her hand and offered them to the man.

He took them and looked at them. He nodded and smiled. "Thank you, your Grace-"

JACOB GRINNED. Who knew it would be so easy to earn a small fortune by robbing a duke? He was about to put the papers in his pocket and instruct Hal and Joss to release the duke when all hell broke loose.

It took him a moment to realise what was happening. The door to the backroom where Lovell and his man were hiding flung open, and several men poured out fanning round the room. Lovell followed with the black-haired giant.

A man in an old-fashioned tricorn and a black jacket, paced into the centre of the room and announced loudly. "You're under arrest for kidnapping, extortion and assault of a peer of the realm."

Jacob looked round at the men ringing the room with a sickening lurch and realised they had been set up. He dropped the incriminating papers and flipped into a roll that took him across the room to the curtained entrance as chaos erupted around him. Lifting the curtain, he fled through the shop and out into the street. He pelted down the street and dived into a side alley and ran hell for leather. He didn't even look back to see if anyone was on his tail until he'd criss-crossed streets and alleys in the dark for ten minutes.

Finally coming to a halt in an alcove, he bent over gasping for breath. When he had his breath back, he swore long and hard at his ill luck and then set his face towards the Globe Tavern. Time he went home and found Genevra, he'd grab her and flee.

London was definitely too hot to hold him now. He hoped the Tavern had done well in his absence. He'd take whatever money they had and run.

∾

By the time Garmon realised the ringleader had gotten away the man had a fair start, he sent two of the constables after him and turned to watch with satisfaction the reunion between Diana and Mowbray. After giving them a moment, he approached and held out his hand to the duke.

Mowbray turned to him and looked at the hand and then back at Diana. With a sudden jolt he realised why Genevra's eyes had seemed so familiar to him when he first laid eyes on her, she had the same startlingly deep blue eyes as the duke. He had sought desperately for a reason why she seemed so familiar, and it had been staring him in the face all along.

Mowbray took his hand reluctantly and Garmon smiled. "I hope you can forgive me, even if Diana cannot. I promise you I relinquish all pretensions to the hell. She is yours."

"Magnanimous of you Lovell," the duke said sardonically.

"Yes I thought so." Garmon grinned. "Perhaps you can solve a mystery for me? My wife has the same blue eyes as you have and red hair, although hers is a lighter copper than yours. Any idea why?"

The duke shrugged. "My grandfather was a notorious rake. I doubt if anyone could trace all of his by-blows, he wasn't in the habit of acknowledging them."

"Whittaker, ring any bells?"

The duke shook his head. "As I said, the old man wasn't in the habit of acknowledging his progeny. He slept with more women than my father and me combined, and we managed an impressive total between us." As he said this, he cinched Diana to his side with an arm round her waist. As if to reassure her that his philandering days were well and truly over.

Diana smiled up at him and Garmon felt surplus to requirements. That look made him miss Genevra, and he signalled to Seb, it was time to head back to the Tavern.

They were about to leave when the constables he had sent after the ringleader came back disconsolate, the man had gotten away. Garmon cursed.

"Ben put the word out to the mudlarks." A man answering his description couldn't hide from them. They'd find him. "What is his name?" he asked turning to the two thugs now handcuffed and being man handled to the door by the constables.

The big man with the tattoos spat, "Tate, Jacob Tate the cowardly prick! May he rot in hell!"

The blood drained from Garmon's head at the name, and he reached blindly for something to hold him up and found Seb at his elbow.

"We had him and he got away?" he whispered, his heart thudding in his ears. "Genevra!" He fought off the shock and turned to Seb. "Genevra may be in danger." He bolted out of the shop followed rapidly by Seb and Stanton and crossed the road to where the carriage they had come in stood waiting for them.

With a hoarse shout to the driver to spring 'em, he clambered into the carriage with the other men and endured the longest ride through the streets of London of his life. His heart thudding mercilessly in his chest and curses tripping off his tongue.

CHAPTER 25

*T*he hubbub of noise in the Tavern was comforting and familiar as Genevra moved between tables wiping up spills and retrieving empty glasses, bowls and plates. Trade was brisk and that was a good thing. Her thoughts skittered over the matter that had taken Garmon out this evening, and she suppressed a shiver of apprehension. He would be fine, he had Mr Rooke with him and both men were very capable of looking after themselves. *Provided the blood thirsty Duchess of Mowbray didn't take into her head to shoot him!*

She smiled at a regular and moved towards the bar with her tray of empties and dirty dishes. Joe looked up as she set the tray down, upending a ceramic jug. "We're out of whisky Mrs Lovell," he said setting down the empty jar.

"I'll fetch some from the cellar," she said, wiping her hands on her apron, which curved over her swollen belly. The babe had popped out somewhat in the last couple of weeks, it was impossible to hide her condition now, not that she wanted to. She smoothed a hand protectively over her belly and headed towards the back hall that led to the kitchen and the cellar.

As she passed the kitchen, she stuck her head in to check on

Mrs Bell. Flushed with wisps of greying hair slipping from beneath her cap, she wiped her hands on her apron and looked up from doling out pork pies, bowls of stew and plates of fresh bread and cheese, ably assisted by Beth, who was in her element. Since becoming mistress of her own establishment, Beth had discovered a latent talent for cookery, and she was soaking up tips from Mrs Bell as fast as the older lady could dispense them.

"Can I help you Mrs Lovell?"

"Just checking you're keeping up with the orders. We have quite a crowd tonight."

"Aye, I've two more trays of pies and another pot of stew, should be fine Mrs Lovell."

"You're a miracle Mrs Bell," Genevra smiled and ducked out again, helping herself to a slice of cheese and bread on the way out. She was ravenous pretty much all the time now that the sickness was past.

Heading for the cellar, she selected the right key off her chatelaine and unlocked the door, lifting the lamp from the wall to light her way, she picked her way down the stairs and set the lamp on a table. Turning to the shelves along the back wall she looked for the jars, checking the labels to find the whisky.

"Mrs Lovell, is it?" the voice sent a shiver of horror down her spine and caused her to drop the crock in her hands. It smashed on the stone floor with a loud crash, splashing liquid over her shoes and skirt and sending pottery shards scattering in all directions. The stinging, peaty aroma of expensive malt whisky rose like a cloud, almost choking her.

The cellar door closed with a snick and footsteps traversed the remaining stairs raising the hairs on the back of her neck. Rigid with shock, she blinked streaming eyes, watching the shadow cast on the wall in front of her as a figure moved towards her.

This couldn't be happening. She must be hallucinating. He was dead. Jacob was dead! She buried his body...

"Turn around." The voice went on, low and menacing. The stuff of nightmares.

How often had she woken in terror with his voice in her head?

Shuddering with fear, she turned stiffly, her hands groping for the shelf behind her to keep herself from falling, her legs felt numb. She blinked again as the man advanced on her, his face illuminated clearly by the light of the lamp.

She tried to swallow, but her mouth was dry. Her heart hammered so hard it threatened to leap from her chest. The babe stirred, and she put her hands over her belly in an instinctive gesture. His eyes glittered in the light; his expression choked the breath from her lungs.

"J-Jacob!" She shook her head. "Y-you're dead."

"Unfortunately for you, no I'm not." He came to a stop barely a foot away, well within touching distance. She could smell him, a mix of sour sweat, damp wool and tobacco.

"I buried your body!" she protested, trying to deny the evidence of her senses.

This couldn't be happening. She was asleep and dreaming.

"Ah you found him, did you? Elijah?"

"Elijah?"

"My brother."

She shook her head trying to make sense of what was happening.

"How far along are you?" he asked nodding at her belly.

This was surreal. "F-five months." She shuddered. Her body was rigid with terror.

"Not mine then." He bared his teeth in a grin that didn't reach his eyes. "I heard them call you Mrs Lovell. You married Garmon Lovell?"

She nodded, her neck felt stiff, her jaw tight.

"So, it's his brat?"

She nodded again, her hands clutching her belly. A kind of whimper seeped between her numb lips.

"We'll have to fix that then, won't we?" he said taking another step towards her.

"No!" She shrieked and dodged as his fist came up knocking her arm out of the way and connecting with her face. Pain exploded as his fist smashed into her jaw and her lip split. Her head snapped back under the force of the blow and her teeth rattled. She tasted blood and with that, some primitive rage took a hold and banished the fear that had held her hostage.

Galvanised, she swung away from him and through a narrowed red haze, her eyes scanned her surroundings for a weapon. Propped against the end of the shelf was an iron bar. What it was doing there she didn't know nor cared. She seized it and swung back towards him, just as he came at her with another fist.

With a blood-curdling scream, she swung the thing with all her strength aiming for his head. It caught the side of his skull and connected with a sickening crunch. His eyes rolled back in his head, and he fell where he stood, crumpling to the floor like a marionette whose strings had been cut.

She staggered, leaning her weight in the table, the bar falling from her nerveless fingers as she fought to breathe, strange sobbing sounds ringing in her ears.

The cellar door flung open and Garmon was there. She stared at him across the body on the floor and put out a hand towards him, as the darkness at the edge of her vision closed in, and she felt herself falling.

"Genevra!"

GARMON SPRINTED across the space between them and caught her as she collapsed. "Genevra!" he repeated, his heart thudding wildly with fear.

He barked at Rooke as he headed for the stairs, Genevra in his arms. "See to it, he doesn't go anywhere."

"Aye, I doubt he will. I think he's done for; she's smashed his skull."

"Then get rid of the body!"

Rooke nodded and bent over the body. Garmon left him to it, rushing up the stairs to the bedchamber yelling at Beth who stood at the foot of the staircase her hands to her face, to fetch the doctor.

"I'll send one of my lads," said Joe from somewhere behind him.

Mrs Bell and Beth followed him up the stairs. Entering the bedchamber, he laid her on the bed and checked her for injury. The blood on her face from her smashed lip and the growing bruise on her cheek made him wild, but he could find no other obvious wounds. He was shaking with a mixture of rage and terror and was surprised to find wetness on his cheeks. Wiping it away he held her hands and muttered, "Genevra love, Genevra, can you hear me? Come back to me love, tell me you're all right..." His voice cracked.

"Garmon?" her voice was a thready whisper.

"Yes love, I'm here, are you hurt, the babe-"

"It was Jacob! He -" she opened her eyes and stared at him terror in their depths. "I hit him."

"I know love, he won't hurt you again, I promise."

She began to sob, jagged sounds that tore at his insides and made him helpless with rage and pain. "Hush love. He'll never hurt you again. He's gone."

"No!" she shook her head. "He wanted to hurt the baby. I couldn't let him do that."

"I know love," he repeated, holding her hands tight with his. "I had no idea it was him. If I'd known, I'd never have let him escape. I'm sorry my darling I failed to protect you." His tears mingled with hers. "Forgive me, God in heaven forgive me!"

She clung to him and sobbed until they were interrupted by the doctor's arrival. Standing back to let the physician attend his wife, Garmon watched and listened. When he was assured that she had taken no lasting harm beyond the blow to her face he slipped from the room and pelted back down the stairs to the cellar.

Here he found Seb with the inert form of Tate still lying on the stone floor.

"Is he dead?" he asked his voice rasping. He was molten with rage.

"He still has a pulse, but its weak–"

Garmon bared his teeth and advanced on the body. "Thank you for leaving him for me!"

Seb took one look at Garmon's face and stepped back. He glanced at the cellar door and went quietly to shut it.

Garmon bent over the body of Jacob Tate and looked at the man who had terrorised Genevra. Objectively he was handsome, except for the bloody contusion on the side of his head. His face was pale, and his eyes were closed, he breathed shallowly but audibly, and a pulse beat visibly in his neck revealed by the open collar of his shirt. Garmon's stomach curdled at the sight of this man and the hatred and anger he had stored up over decades for all the injustices he had witnessed or experienced came boiling to the surface. This man epitomised it all.

He pulled him up by the shirt and shook him. Tate's head rolled on his neck.

"Wake up you fucking bastard! I want to kill you while you're awake to know about it!" roared Garmon in his face.

Tate's eyes fluttered and opened. He squinted and groaned, putting a hand to his head.

Garmon grinned at him. "My wife did that to you! And it's nothing less than you deserve you prick! To think I had you within my reach and I didn't know! You're going to pay now for everything you did to her!" Garmon grabbed his throat and squeezed. Tate gurgled something unintelligible. His hand scrabbling at Garmon's grip.

REVENGE ON THE DEVIL

Garmon laughed and let him go. Tate flopped back onto the stone floor. "Don't worry, you're not going that easily!" He glanced at Seb. "Find me some implements."

Seb nodded and left the cellar quietly.

Garmon turned back to Tate who still lay on the floor. Blood seeping from the wound in his head was beginning to pool in the mortar between the floor stones, the metallic smell of it coated Garmon's tongue.

Tate's laboured breaths were the only sounds in the room as Garmon contemplated what he was going to do next.

Tate opened his mouth, and a gasping wheeze came out. Then words tumbled out, falling over themselves in their hurry to plead his cause. "I was trying to do you a favour Lovell, get the hell back for you..."

Garmon lunged at him and grabbed his face in a tight grip. "Shut up, you worthless worm! If I'd known who you were then I'd have killed you on the spot! What kind of man hits a woman? What kind of monster hits the woman carrying his child? You cost her two babes, and you blamed *her* for it?" Garmon spat in his face, dropping his head back onto the stone. "You're going to pay in pain for that, before you die. My face is the last thing you will ever see, and it will accompany you to hell where you will burn for eternity!"

The cellar door opened, and Seb closed it quietly and came down the steps. He held out a range of implements to Garmon. A sharp knife, a pair of pincers and a hammer.

Garmon smiled and took the pincers. Turning to Tate he said, "Hold him Seb, this is going to get messy!"

GENEVRA WOKE SOMETIME LATER with her husband's arms around her, his head on the pillow beside hers. Her face ached and her cracked lip stung. The horrors of a few hours earlier came

259

crashing back in, and she began to shake. A sob rose in her throat, and she tried to swallow it, closing her eyes.

"Hush love," he murmured stroking her back. "Don't cry my darling, I have you safe now, nothing can hurt you like that again. He can't hurt you; he's gone."

"G-gone w-where?" she sobbed. "Is he dead? Did I k-kill him?"

"No, I did. Mr Rooke disposed of the body. As far as the world is concerned, he's been dead and buried for months. I'll pay off anyone who knows different. No one here will betray us love. You're safe."

"He threatened the baby, I had to-"

"I know love. I had him in my reach at the printery, if I'd known who he was -. You should never have had to confront him like that. I don't want you to carry this. I killed him. He's gone, he can never hurt you again I promise. " He hugged her tight and she subsided into this embrace.

"I thought I was having a nightmare; I couldn't believe he was back." she shuddered.

She sighed and after a bit she said brokenly, "my babes are avenged now. I didn't know how angry I was until he threatened me again. I did it for them."

"There are some things that can never be set right, but his black soul will pay for what he did for eternity. You have nothing to feel guilty for my darling. He did not deserve to live."

She nuzzled into his chest, and he held her close. "Sleep sweetheart, I'm here and will never leave you."

The tension leached out of her body as fatigue took its toll, and she slipped into sleep, a measure of peace in her heart.

THE NEXT MORNING Genevra stirred when her husband brought her tea and toast in bed, and she struggled into a sitting position to drink the refreshing brew and nibble on the hot buttery toast.

"So, what happened last night with the duke, did you liberate him from the extortionists?"

Garmon helped himself to a slice of toast and nodded. "Yes. And I think Diana might forgive me eventually, although I wouldn't put money on it."

"I was afraid she was going to put a bullet through you."

"So was I. My niece is a fierce woman." He finished the toast and poured himself a cup of tea from the pot.

"Something else I discovered last night."

"Hm?" she took a sip of tea.

"I suspect, but I can't prove it, that you may be related to the Duke of Mowbray. When I first met you, I was struck by the familiarity of your eyes. I was sure I'd seen them somewhere before. You have the same deep sapphire blue eyes as the duke. He has red hair too, but his is a much darker red than yours."

Shock made her heart skip. "You're not suggesting I'm his daughter? Mama would never-!"

"No. That's impossible you're much the same age. But someone in your lineage may have been a child of his grandfather. The old Duke was a notorious rake, and apparently he had numerous children he never acknowledged. Do you know how far back the red hair and blue eyes go?"

"Papa's mother had them. He always said I resembled her, and Great Aunt Maddie said the same." She looked thoughtful for a moment. "I shall write to Great Aunt Maddie and ask her, I suspect she may know the truth, but she would never say."

He nodded. "Well, that's one mystery solved." he sighed. "I still can't find any trace of Connor."

She squeezed his hand. "I'm so sorry." He shook his head and wrapped an arm round her shoulders, kissing her hair.

"I have everything I ever wanted right here with you, and our child. My hope is that Connor has found what he wants, and no harm has come to him."

She smiled. "You seem more relaxed this morning."

"Do I?" He paused. "I think I let go of something last night. Something I'd been carrying for a long time. My rage against the injustice of the world." He paused again. "I know there will still be injustice in the world but finishing Tate off last night–it made me feel as if my personal injustices were paid up.

"I avenged you. It was satisfying. All along I thought I needed to avenge myself against Mowbray, but once I met you, that began to mean less and less. I thought the hell was so much a part of me I couldn't be me without it. Turns out I was wrong. I don't need the hell, all I need is you."

"Oh Garmon!" She wiped tears from her eyes and flung hr arms round his neck. "I didn't think I could love anyone without losing myself. But you let me be me and still love me. You don't know how much that means to me."

"Yes I do love. I kill people and you still love me. I didn't think that was possible."

"Killing Jacob makes me love you even more." she murmured kissing him. "The only thing I'm sorry about is that I didn't get to see the body, so I can know absolutely that he's dead and gone."

He shook his head. "You wouldn't want to have seen it love. It was–messy!"

"Oh!" her eyes widened. "Did you torture him?"

"A bit." Garmon compressed his lips. "I'm not giving you the details, you don't need that in your head. Just rest assured he's never coming back to hurt you ever again."

"Oh Garmon," she said softly. "I do love you so much!"

EPILOGUE

Four months later

Garmon paced to the parlour window and back for the umpteenth time, his ears straining for any tell-tale sounds from above. His nerves were strung tighter than a harp string and if something didn't happen soon, he would not be responsible for the consequences. The tension was unbearable.

He turned and almost ran into Seb who shoved a refilled glass of whisky at him. "Here," he said with a sympathetic smile.

He took the glass, his third in as many hours and sipped the fine malt brew. It didn't seem right to get sotted while his wife suffered all the pain, but his own internal terror needed something to sooth the clawing panic inside him.

The doctor and the midwife had both explained to him that it could be hours before anything happened, which he well knew from his days living in the brothel. But recalling those days didn't help his anxiety as he also knew firsthand some of the things that could go wrong.

He had spent the day putting up new shelves in the cellar and unloading and doing a full inventory of the new order that arrived that afternoon. Having run out of distracting tasks he was reduced to pacing and sipping whisky in a vain attempt to stop his world from flying apart. *How did other men stand it? The helplessness. The waiting. The worry and the risk.*

He had never thought himself risk averse before this. But he realised with a sickening sense of horror, he had never had anything he really feared losing before. The truth was if he lost Genevra and the child she struggled to bear, he didn't know how he would survive it. The thought of losing either or both rendered him a gibbering mess on the inside.

He glanced at the clock. It had been over twelve hours of torture now, surely it couldn't be much longer? A sudden loud shriek from above stairs, brought him to a standstill, panic seizing his bones.

He flung the whisky glass aside and strode to the door, wrenching it open and running to the foot of the stairs. 'What is wrong?" he bellowed unable to contain his anxiety any longer, he set a foot on the stair and stopped halfway up as Beth appeared at the top of the flight. Her hair hung in wisps about her flush and shiny face. Behind him Sebastian bracketed the stairs.

"The mid-wife says the baby's head is crowning." Her words were almost drowned out by another agonising shriek.

Garmon gripped the banister and tried to breathe. "Is she alright?"

Beth nodded. "The mid-wife says she's doing well. It won't be long now."

Garmon swallowed, his legs feeling weak from the sudden loss of tension. He staggered backwards and felt Sebastian's steady hand at his back.

Beth returned to the bedchamber and Garmon clung to the banister rail, listening to the sounds coming from behind the door. A groaning noise was followed by silence, and then the blessed sound of a baby's wail brought tears to his eyes, as he turned to Sebastian and hugged him blindly.

He then staggered up the steps to the top and knocked on the door.

He wiped his face and sniffed, his voice croaky as he asked, "Can I see my wife?"

"Just a minute!"

Garmon ignored that and pushed the door open. The room was warm with a fug of blood and bodily fluids. Genevra lay back against the pillows, her hair lank and damp, her skin sheened with sweat. In her arms was a swaddled bundle absorbing all her attention.

Beth had a bundle of bloodied sheets in her hands and the mid-wife glowered at him as he crossed the room to Genevra's side.

"We've the placenta to deal with yet, Mr Lovell, you shouldn't be in here."

He ignored her, his whole attention on Genevra and that bundle.

"Gennie," he said softly, dropping to his knees by the bed.

She looked up at him, a weary smile lighting her eyes. "Isn't she beautiful?" she whispered.

Garmon swallowed the lump in his throat. *A girl! His daughter.* He took in the pink crumpled face and tiny perfect fingers curled near her rosebud mouth.

"Perfect," he breathed and kissed his wife's hair. "My perfect girls."

Genevra gasped, her body tensing and the mid-wife said sharply, "the placenta! Out Mr Lovell, now!" He opened his mouth to protest at being evicted, but caught Genevra's eye. She shook her head and motioned for him to leave, so he rose to his feet as Beth swooped in to take the babe from Genevra and followed him out into the hallway shutting the door behind her.

"Do you want to hold her?" she said with a beaming smile.

Seb hovered in the background and Garmon took the little precious bundle from Beth gingerly. It had been many years since he had held an infant, but he'd been no stranger to it or the birthing room in his days at the brothel. Amazing how it all came back to him.

He held his daughter in his hands, her tiny form swaddled in the white blanket and as she stared up at him sleepy and solemn, he felt his heart leave his chest. This tiny thing had reached in and grabbed it with her small fists and would never let go.

A little while later he was allowed back into the bedchamber and set his daughter in his wife's waiting arms. Genevra looked a bit less dishevelled and grinned at him in triumph.

They had discussed names, but not settled on anything firmly. He sank onto the chair by the bed and took her hand and kissed it, one finger tracing the soft skin of his daughter's cheek, unable to tear his eyes away from her mesmerising beauty.

"Elizabeth Mary Beth," said Genevra.

He nodded and smiled. "Thank you, my darling, for this wonderful and most precious gift. She is a treasure." He smiled at his daughter and whispered, "My darling Lizzie you will want for nothing, I promise to dedicate all the days of my life to your protection and happiness."

Genevra sighed and settled back against the pillows, squeezing his hand. "I am so happy Garmon."

"I am too." He said and kissed her hair, smoothing a lock behind her ear.

"Perhaps next time it will be a boy?" She murmured.

Garmon wasn't sure he could survive a next time but kept his misgivings to himself. "If she is our only blessing it will be enough Gennie."

Genevra squeezed his hand, and he knew his cup was entirely full.

∽

266

6TH OF JUNE 1815

"Sleeping beauty is awake!" the husky feminine voice cut through the pain in his head like a razor blade. "Better let the captain know."

Connor's head was pounding worse than any hangover he had ever had, and his stomach was rolling ominously. *I must have tied one on severely last night?* He cracked an eyelid and blinked, his eyes watering as sunlight hit them with blinding force. He closed them quickly and groaned, making a second discovery, his limbs were confined by ropes, tying his hands and legs together in front of him and forcing his knees up near his chest.

He was lying on something hard and a strong smell of salt, fish and something rotten assailed his nostrils, making his stomach heave.

"Oh, there he goes!" said another female voice as he rolled onto his knees and vomited. "You'll have to clean that up mate, you realise!" his tormentor chastised. But he was too miserable to care. He just wanted to die. He would never drink again. *Never again I swear!*

His stomach stopped heaving, and he rolled back onto his side away from the mess.

"Hey Dev, bring a bucket and mop, better get this cleaned up before the captain arrives."

Connor ignored the activity around him, preoccupied with his stomach and the state of his head. Vaguely it occurred to him to wonder why he was tied up and why his tormentors appeared to all be female, *perhaps he was in a whore house?*

The End

TO FIND out what happened to Connor look out for Book 4 of the Villain's Redemption Series Seducing the Sea Devil.

BETH AND SEBASTIAN'S story can be found in Book 3.5 Saving Mr Rooke.

AFTERWORD

It is always fun to add historically accurate touches to stories. Queen Anne's Bath actually exists in St Giles and was used by the locals as a hot spring bath.

The Globe Tavern also actually existed in the location given in the story and the location given for Whittaker's Brewery is the site of the great beer flood of 1814, when the largest beer fermentation tank every built broke and flooded George St and New Street in St Giles Rookery killing at least eight people.

There is a printery in Monmouth Court in Seven Dials where Garmon's headquarters are located. Hart Street, where Garmon lives no longer exists, but it did in 1815.

If you want to know what happened between Beth and Sebastian look out for Saving Mr Rooke, book 3.5 in the Villain's redemption Series.

Connor's story is told in book 4 Seducing the Sea Devil.

I hope you enjoyed this love story between Genevra and Garmon, it was fun to write and kept me sane when my life was falling apart.

Wren St Claire

ALSO BY WREN ST CLAIRE

Villain's Redemption: Steamy Regency Romance

The Devil's Mistress Book 1

Taming the Devil Book 2

Revenge on the Devil Book 3

Saving Mr Rook Book 3.5

Seducing the Sea Devil Book 4

Printed in Great Britain
by Amazon